STONE
& SILT

to Irene,

Harvey R Chute

HARVEY CHUTE

Stone and Silt
A Red Adept Publishing Book

Red Adept Publishing, LLC
104 Bugenfield Court
Garner, NC 27529
http://RedAdeptPublishing.com/

First Print Edition: July 2013
ISBN-10: 1-940215-04-8
ISBN-13: 978-1-940215-04-4
Library of Congress Control Number: 2013940601

Cover and Formatting: Streetlight Graphics

For Carrie, who puts up with my various projects and pursuits, who is everything I could wish for in a caring wife and loving mother of my daughters, and who—most of all—is my best friend.

CHAPTER ONE

Fort Yale
Colony of British Columbia
1863

"YOU DIRTY CHINAMAN! WHERE'D YOU get those city boots?" Nikaia stopped. The rough words had risen from behind the chokecherry bushes separating the cedar-planked schoolhouse from its dirt playing field. She recognized the speaker's voice: Joshua Doyle. His menacing had started early. The first classroom lessons of the year had ended only moments ago.

Nikaia pulled her hand from her sister's fingers. "Klima, head on home. I'll come soon."

Klima hesitated. "No, I want to stay with you." At fourteen years old, she was only two years younger than Nikaia. But she could cling like a thornbush, especially when trouble seemed afoot.

"Go on," Nikaia said, keeping her voice low. "I won't be far behind. I might even beat you home." Without waiting for a protest, Nikaia crept over to the bushes. She held her pigtails back from the serrated leaves and peered through the branches.

Joshua Doyle—unmistakable with his greasy black hair and ragged pants—stood in a small circle with the Cox twins, Edward and Henry. Joshua stood a good half-head taller than the Coxes, and his arrow-thin frame contrasted with their stout middles. Nikaia had seen the boys huddled together earlier that day, Joshua smirking while the dull-witted Cox boys nodded in support of whatever schemes he was hatching. Perhaps Joshua's crafty ways were what earned him their loyalty. Whatever the reason, the twins followed his lead like stray mongrels.

A dark-haired boy stood in the midst of the trio. The coarse talk soon led to pushing, and before long, the smaller one lay on the ground. Edward and Henry held down his arms.

"I'll have these!" Joshua cackled as he worked the leather laces on the black calfskin boots. "You can always get more."

Nikaia got a good look at the target of Joshua's tormenting: Yee Sim, who worked in his family's small general supply shop, Yee-wa. The store lay only steps away from the cabin Nikaia shared with her sister and parents. She often saw Yee Sim stocking shelves with his mother, Yee Sun, while his father tended to customers.

Nikaia had rarely seen him outside of the store and was surprised when he'd entered the classroom that morning. Most Chinese in Fort Yale sent their children to the smaller school in the Chinatown district. Yee Sim had flattened his windblown black hair and glanced around the classroom, which was already full of students wearing their first-day-of-school clothes. His eyes met Nikaia's, and she thought he probably recognized her, though they had never spoken. He headed straight to a desk in the back, where he kept to himself the rest of the schoolday. Nikaia had noted the unwelcoming looks of the girls in her row and wished she was bold enough to offer him a friendly face.

Yee Sim pumped his legs to thwart Joshua Doyle's unlacing. Edward and Henry jostled and bounced as they countered the flailing of Yee Sim's arms. His struggles were no match for their combined weight.

Nikaia glanced back at the schoolhouse. Mrs. Trey had closed the door and was nowhere to be seen. Nikaia pulled in an unsteady breath then stepped forward through a break in the chokecherries. "Leave him alone!" The sharpness of her own voice surprised her.

The three boys wheeled around.

"Says who?" Edward asked. "Go home, squaw."

The other boys guffawed.

"Just leave him alone!" She felt her throat tighten, lifting the pitch of her words.

Joshua Doyle stood and stepped toward Nikaia. His face contorted into a sneer. She froze. Out of the corner of her eye, she saw Yee Sim scramble to his feet and bolt away, the loose laces whipping about his legs.

In the next instant, the boys were on her. With a shoulder shove, she was pushed to the ground by Joshua Doyle. She tried to twist onto her side, but Joshua's weight settled on her as he straddled her torso. She reached out to push him away. His rough fingers clamped onto her wrists, pinching her skin. With a sudden jerking motion, he brought her arms up on either side of her head and pinned them down to the clay. The small rocks in the clay dug into her arms.

"Get off of me!" Nikaia cried.

From behind Joshua, the face of Henry Cox came into view. He leered at her as she struggled, his mouth open and his eyes dancing with callous delight. Nikaia felt a surge of shame and outrage at being seen that way.

Joshua shifted forward, settling his rump on her chest. His hands gripped her wrists more tightly, and his knees pressed into her upper arms. He laughed, cold glee in his eyes. "You should keep to your own business, half-breed."

The cruel taunt was one Nikaia had heard before, and not just from Joshua Doyle. It always stung. "Can't breathe." She squirmed, but it only caused him to drive his knees forward. Her upper arms burned under the added weight. "Get off me!" She tried to buck him to the side. "Please."

"You just cost me a fine pair of boots." He brought his face closer to hers, easily containing her struggles.

Nikaia recoiled from his stale breath.

"Half-breed," he hissed. "What're you gonna do to—yow!" He winced, and something fell from his hair.

She turned her head to see a smooth rock, no bigger than a cat's paw. Joshua brought his hand up to the back of his head, turned, and looked over his shoulder, but not before she saw his face redden. Nikaia followed his gaze and saw Edward and Henry also rubbing the backs of their heads. They spun around to find the source of the stones. Nikaia spotted Yee Sim at the end of the line of bushes, running across the field toward the riverbank.

"Get him!" Joshua yelled.

The three of them scrambled toward the water, leaving Nikaia suddenly free. Keeping her eyes on the boys, she stood up cautiously. Her heart hammered in her chest as she rubbed her aching arm muscles. She straightened her skirt and circled the bushes to go back to the school path.

Her sister was nowhere to be seen. *Good girl*, Nikaia thought with relief. It would have been humiliating to have Klima see her struggling with the boys. She started down the path, and something caught her eye in the alder shadows. *If that's Klima, I'll shake her like salmon in a net.*

Yee Sim hopped out into the afternoon sun. Nikaia wondered how he had evaded the boys. She opened her mouth to speak, but before the sounds could form, she heard excited voices approaching.

"They're coming back this way!" she said. "Quick, follow me!"

They charged to the far end of the chokecherries, Nikaia in the lead. She glanced back to see Yee Sim pumping his legs in smooth strides to keep up. Nikaia knew an animal trail that threaded through the firs and cedars, running parallel with the riverbank. The calls of Joshua Doyle and the Cox boys faded away as she and Yee Sim darted over roots and stones toward the north end of town.

They soon reached Front Street and slowed to a walk, short of breath. Nikaia felt safer among the bustle of busy hotels, saloons, and gaming houses.

Crossing Albert Street, they saw a group of Royal Engineers stringing survey lines over a flattened lot. Nikaia had heard her parents talk of a church to be built on that site. It would replace the nearby tent that presently served as home to Fort Yale's Anglican ministry.

A foreman in a red-checkered shirt looked up from his papers and watched the two of them pass. Nikaia suddenly became conscious of the dirt marks on her skirt.

From Albert Street, it was a short walk to the outskirts of Fort Yale, to Yee Ah's supply store and, slightly beyond that, to Papa's cabin. Joshua Doyle and his gang must have lost interest or found some other target to menace.

When they reached the supply store, Yee Sim headed for the door with a low wave of his hand.

Nikaia walked on a few steps then turned back. "You have a good throwing arm," she called.

Yee Sim looked at the ground but allowed a small grin. "Yes."

"Thank you, Yee Sim."

He seemed mildly surprised that she knew his name. He raised his dark eyes and looked directly at her. "Thank you." Then his face turned serious again. "Next time, I'll pelt them with rocks like rain."

Nikaia rubbed the pangs out of her arms as she walked the last few steps to home. She tried to shake the shame and fear of Joshua pinning her to the ground and felt grateful that Yee Sim had not abandoned her. But there was no one to shield her from the cruelty of Joshua's words. *Half-breed.*

She pictured her mama and papa sitting near the woodstove that morning. They loved each other, Nikaia knew, but surely they must have known their marriage would produce children who landed in the void between two wildly different peoples. Perhaps in their youth they were too foolish in love, too deep in longing for each other, to worry about the future. It hadn't mattered then that he was a Welshman and she a native Indian. The mocking names she sometimes heard in the schoolyard were bitter reminders of her own longing... for what? She wasn't sure. To fully belong, perhaps.

Nikaia looked down at the brown wool of her skirt. The front and sides of it were smeared with clay. She swept her hand behind her; the back was equally a mess. She spied a straight twig and used it to scrape the skirt. Futile. She tossed the stick aside and felt a cool dampness between her shoulder blades. The clay had seeped through the back of the button-up blouse Mama had unfolded for her that morning. *I'm in for a talking-to today.*

She was in no spirit to discuss the schoolyard encounter or to hear Klima prattle on about how Nikaia could have walked away and avoided any trouble. She approached the door to her family's simple home and let out a sigh of relief when she heard the scraping of Papa's planing blade coming from his woodshop. Papa always ended his day by sharpening each tool he had used, and the family could time his arrival home by the sounds of his routine.

Nikaia softly closed the cabin door behind her. Klima looked up from the corner stool, a heavy book open in her lap. Nikaia ignored her inquisitive stare.

Mama knelt with her back to the door, working to rearrange a piece of wood aflame in the cabin's stove. Her braid, thick and black, lay along her spine like the shimmering mane of a pony. Nikaia started to walk past, hoping to change into different clothes.

"Smells like you and mischief met up again," Mama said, still facing the woodstove.

Nikaia haltingly related the encounter while Mama added small cedar cuttings to the fire. A waft of smoke twisted from the firebox, and Nikaia blinked to keep her eyes from watering. Her voice broke when she told of Doyle's jeering.

Mama turned to her. "Better to be a half-breed than a half-wit like Joshua Doyle," she said evenly.

Papa stood in the doorway, wood shavings sprinkled throughout his springy brown hair. "Daughter, you are not half of anything." He brushed his thick fingers along the shoulder of his wool flannel shirt, releasing small curlicues of cedar.

Nikaia did not know how to express the turmoil inside her. Finally, she choked out, "Half plus half makes *neither*!" Hot tears spilled onto her cheeks.

Mama rose from the stove and held out her hand. "Child, walk with me."

They stepped outside. The fall air, cooled by the river, felt fresh against Nikaia's face. She followed Mama to the waterline, where the lowering sun held off the advancing shadows of the fir trees. The Fraser River's brown waters, flowing swiftly and saturated in silt, scrubbed the bank with a gentle hissing. Her mother liked to call the soft sounds "river whispers."

Mama pulled off her deerskin shoes and motioned for Nikaia to do the same. She took Nikaia's hand and waded into the eddy, soaking the hemline of her dress and pulling Nikaia behind her.

"Mama?"

"Don't be afraid," Mama said.

"It's wet!"

"Yes. The river is quite wet today." Mama let out her soft laugh.

Nikaia had to smile at the absurdity of it. She hoped no one was watching from the banks.

Mama took a series of steps deeper into the river, tugging Nikaia behind her. The opaque water concealed whatever rocks and snags might lie below its surface, and Nikaia felt her way with each footplant. They approached the eddy line, where the water curled against the main flow like a swirling nest of snakes that pulled at their skirts. Nikaia flexed her knees and leaned into the current to keep her balance.

Mama released her grip on Nikaia's hand. Nikaia sculled her hands through the water to steady herself, shivering from the Fraser's cold. Mama leaned forward and plunged her arm into the river. Holding up her black braid with one hand, she traced a series of circles in the water with her other hand.

After a moment, Mama lifted up her open palm and presented its contents to Nikaia: a single river rock, black and gleaming in the late-day sun. Its edges were rounded into a near-perfect oval, and a thin white vein ran through its equator. There were many like it along the banks and in the river shallows.

"See this?" Mama wiped it with her thumb and held out the glistening orb pinched between her thin brown fingers. "It faces the river currents. Every day, rough water. Not so easy a life for a rock, being ground up by the flow and the silt." She studied its dark surface. "But after a time, the river has done all it can do. The rock is transformed into something so strong, so smooth. So beautiful."

Mama pressed the rock into Nikaia's palm. Nikaia closed her fingers around the cool curves of the stone.

CHAPTER TWO

"LIFE GRANTS NOTHING TO WE mortals without hard work."
Yee Sim enunciated the words in a dead-on mimicry of
Mrs. Trey's Irish accent.

Nikaia snorted and glanced behind her to confirm they were
out of earshot of the one-room school's teacher. She tried to put
on Mrs. Trey's brogue. "Beware dull minds with no edge to cut
through the world's complexities." She knew her attempt was far
from the mark, but Yee Sim laughed.

"Bewahhhhre," he said, digging deep on the long Rs that
colored Mrs. Trey's speech. "The whaaarld's complexities."

Nikaia let Yee Sim entertain her in his quiet way as they
walked toward home. She was enchanted with his gift of mimicry
and marveled at how someone who grew up speaking Chinese
could have such a command of English. Perhaps the exposure to
customers in his father's supply store had helped him grasp the
language. His speech reflected a mix of the British and American
accents that he heard daily.

In the days that had followed the scrap with Joshua Doyle,
Nikaia found frequent reasons to go to the Yee-wa General Supply
Store. News had arrived from Lytton that Auntie Tsaht-koo had
taken sick with an awful skin ailment. The cramped quarters of the
cabin had become tense as Mama fretted about her sister.

Nikaia wondered if it was the same disease that afflicted Duncan
Charlie's Uncle Richard. Duncan had told her in a hushed voice
that his uncle suffered terribly from boils that erupted and split
his skin. The illness was creeping into the Indian settlements, he

said, leaving white people largely untouched, and it spread easily from one native to another.

The past few nights, Nikaia and Klima had heard Mama and Papa from their bedroom—low voices, talking late into the evenings. A blanket of worry cast a weight upon the household.

Nikaia walked out of the cabin, swinging a small galvanized pail by its handle. Anticipating a meal, Rooster shuffled his front hooves in the dust.

Slow and nearly blind, Rooster had been retired from his work on a cargo mule team. The animal was a bartered payment from Barnard Express for a set of four wagon wheels Papa had built shortly after the family's arrival in Fort Yale. The Express, or BX as Papa called it, ran the largest stage train operation in Fraser Canyon.

Nikaia recalled the day Papa had secured the wagon wheel order. He announced the news with jubilation at the dinner table and opened a tankard of beer. He even poured a finger's width of the yeasty brew into tin cups for Nikaia and Klima, ignoring Mama's disapproving look.

"To the Wales wagon wheel business!" he said as he raised his glass. "Toughest wheels in the canyon."

Nikaia clinked her cup against his and sipped the foul-smelling liquid. She and Klima exchanged winces of distaste and giggled. Mama's glare had deepened when Papa revealed that the payment for his work would not be in cash but in the form of a mule.

"You have the good life now, don't you, Rooster?" Nikaia stroked his graying cheeks as he dug into the mix of alfalfa and oats. The mule snuffled with pleasure.

She had heard stories of mules and horses slipping off the gravel road on its narrow stretches and cartwheeling down the steep canyon walls to their deaths or panicking when crossing the rickety trestles tacked onto the canyon walls, high above the river. While the road was much improved, Nikaia remained thankful that

Rooster's work duties had become limited to the occasional pulling of the cart for Papa's wagon wheel deliveries.

Mama had groaned in the first early mornings after Papa brought the mule home. The animal had a habit of braying noisily well before sunup—an insistent call that went on until silenced by a fresh pail of barley.

After a week, Mama complained. "That beast is at it again! Are we going to awaken to that every day? He could raise the dead from their graves. Truly!"

Papa laughed and planted one of his gentle pokes in Mama's side. He had a soft heart for the animal, who always seemed to gain calmness in Papa's presence. "Well, I suppose we'll never want for a rooster," he said, stroking the brown bristles of his chin.

And from that day forward, the family called the mule Rooster, replacing the generic name of Blackie that his coach drivers had used. Mama had a deft hand with animals, but to the amusement of the girls—and Papa—Rooster rarely cooperated with her. As a result, feeding and grooming chores often fell to Nikaia.

She held the pail high and rested her cheek against the old mule's enormous head. Rooster flicked an ear at a fly. He bore his muzzle down hard on the bottom of the pail.

She heard Mama and Papa's worried voices inside the cabin. The old metal coffee pot clanked against the surface of the woodstove. While she couldn't make out their conversation, it was likely the beginning of another day of distress and concern.

She set the pail in the dirt and looked over toward Yee-wa. *Maybe Yee Sim's finished with his chores.* She looped Rooster's lead through the iron ring bolted into the cabin's outer logs, secured it with a double half-hitch, and crossed the small clearing toward the supply store.

She peered through the front window, looking between the signs heralding New Shipments of Dungarees and Reduced Prices on Cash Boxes. Aside from the Yees, she knew no Chinese people in Fort Yale. Almost all of them lived in Chinatown, a cramped district that huddled east of Front and Douglas streets, between the Indian reserve and the white community. Chinatown was a separate world, complete with its own restaurants scenting the air with unfamiliar spices, open food markets, doctors, and laundry services.

Two years before, Nikaia had watched in curiosity as Yee Ah constructed his store close to their cabin. At dinner one night, Papa commented that Yee Ah had been wise to choose that location close to the Front Street businesses. The small store ran year-round, selling garments, prospecting supplies, and fur-trade gear. Eventually, Yee Ah moved his family from Chinatown to a compact room built onto the rear of the store.

Nikaia pushed on the heavy door. "Good afternoon, Mr. Yee," she said brightly.

Yee Ah was bent over the counter at the rear of the store. He nodded and continued drawing his strangely shaped figures into a records book. Beside him on the counter was a small set of gold scales.

Nikaia walked the store's narrow aisles, running her fingers along the neatly organized items: a pair of brown braces, a neat pile of split-bamboo kitchen whisks, fire-starting flints, gloves, brimmed hats, stiff shirts—all of rugged quality for use by the incoming miners. In a corner near the door, a collection of spades and pick heads splayed out from a wooden barrel.

She turned into the middle aisle. A man wearing a shabby blue plaid shirt and torn dungarees pulled a pair of black trousers from the shelf. He brought them to Yee Ah's counter and retrieved a weathered pouch from his carry bag. Nikaia kept her distance but watched with interest. Most patrons of the store paid in cash, either British pounds or gold coin. Occasionally, American currency would be used, making its way up to Fort Yale in the pockets of San Francisco miners. But raw gold, carried from the claims by the Fraser River miners in doe-skin pouches—or pokes, as they were commonly called—was also accepted by most Front Street merchants.

Yee Ah retrieved some tiny weights from below the counter while the miner untangled the leather drawstring of his pouch. The weights resembled miniature versions of the pawns from

Papa's wooden chess set. Yee Ah placed two of the smallest ones on the scale. On the other side of the scale, the miner shook out a pile of fine gold dust, almost flour-like in its consistency. Nikaia imagined it could all be blown away with a light sneeze. The miner tickled a few more flakes out of the poke until the scale found its equilibrium and the plate with the pawns lifted.

Muted words of Chinese from the far aisle distracted Nikaia from the transaction. She walked to the far aisle of the store and found Yee Sim with his mother, Yee Sun. He was arranging orderly piles of candle boxes with quick, short movements while his mother scratched out markings on a chalk tablet. Yee Sun had a thin braid that dropped to the middle of her back and wore her usual white tunic. Nikaia thought it must be terribly uncomfortable with its stiff material and buttons that led all the way up to a closed collar.

Yee Sim looked up and spotted Nikaia. His dark eyes flashed with delight, and she gave a small wave. He conferred briefly with his mother in Chinese. She peered at Nikaia, scanning up and down as if examining a cut of beef at a market stall. She gave a slight nod to Yee Sim. Nikaia felt her wary eyes watching them as they left the store together.

Nikaia and Yee Sim crossed the Front Street boardwalk and ventured into the thickest woods near the river, where cool gusts of air whipped against their faces. At the fringe of the trees above the eddy, Nikaia heard a low grinding sound and gazed up at the Creaking Fir, one of the broadest trees on the riverline. At the midpoint of its height, twin trunks split off then crossed each other in a twisted embrace that shifted in the wind. The overlapping branches brought to mind the image of an ancient couple, groaning as they helped each other stay upright.

Nikaia tugged on the shoulder of Yee Sim's cotton shirt. "Come on, let's go hunt."

They followed animal paths under the forest's canopy of fir and cedar, pretending they were in the deep wilderness on a mission of survival. Nikaia had enjoyed the activity since she was a small girl, and sharing the game with Yee Sim gave her a new sense of joy in it.

"Yee Sim, look!" Nikaia crouched in the brown bed of fir needles that matted the trail. She brushed aside the thin strands of bunch grass that spotted the path in pale green clumps and pointed at an impression in the underlying dirt. "Black bear."

Yee Sim squatted beside her. "Could it be grizzly?"

"No. A grizzly would be much bigger and have claw marks ahead of each pad. It's a black bear, probably full-grown."

Nikaia leaned over to study the print, trying to gauge the depth of the impression. One of her plaited pigtails slid down and settled in the dirt. Yee Sim gently moved it back over her shoulder.

"That is brilliant," Yee Sim said softly.

She pretended not to notice his nearness, but heat rose in her face at the praise. Papa had taught her how to identify tracks, a skill he was expert in from his fur trading days. Nikaia felt deliciously clever.

She imagined the scorn her schoolmates would heap on her for playing such childish forest games. After all, at sixteen, she was almost a woman, close to the age where many girls married and took up house. Those changes and responsibilities seemed far off to her. Even so, she had to admit that part of the reason she loved such afternoons was that they gave her exclusive time with Yee Sim. She delighted in impressing him with her tracking skills.

They climbed to the flat bench of land above the river and walked past the old Indian graveyard. The warm fall air carried the sweet aroma of fir as their feet crushed the pathway's bed of dry needles.

She noted the recently scraped ground where white settlers had extended the clearing to bury their own dead. The graves were marked with simple stone flatrocks and wooden crosses. She fingered the words on one weathered cross inscribed with only a name—Lydia Hastings—and the dates of birth and death. A poor summary of a woman's life, Nikaia thought. She imagined the many happenings, the loves gained and lost, and the victories and heartbreaks, all reduced to a few simple etchings fading into nothingness as the weeds grew over the grave.

She could easily identify the older Indian graves. Most were adorned with jade laid out carefully at each gravehead or lining the perimeters of the mounds of dirt. In the afternoon sun, the smooth stones took on a translucent appearance, almost seeming to glow. They gave the illusion of having their own lifeforce, and it somehow added a glint of promise to the dreary graveyard setting.

"What is it your mother calls this place?" Yee Sim asked.

"The Garden of Heaven." She tapped a green stone with her foot. "They decorate with jade in the Lytton gravesites, too."

She knelt and brushed her hand against the coolness of one of the larger stones. As young girls, she and her Lytton friends had scrambled along the rocky banks of the Fraser, delighting in finding small emerald-like pebbles in the sand. She would present them with pride to Mama, who sifted through them with great seriousness, commenting on their shape and lustre. "My grandfather is buried up there. Mama says that Grandma laid jade alongside him, right in the grave."

A scraping sound caused them to turn toward the river side of the cemetery. A solitary man, darkly dressed, shoveled dirt off in the distance.

"That's Mr. Collier," Nikaia whispered.

The gravedigger's thin frame was all joints and angles as he leaned into his shovel. She could see no coffin but wondered if the grave was for Duncan Charlie's uncle. Burying the dead was no doubt becoming a steady business as the white man's disease took hold.

"Come on," Yee Sim finally said. "Let's go around, back to the river."

CHAPTER THREE

"**C**ARE FOR A ROW, GOOD sir?" Nikaia raised her arm and bowed in a fancy-lady flourish.

Yee Sim gave her an inquiring look. She led him through the sandy dunes to a muddy path that wandered alongside the purple-petaled salmonberry bushes. Nikaia looked back with bemusement as Yee Sim stepped carefully to avoid scuffing his blackened boots. They reached the river at the upstream edge of the back-eddy that dominated the riverfront.

Nikaia lifted a protective nest of alder branches to reveal a small rowboat. "Papa built this," she said, reaching for the bowline. Back in her thirteenth year, she had watched in fascination as the boat took shape under the hands of Papa and his young helper, Albert George.

Nikaia had become close to the George family, who lived outside of town on the reserve. As with many Indian families, they relied heavily on sockeye salmon for food. The Georges used a canoe to set up and maintain gill-nets in the eddies north of town. Nikaia had seen Albert and his sisters cart basketfuls of salmon from the river. Albert would sometimes bring a salmon up to the cabin and present it, still dripping with river water, to Mama. He refused any kind of payment or trade.

Mama had once explained to Nikaia how, in the native tradition, no person could own the Fraser's waters, but that gill-net location was a coveted asset for the native families along the river. "Just like a salmon comes home from the sea to its original waters," Mama said, "the same families go back, every fishing season, to the eddies of their ancestors."

Nikaia had overheard, though, that the Georges' gill-net site was in dispute. Grace Thompson had stopped by the cabin, bearing a pail of fresh blackberries and a lungful of gossip.

"Shameful," she said over tea with Mama. "The fights and arguing between the Georges and the Thomas brothers." Mama smiled politely, and Grace went on. "The Georges have used that eddy for generations, and Mima George's marriage to Samuel Thomas doesn't change that. And the burning last week of the Georges' canoe… awful! I'm sure I don't know what to think."

For a time after that, Albert and his sisters would work the gill-nets without a canoe, laboriously pulling the nets in for retying or, when the waters were low enough, wading daringly into the Fraser to access the salmon ensnared in the knotted mesh.

Yee Sim ran his hand along the smooth cedar of the boat's gunwale.

"Grab a thwart," Nikaia said, "and help me tug it into the water."

The hull scraped along the moist ground. She recalled how Papa had told Albert that he had a special order and would need his help more often in the shop. When Albert turned to pull his apron from the wall hook, Papa gave a secret wink to Nikaia.

Papa guided Albert through the selection of cedar, which they took to Lawson's sawmill to be cut into strips. Papa pulled his hand plane in draw strokes over the strips, and the wood curled away, seemingly as soft as goat butter. The shavings piled up on the floor and covered Papa's shoes.

Working from opposite ends, he and Albert sanded the wood strips until they lay as flat and smooth as a baby's cheek. Nikaia enjoyed watching the two of them at work. They exchanged few words except for Papa's occasional instructions. Papa's patient manner and Albert's willingness to learn gave them a natural tradesman-apprentice relationship.

Nikaia would bring a book into the shop and sit cross-legged to read while her father worked. She would sometimes become aware of Albert staring at her as his wiry arms worked the sanding cloth against the strips. When Nikaia met his eyes, Albert flinched and returned his gaze to the wood. At thirteen, Nikaia had held little interest in boys. It amused her to see Albert's discomfort. Still, she had to admit his soft brown eyes and sharp cheekbones were pleasant to observe. And she appreciated his shy and respectful ways around Papa. She heard a voice in her head that said, "Maybe someday."

She wanted to share with Yee Sim her pride in Papa's craftsmanship. "Papa and his helper soaked lengths of cedar in tubs of river water and weighed them down with iron weights to curve them." She was unsure why, but she didn't care to refer to Albert by name as she described the building of the boat. "He made a hull jig out of thick blocks of fir and laid the strips inside it. Then one by one, he removed each strip and brushed glue onto its edges."

Nikaia had been fascinated as the skeleton of the boat took form, secured by cross thwarts that doubled as seats. Papa finished the rowboat with marine varnish and screwed in the metal oarlocks. The project had taken most of the summer, with Papa splitting his time on the boat with other more urgent jobs on stagecoach wheels.

"You hold the line, and I'll hop in," Nikaia told Yee Sim.

The river gave a small surge that lifted the boat as she swung the oars out toward the water. Yee Sim gave a push and leapt into the stern. Facing him from her seat on the thwart, Nikaia pulled smoothly on the oars. The boat scraped its way off the graveled bank.

Nikaia recalled with pride the day of the giving. Albert had arrived at the shop early in the day and pulled one of Papa's leather aprons from its wall hook.

Papa reached out and held the apron. "Hold on, Albert. No work here today." He walked to the back of the shop and pulled back a sheet of burlap to reveal the finished boat gleaming in its newness and outfitted with two fine oars shaped from Douglas fir. "It's yours to use. You've put good work into it, Albert. Now let it work for you."

Albert stared at the boat and then back at Papa. He had nodded, his eyes shining.

"Papa gave the boat to the Georges, and they used it for two fishing seasons, I think," Nikaia told Yee Sim. "They must have preferred the old ways, though, because after a while they got a canoe and didn't use the rowboat anymore."

She had seen Albert, his father and mother, and his two sisters, cart the rowboat back to Papa's shop. In the boat were two large woven baskets filled with dried salmon. They laid the baskets on her family's small porch. Mr. George, a heavyset man with a well-worn face and long coarse hair, approached Papa and Mama.

For a moment, he simply looked at Papa with a solemn expression. "Kwoks-chams," he rasped. That was one of the first Nlaka'pamux words Mama had taught Nikaia: *Thank you.*

After that, Papa kept the boat tied near the river, a few yards upstream from the eddy. He loaned it out so often to various miners and fishermen that most had come to consider it community property. Sometimes Nikaia would see strangers using it to ferry supplies from the sternwheelers back to shore. Papa seemed to delight in that. He took to calling it the *Anybody Boat.*

Papa would not be pleased, however, to see his daughter rowing on the river without his supervision. And Mama would be apoplectic. River drownings were alarmingly common in the Fraser Canyon. Nikaia would occasionally sneak out for a short row on hot summer days. Sometimes she brought Klima and let her sister handle the oars in exchange for sworn secrecy.

Yee Sim laid his arm over the gunwale and dragged his hand through the water. Nikaia took care to stay within the eddy, working the outside oar to keep the boat within a few lengths from the rocky beach. The forward pulsing motion of the boat was rhythmic and mind-lulling. Yee Sim closed his eyes against the upstream breeze. The wind parted his straight black hair, washing over his fine features. He looked to be the very essence of calm and contentment.

It occurred to Nikaia that Yee Sim had never touched her before his re-arrangement of her braid. The action had taken but a second, yet it had filled her with thoughts she wasn't quite willing to explore. She rowed on, timing the drop of her oar blades to match the smooth movement of the boat.

She was studying Yee Sim's face when the bow of the boat jerked sharply sideways. *Oh, curse me. I've crossed the eddy line.* She knew from Papa's warnings that the Fraser could be treacherous once its main flow caught hold of a vessel. The upstream edge of the boat tilted down toward the water, knocking her to the side. Yee Sim jolted forward and looked at Nikaia.

"Sorry! I was daydreaming." She tucked the downstream oar under her knee and pulled hard with both hands on the handle of the upstream oar. The boat swung about in response, its stern now facing shore. She then pulled on both oars, straining to free the boat from the current's grip.

Yee Sim looked downriver, his eyes widening. The safety of the rocky bank shifted further away as the boat slid downstream. "Can I help?"

"No. Well... yes. Yes, come to the middle of the boat." She hoped that with less weight in the stern, the boat would pivot more easily.

Nikaia doubled over as she drew the oar handles as far in front of her as she could reach. Her hands slippery with sweat, she squeezed hard to keep her grip on the oars. She braced her feet on the forward thwart and pulled back hard with both arms. The force of the motion caused her body to lift from the seat. The boat lurched toward the bank, cutting a jagged course as it broke the eddy line.

Nikaia puffed out her cheeks and exhaled harshly. "That was too close. Sorry, Yee Sim."

He raised his arms and stretched like a cat. "I think I almost got a free ticket to New Westminster."

Nikaia's embarrassment washed away, and she laughed with him.

After pulling the boat back into its resting place, they wandered back through the shadowed woods. The trails led them back to Front Street and to Yee-wa.

"I want to show you something," Yee Sim said as they approached the store. Nikaia glanced over at her family's cabin a few steps away and heard a pot clank against the woodstove. She hesitated. *A few minutes more with Yee Sim, then I'll go help Mama with dinner.*

He led her to an open-ended barrel outside the side of the store, near a small pile of empty bottles and jugs. Lifting the barrel, he uncovered dozens of rounded rocks, all smooth-edged. Some were the size of eggs, others almost as large as Nikaia's fist.

"My throwing rocks," he announced. "I find them by the river." He shrugged, but Nikaia sensed the pride in his voice.

Nikaia squatted to examine the collection. "Can I try them?"

He nodded and looked pleased. "Let's set the bottles up on the stumps." He pointed at a row of fir chopping blocks arranged in the dirt.

Yee Sim had gathered the empty bottles from the saloon boardwalks on Front Street, where they were in abundant supply. His collection included blue bottles with graceful curved shoulders, others with brown glass and slender tapers, as well as the black stubbies used for ale. A vague odor of stale beer and spirits hung over the assortment. Nikaia balanced the bottles on the uneven stumps, while Yee Sim counted out fifteen paces and laid the rocks on the ground. He walked back and switched a few of the bottles to line them up according to size.

They took turns pitching the stones. Yee Sim loaded one stone in his right hand and several in his left. Each successive throw burst from his grip, the rocks flowing easily from his left to his right hand. Nikaia observed his smooth movements with admiration.

Nikaia wished her throws were as impressive. She tried to hide her embarrassment as her shots either rose high above the bottles or popped up blasts of dirt in front of the stumps. She heard a giggle and turned to see Klima lurking beside the cabin and holding her hand over her mouth.

"You try, then!" Nikaia said.

Klima strode to the pile of throwing rocks. She sorted through them in an analytical fashion and chose three. She walked up to stand between Nikaia and Yee Sim. "Working space, if you will," she said, her eyes on the bottles. Her phrase was one that Papa used often in the shop.

Yee Sim stepped back, and Nikaia followed suit, ready to mock her sister's attempt. Klima pulled her arm back and gracefully threw the first stone toward the leftmost bottle, a large blue one. It didn't just topple; it shattered. Nikaia watched, stunned, as Klima dropped the other stones to the ground and strode away, her braided pigtails bouncing with each step.

Maybe I've underestimated Klima. Nikaia was more than a little annoyed at the impressed look on Yee Sim's face as he watched Klima strut until she disappeared around the corner of the cabin.

She and Yee Sim continued throwing. Gradually, Nikaia's rocks hit nearer to their marks.

"Let's bring the throwing rocks next time we play Hunt," she said.

Yim See seemed pleased to agree.

One day, Nikaia promised herself, *I'll bring a dead rabbit back to Papa. And hopefully before Klima does the same.*

Nikaia poured the last of the kettle water into the clawfoot bath that hugged one wall of the kitchen. She lined up two chairs alongside the tub and draped a towel and a fresh change of clothes over them. The chair arrangement formed a rudimentary privacy barrier as she slipped out of her deerskin dress and unbuttoned her blouse. She pulled off her chemise and underclothing and laid them on one of the chairs.

Even with the woodstove lit, the cabin air was cool, and she clutched herself, shivering. She slid into the steaming water and unwrapped the twine ties at the ends of her pigtails. Her hair free, she sank into the bath, submerging her head. The water soothed her chilled skin like a caress.

She sat up and reached for the lumpy bar of soap atop the tin tray at the end of the bath. Working it underwater between her hands, she coaxed a weak lather out of it. She spread the suds along her arms and shoulders, and laid back to rinse off. She dug her fingers through her hair, enjoying the light scent of the soap as it cleared the grime that had built up since last week's bath.

She laid her hair out flat against her skin, thick black strands that reached down to her lower ribs. She settled back under the warmth of the water and realized she could hear Mama and Papa's voices coming from their bedroom. She thought she caught the sound of her name.

"Well, she is sixteen and not so far from being a woman," Mama was saying. "She won't be living with us forever. Some girls her age are already married."

Nikaia lay still in her bath, straining to hear.

"That seems a ways off for her," Papa said. "Even so, I'm not sure about her going off unescorted through the woods like that. With any boy."

Mama's voice softened. "We weren't so much older when we took our own long walks."

"That's what I'm concerned about."

"It's part of her growing up. There are times when I've despaired about her finding a good man. She hasn't outgrown being such a tomboy."

Nikaia felt her cheeks grow warm upon hearing her parents discuss such things. *I may be sixteen, but I've no desire to be married.*

Her mama continued, "It's almost a relief to see her spending time with a boy."

"A Chinese boy."

"Yes."

"That doesn't concern you?"

Mama's voice hushed, and Nikaia leaned forward to hear. "Yes, of course. It wouldn't be an easy life."

"I think Yee Ah has a good family and a solid, honest business. His boy seems a decent sort. It's just that life is hard enough as it is. I wouldn't want Nikaia to needlessly live with all that comes along with that kind of marriage. I've seen what you've had to sacrifice, with your family, when you married an outsider."

"And yet, I wouldn't go back and change that even if I had the power," Mama said.

"Nor me."

"I think we fret too early. She's a pretty girl, and there'll be other boys. As you like to say, one swallow does not a summer make."

Nikaia laid the soap back into its tray. *Marriage! I want to finish school and, after that, train to be a teacher. Mrs. Trey says that if I keep up with my lettering and arithmetic, I'd be well-suited for that. And I enjoy it when she has me help students in the younger grades. Being a teacher would give me a life of choices beyond Fort Yale. Why should I put all that aside and submit myself to being a wife and mother?*

She leaned forward to squeeze and twist the water out of her hair. *Why should I yearn for someone to lord over me? Or who wants me to be a brood hen then raise his offspring? When the time comes, I want a marriage like... well, like Mama and Papa's, I suppose. The man I marry will be a friend.*

Klima walked out of the bedroom she shared with Nikaia, her school reading text in hand. She looked over at the tub. "Can you save the hot water for me?"

"Yes. It's getting cool, though. Best to put another kettle on to warm it up." Nikaia stood and reached for her towel. She dried herself off and tried to sort through her tumbling thoughts.

CHAPTER FOUR

"**N**IKAIA WALES, ARE YOU WITH US?"

Mrs. Trey's voice cut through Nikaia's daydream. She snapped to an alert posture, her face growing warm. "Yes, ma'am."

Molly O'Scanlon and Lillian Dirth giggled from their desks beside her. Mrs. Trey shot them a stern look. Molly ducked her head, while Lillian retied the blue-and-white-striped kerchief wrapped over the waves of her chestnut-colored hair.

"I asked if you could name the members of our royal family." Mrs. Trey's forehead crinkled as she approached Nikaia's desk.

Oh, please, no. Nikaia was horrified that the schoolteacher might look at her papers. She leaned forward and covered the loose pages with her arms. Her mind had indeed been wandering that morning. She had stared at the empty desks in the room and thought of how few of her schoolmates were left. A few had died, from various ailments. Lucas Craner, with his bright blue eyes and shy smile, had drowned the past July after deciding to cool off from the canyon heat with an ill-thought swim in the Fraser. Some of the other boys had left school to take on jobs with the coach houses, which clamored for drivers and horse-handlers.

But the biggest reason for the empty desks was that the girls were starting to marry and have families. Just last month, quiet Agnes Druthers had married Mr. Hawkins, a hotel owner. The man must have been fifteen years older than Agnes, and he never seemed to smile. Nikaia wondered what on earth the two of them would have to talk about. *Did they ever laugh together?*

Her mind had then leapt to Yee Sim, who at that moment was sitting six rows behind her. She thought of the conversation she had overheard between her parents and considered how he would do as a husband. She almost laughed aloud at the thought. *Marrying a Chinese boy?* They would be the scorn of the whole town. Surely, Mama and Papa would die.

Still, he does make me laugh. And he is kind and gentle. We always have a lot to talk about. And when we're quiet, it's still pleasant to be with him. Would he stay that way as he grew older? He's almost sixteen, essentially a man already. Do people even change after that age?

She thought of the two of them as a couple walking through the woods. It made her think of stories Mama had told her and Klima about the days when Papa was courting her. At the time, Nikaia had listened with only mild interest. But now she was curious. She wanted to know more about those early times that had led to Mama's marriage to Papa.

How difficult it must have been for Mama to marry outside of her culture. And then to take her husband's name—how strange! It would be like putting on new skin.

She considered Yee Sim again. Like most Chinese, his family placed their surname first. If she were ever to marry him— *ridiculous!*—she would become Yee Nikaia. That sounded even more drastic and ludicrous than her mother adopting the family name of Wales. *Yee Nikaia.* The notion of such a name bemused and intrigued her.

Nikaia untied the ribbons around her paper bundle. She picked up her cedar pencil. *Yee Nikaia.* She printed the letters carefully and stared at the page. She wrote it again and then a third time. It seemed less strange with repetition. When Mrs. Trey called on her, she had been imagining the moment when she might be asked for her hand in marriage.

"And your answer would be?" Mrs. Trey asked.

Nikaia gathered herself and her straying thoughts. "Queen Victoria, ma'am. And her husband, Prince Albert, who died the winter before last. Her eldest son is Edward the Seventh."

"Yes, the heir to the throne. And her other sons?"

Nikaia knew the names well, both from school and from Papa's discussions of current news. "Prince Alfred, Prince Arthur, and Prince Leopold."

"Very good. Correct." Mrs. Trey walked backward to her desk as she addressed the class. "And who can name the daughters of the queen?" Mrs. Trey pointed in turn to the different hands in the air.

"Princess Victoria," Klima called out confidently from the third row.

"Princess Alice, ma'am," Harriet Williams's soft voice responded to Mrs. Trey's pointed finger. The teacher continued around the room.

"Princess Helena."

"Princess Louise."

Nikaia blew out a full breath and folded the paper on her desk into halves then quarters.

After school, Klima ran ahead while Nikaia walked more slowly with Yee Sim. She and Yee Sim parted ways outside the store, and she continued home alone.

Nikaia knew immediately upon opening the cabin door that something was amiss. The air smelled of distress. Her sister sat alone at the kitchen table, her eyes full of worry.

"Klima, what is it?"

"I don't know. Something terrible." Klima glanced toward the small bedroom at the back of cabin.

Nikaia could hear Papa's voice, low and soothing, and anguish in her mother's muffled responses.

"I think it's Auntie Tsaht-koo," Klima said.

Nikaia sat beside her sister at the table. They waited anxiously, aware of every small sound emanating from the bedroom. The hushed voices were soon obscured by the scraping of drawers opening in Mama's clothes chest.

Nikaia stood. "Come on. The stove pile needs restocking."

Outside, Nikaia loaded the split fir into Klima's arms then filled her own. They shuttled between the orderly woodpile and the stack of stove-lengths in the kitchen. She was relieved to be busy and could tell her sister felt the same way.

Nikaia thought back to the last time she'd seen Auntie Tsaht-koo, four summers ago. Her aunt was always up for jump rope, and her bright laugh was never far from her lips. She taught Nikaia and Klima how to play knucklebones. Sitting with them in a tight circle on the floor, she would expertly flip the five wooden jacks from her cupped palm to the back of her hand and over into her palm again. Then she would press her childlike hand against Nikaia's fingers, curving them into a proper cup shape. When Nikaia finally flipped all the jacks successfully, her aunt had waved her arms over her head and whooped in celebration.

Her hands. Nikaia remembered them as soft and brown and beautiful, a high contrast to Mama's hands, which were lined and roughened from the labors of raising a family and keeping up a home. Auntie Tsaht-koo was in her twenties but had not yet married. She lived with Nana Klat-su, Nikaia's grandmother.

The kitchen woodpile was usually kept small, but she and Klima piled it almost to the level of the stove's top. Finally, Mama came out of the bedroom, her eyes red and swollen. Papa followed, folding a letter and sliding it into the back pocket of his trousers.

"Girls," Papa said, "Auntie Tsaht-koo is not doing well. Mama needs to be with her. She's leaving in the morning."

Klima turned to her mother. "How long will you be gone?"

"Probably not long." Mama raised her head to meet their eyes. "Your auntie needs your prayers, girls."

"Is it... the pox?" Nikaia whispered. She knew it was an indelicate question, but she wanted to know.

Mama pulled in a fluttery breath. "Yes, it seems it is."

"Is anyone else up there sick from it?" Nikaia asked.

"I don't know."

Klima cut in. "Mama, what if *you* catch it?"

"Oh, I don't believe that will happen. I'll be careful." Mama's voice was light, but Nikaia saw concern in Papa's gray eyes.

Papa met Nikaia's gaze and seemed to make an effort to compose his features. Nikaia's senses sharpened, and she felt a tightness in her stomach. She rarely saw Papa unsettled.

Klima kept up a steady stream of questions about the strange illness. Mama answered patiently. Nikaia pictured Auntie Tsahtkoo's suffering, that creamy brown skin being ravaged and blemished with sores.

"How long will it take her to get better?" Klima asked.

Mama shook her head and rubbed her hands down the front of her skirt. "Child, there are some things that only the river knows."

That was what Mama said when it was time to stop asking questions. Nikaia wished there was something she could do or say to help matters. But Mama's worries seemed far beyond the reach of any comforting words she could offer, even if she had the wit to summon them.

"You girls get the fire started," Papa said.

The next morning, Rooster brayed earlier than usual. Klima stirred beside Nikaia then buried herself up to her nightcap in the coarse blankets. *That girl can sleep through anything*, Nikaia thought as she got out of bed and pulled aside the burlap curtain covering their bedroom window.

Outside, the cart creaked as Papa settled Mama's clothes bag into it. Rooster shuffled restlessly at the hitching post, pawing the dust with his forelegs. The mule knew that when Papa pulled the cart from the woodshop, he would soon be harnessed to it.

Nikaia tossed her nightcap onto the bed and pulled her sleeping gown over her head. She put on a white chemise and donned a woolen skirt and a cotton shirt. She wiggled her toes into cotton stockings and stepped into her deerskin shoes. As she threaded the row of buttons on her shirt, she twisted her feet on the floor until her heels worked their way into place inside her shoes. As she walked from the room, she inspected the string wrappings at the ends of her pigtails.

In the kitchen, Mama stood beside the table, dressed in the long gray skirt she wore on Sundays. She stacked pieces of bannock into a woven basket. Her knitted shawl and three-quarter-length cape lay folded on the bench behind her. She had a full-day journey ahead.

"Is Papa taking you to Lytton with Rooster?" Nikaia asked.

"No, no. Just to the express station. I'll be taking the passenger stage."

Nikaia helped load the basket with potatoes and apples. Mama laid a candle and some flint alongside the food. Klima stumbled in, still clad in her cotton nightgown and wiping the sleep from her eyes. She looked bewildered at first and then troubled as she took in the sight of Mama in her formal clothes, the packed basket on the table.

Papa walked in and picked up Mama's cape. "If you're about ready, love, I'll get Rooster hooked up."

"I'm ready," Mama said, closing the basket lid. "Nikaia, I've left a salmon for your dinner tonight." She motioned toward a bucket in the corner. "And some potatoes."

Nikaia followed her mother outside, where Papa led Rooster to the cart. He buckled the belly band around the mule and guided the wooden cart shafts through the leather loops of the harness. After untangling the long leather traces that extended from the rear of the harness, he attached them to a crossbar and pulled them back to Rooster's hind end. He unwrapped a chain from the crossbar and passed its links through a hook screwed into the front of the cart.

He walked to Mama, took the basket, and swung it into the cart beside the clothes bag. Mama stepped up into the bench seat at the front.

Klima skipped out from the cabin, fully dressed and with her pigtails tightened. She planted her feet in front of Rooster. "I'm coming."

Mama covered up a small smile with her hand, while Papa eyed Klima with surprise.

"Well, I'm coming too, then," Nikaia said and climbed into the back of the cart.

Papa looked at Mama. He shook his head and chuckled softly as he untied Rooster's lead. "You can both come as far as the express station."

Klima leapt in beside Nikaia.

"Hup!" He eased the reins, and Rooster started plodding toward town.

Nikaia held the short sidewall of the cart as it bumped through the gravel. They passed Yee-wa and the darkened windows of the Front Street gaming houses. The boardwalks were empty except for one saloon keeper who was splashing a pail of sudsy water onto the planks leading into his establishment.

Papa directed Rooster toward the coach station above the eddy. Inside the fenced loading yard, teams of horses whinnied as hostlers worked, bending the horses' legs to check their shoes. Papa spotted an empty hitching rail and pulled up on the reins.

Across from them, a driver examined his coach harnesses. He turned toward the Wales family. "All aboard the jerky!"

Nikaia thought the name aptly described the clunky-looking two-horse stage. Papa reached up to put Mama's clothes bag into the cargo storage above the passenger compartment, sliding a miner's packsack to the side to make room. The stage tilted on its springs under the weight of the luggage. It seemed alarmingly top-heavy to Nikaia.

Inside the coach, a trio of youthful miners waited, sporting unwrinkled workshirts and clean trousers. They stopped speaking as Nikaia approached the cart with Mama's food basket. She wondered if they had seen a family of mixed race before, and she felt uncomfortable under their stares.

Mama set the basket inside the coach and pulled Nikaia and Klima tight to her. "Klima, I'll be back before long. You keep up with your schoolwork. And your chores."

Klima nodded glumly. Mama kissed Nikaia's cheek. Nikaia caught the scent of the lilac water her mother dabbed behind her ears. She embraced Mama's neck and lingered in the fragrance.

"Mind the fort while I'm gone," Mama said. "Watch your sister. Help Papa when he needs it." She brushed Nikaia's nose with her finger. "And stay clear of trouble, little Mischief."

Mischief. Nikaia hadn't heard that nickname in some time. It triggered a memory from her childhood in Lytton. After a pow-wow, Mama had brought home an elaborate beaded headdress. It belonged to Mama's cousin Samson, who had asked her to repair some beadwork that had partially detached.

Nikaia had stared in fascination at the headgear, with its bold colors and striking eagle feathers. When Mama and Papa were seated in the kitchen with their cousins, Nikaia stole into Mama's bedroom then walked out to the kitchen, the headdress hanging low on her ears. Mama gave her a stern look and stood up, but the cousins simply looked amused. They encouraged Nikaia to dance.

Nikaia had seen the pow-wow dancers and was happy to oblige. But rather than the twirling circles of the female dancers, she danced like a warrior, kicking to the rear with bended knee and spinning backward in tight turns. Papa tilted his head back and let out his throaty laugh. The cousins clapped and chuckled, and soon Mama gave up trying to be serious and shook her head in laughter.

That performance had earned her the nickname *Miss Chief* from Mama, but Papa took to calling her *Mischief,* always with a twinkle in his eye. Nikaia enjoyed the attention, as well as the good humor it spawned in her parents. And she had to admit that both names fit her quite well.

Papa hugged Mama and helped her step up into the coach with her basket. His face was grim. "When you're with Tsaht-koo, keep the windows open. Don't touch her if you can help it."

"I know," Mama said softly.

"And if you must touch her, wash yourself well. In steaming water."

Mama put her fingers to Papa's cheek.

"Please, Kate," Papa said. He rarely called her by name, usually just saying Mama or something tender like Sweetness. Actually, Mama's true name, her native name, was Ke-mat-pa. The Anglican ministry in Lytton had re-christened her and, for good measure, had assigned her whole clan the family name of Paul. So Ke-mat-pa grew up as Kate Paul to the white community.

"You're a good man, John Wales," Mama said. "I'll be fine. I'll send word as soon as I can."

The driver touched his cap. "Off!" he called, loosening his pull on the reins and releasing the hand brake.

The stagecoach lurched forward. Nikaia watched as the buggy creaked and tilted in the ruts, heading to the end of Albert Street and onto the winding wagon road to Lytton.

CHAPTER FIVE

WITH MAMA'S ABSENCE, THE CABIN seemed strange and vacant, its natural rhythm of meals, schoolwork, and chores disrupted. Papa returned to his woodshop, shaping spokes for an order of freight wagon wheels, and Nikaia realized she would have to be an adult for a while.

She adopted a motherly tone with Klima as she oversaw their first supper without Mama. "Get the flint, please, and start the kindling."

Her sister assembled a pyramid of fine-cut sticks in the stove. Nikaia pulled the speckled sockeye from the bucket of water. It shimmered green and blue as she held it suspended over the bucket, water spilling from its gills. When the dripping slowed, she laid the fish on a wooden cutting board—tail to the left, as Mama had shown her many times.

"Add some dry leaves in the center," she told Klima. "Otherwise that wood won't take to the spark."

Nikaia took Mama's adze from the shelf. She palmed the rounded end of the mottled green stone and examined the edge. Steel knives were readily available in Fort Yale—Yee-wa had several varieties—but Mama preferred her traditional cutting knife. She had told Nikaia how her own mother, Nana Klat-su, had patiently scraped the midpoint of a rounded jade stone with wood and quartz sand. Eventually the center of the stone thinned until only a sliver of connecting rib remained between the halves. Then she split the stone in two, creating a pair of wedge-shaped pieces that made for effective cutting tools. The honed blade, almost translucent, held its edge brilliantly.

Nikaia had often watched Mama gut and fillet salmon after the dip-netters brought round their haul. One day, midway through a pile of six salmon, Mama flipped the adze in her hand and thrust the handle at Nikaia. "Daughter, your turn. A woman needs to know how to handle a knife." Nikaia had worked diligently at it, absorbing Mama's few words of instruction and encouragement.

Nikaia's hands moved expertly over the fish with no wasted motions. She pushed the adze into the underside of the fish, above the vent, and cut along the centerline toward its head, revealing the pink inner flesh. She took care not to plunge the edge too deeply so as to keep the internal organs intact.

She set the adze in a crossways position behind the pectoral fin and leaned on the knife until it stopped at the fish's backbone. She flipped the fish over and repeated the cut on the other side.

Klima exclaimed with satisfaction as the leaves caught fire in the stove.

"Good work," Nikaia said. "Do you need to add more kindling?"

"No, it'll catch. I feathered the sticks."

Papa had shown them how to draw a knife through the small pieces of wood, creating curls to expose more surface to the flame. Nikaia leaned harder on the adze and severed the fish's head from its body. She bent toward the wash bucket and dropped the head with a splash. The head dipped and twirled as it floated downward. Then with her hands, she spooned its innards into the water, pulling at the slippery guts to release them from the surrounding tissue. At one time, that step had been repulsive to her, but with repetition, she had lost any aversion to it.

A column of smoke rose from the stove door. Klima scurried to the cabin door and pushed it a hand's width open, allowing the outside air to pull its way into the stove and up the chimney. It occurred to Nikaia that Klima was trying hard to demonstrate her competence to her older sister.

She resisted the urge to criticize or overdirect her sister's actions. "She's off to a good start now!" she said, nodding toward the stove.

Nikaia returned the fish to the cutting board and carved out the dark red ribbon of kidney that lay along the backbone. She held the fish upright and cut off the remaining fins. At that point, Mama would sometimes slice the fish up into steaks, but Nikaia chose the more difficult technique of filleting the meat. She sawed the adze along the length of the backbone then flipped the fish over and repeated the cut on the other side. "Klima, can you set the fry pan on the stove?"

Klima put the cast iron pan in place. The fire crackled energetically.

"You work that knife like your mother," Papa said from the doorway.

Nikaia felt a surge of pride as she sliced into the fillets to remove the remaining rib bones. Papa walked over to the stove and warmed his hands. He pulled the stove door open and peered into the firebox. Nikaia glanced over as the flames lit up the angles of his face.

"And that is one fine cooking fire," he said. The lines around his eyes deepened as he smiled.

Nikaia had never thought of Papa as handsome, but in that light, she could see why Mama might have thought him fetching as a young man, with his caring face and boyish grin. "That was Klima's doing," Nikaia said.

Before long, the fillets were sizzling in the pan, and the potatoes had softened in the boiling water. They dished the food into black enamel bowls. Nikaia pulled the rest of the fillets from the pan and carried them to the table on a smooth cedar plank.

"Mmph—good salmon," Papa said. "Just like Mama's."

The twin prongs of their forks scraped along the bowls as they ate. Nikaia looked at the empty chair closest to the kitchen and felt a pang at Mama's absence. Mealtimes were usually accompanied by her mother's questions about the girls' activities or her discussions with Papa regarding family matters and affairs of the town. More often than not, one of Papa's dry comments would bring out her musical laugh. Nikaia loved how Mama's nose would wrinkle in such moments, and she would sometimes practice the same expression in the looking glass that hung on her parents' bedroom wall.

"Let's have a few more taters, shall we?" Papa said.

Klima's chair clattered as she pushed it back. She brought the warm pot from the stovetop and set it on a dishcloth in the middle of the table.

Papa reached in with his fork and stabbed a potato. "You hear that?" Papa suspended his fork halfway to his bowl. "Listen."

Klima and Nikaia stopped their scrapings. The distant hoot of an owl sounded through the cabin window.

Papa winked at Nikaia. "Your guardian spirit is close by tonight."

Nikaia looked toward the window. In her coming-of-age ceremony six months before, the owl had become her special animal. She thought of the great winged creature as her spiritual guide and protector.

Papa placed a potato in his bowl and leaned forward in his chair. "Did I ever tell you girls about Charlie Ray?"

Nikaia shook her head.

"Charlie was new to Lytton when I met him, freshly arrived from Fort Langley. He asked if he could join me when I cleared my trap lines in the Stein." Papa cut his potato into slender discs. "It was in the fall, and an early snow had come. I was happy to accept his help, even though Charlie was a bit of a tenderfoot. I don't think he'd spent a night in the bush before. Pass the butter, if you will."

Nikaia delighted in Papa's stories, told in his lively voice and with animated gestures.

"The lines were full," he said, "and our packs heavy with beaver pelts by the time the light fell. We found a clearing, and I showed Charlie Ray how to pitch the canvas tent. I got a fire going and asked him to fetch a kettle of water from the Stein. So off he went.

"Some time passed, and Charlie hadn't returned. I figured to follow his tracks to the river, and that's when I saw cat prints in the snow." He set down his fork and reached for more salmon from the serving plank.

"Bobcat!" Klima said, her eyes wide.

"Ah, I would have wished it were so!" Papa leaned his head toward Klima and dropped his voice to a lower register. "Cougar. And I could see yellow spots in the snow, all about. It was marking its territory."

"Where was Charlie Ray?" Nikaia asked.

"I didn't know. I followed his tracks further and came around some pines to see the snow disturbed. Signs of a struggle. And then blood stains, deep red in the snow."

Nikaia stopped chewing her mouthful of potatoes.

"And there before me was a young deer, a fresh kill. One leg was completely separated from its body, and all around it were pad tracks and urine markings."

Oh, poor deer. Nikaia imagined its terror as it fought for its life against its predator's fangs.

Papa drew his eyes upward and tilted his head toward the cabin's knotted ceiling. "Overhead, all I could see were the darkening tree branches. I walked on, half-expecting to feel claws landing on my neck at any time. I decided it best to not call out for Charlie—no sense drawing attention from the cat. So I followed his boot prints, and every few steps, I'd let out an owl call."

Papa put down his fork and cupped his hands. He parted his thumbs to form an aperture, and bringing his hands to his face, he blew across the opening. A loud and reedy triple-hoot sounded. Nikaia had seen him do that many times. Sometimes he would flutter his fingers as he blew, making a rise and fall of notes like the haunting call of a loon.

Klima cupped her hands and blew hard into them. Nothing resulted but a blast of wet air mixed with a few salmon flecks.

"Oh, you mess!" Nikaia laughed and threw her cloth hand rag toward her sister.

Papa let out a chuckle. "Let's get these bowls cleaned and some coffee boiling."

"Wait. What happened to Charlie Ray?" Klima asked as she wiped her face with the rag.

Papa gathered his bowl and utensils and walked into the kitchen. "I followed his tracks until it was near dark. Finally, his path led me back to camp, and there he was by the fire, wild-eyed and shaking like a spooked pony. I asked him if he'd seen the deer kill."

Nikaia took Papa's bowl and dipped it in the washbucket. She handed it to Klima to dry.

"Charlie Ray nodded," he said, "and told me he'd seen the cat tracks, too. And then..." Papa's shoulders bounced as he suppressed his laugh. "Then Charlie said 'Not only that, I could hear an owl following me, relentlessly, all the way back to camp! Those things will tear your hair out!'" Papa threw his head back and roared.

His buoyant mood washed over the girls, and they laughed along with him while finishing the kitchen chores.

Papa loosened the buckles on the leather braces that draped over his shoulders. He picked up a book and settled in his rocking chair next to the stove. Nikaia selected *Don Quixote* and sat on a nearby chair. She slid over to make room for her sister as Klima sidled in lugging the leatherbound *Robinson Crusoe*. The simple cabin had few luxuries, but Papa's small shelf of books was one of them. His collection was varied, the result of his willingness to take books in barter when customers lacked the money to pay for his work. The titles included adventure stories, like *Moby Dick* and *The Woman in White,* and various books of poetry. Over the years, Nikaia had listened as Papa read them aloud in the winter evenings. Mama would sit nearby, occasionally interrupting to offer her perspective on some passage. Nikaia remembered crowding onto Papa's lap with Klima, holding the book balanced in her lap. She could feel his deep voice rumble in his chest. She absorbed the lyrical words along with the cedar scent of his flannel shirt, which seemed to never be completely cleared of wood shavings.

They had eventually gotten too old for Papa's lap and could read the books on their own. Nikaia reveled in the faraway lands that sprang from the pages, worlds that seemed as far removed from Fort Yale as the planets were from the moon.

Papa was particularly fond of poems, and he was proud of his well-used copies of works from Elizabeth Barrett Browning and John Greenleaf Whittier. Nikaia's favorite was Longfellow, the newly famous and popular poet from the United States. His poems were straightforward and easy to understand, flowing with a pleasurable rhythm. She and Klima took delight in reciting memorized lines for Papa, who would pull on his pipe and listen with great solemnity to their efforts.

After a time, Papa lowered his book. "You girls can come with me to the river tomorrow. I'm expecting a load of iron plates."

Klima jumped from her chair, *Robinson Crusoe* spilling from her lap. "From a sternwheeler?"

Papa grinned. "Yes, ma'am."

"Oh, yes!" Klima squeezed Nikaia's upper arm.

Nikaia shared her glee. Riverboat arrivals were an entertaining novelty, and she delighted in the bustle that surrounded the arrival of the great boats.

Nikaia placed her book back on the shelf with the others. The exotic settings described by Defoe and Cervantes could wait, for tomorrow would be a day of great excitement in Fort Yale.

CHAPTER SIX

"**N**IKAIA! LET'S GO!" KLIMA HOPPED in place like a robin looking for a worm.

"Patience, sister," Nikaia said, acting like an elder, even though she was equally excited. She placed a handful of carrots into her cloth haversack, a snack for later in the day.

The sternwheeler *Umatilla* was expected soon. Nikaia recalled the day the boat had first appeared in the town's eddy, shortly after she and her family had moved from Lytton. The first boat to churn its way up the Fraser River to Fort Yale, the *Umatilla* ran a regular round trip between the town and the Fraser's southern outlet to the Pacific.

Nikaia pushed open the cabin door and looked out into the yard. Rooster scuffed the dust as Papa buckled his harness. The small cart behind Rooster would carry the shipment of iron plates back to Papa's shop.

"Wait here," Nikaia whispered.

But Klima was already stepping through the doorway. "I'll wait outside. Papa's almost ready."

Nikaia slipped into her parents' bedroom with her haversack and opened Papa's wooden chest. She held back the hinged lid and inhaled the pleasing fragrance of old cedar. A shallow removable tray lined in red velvet was fitted into the upper part of the chest. It bore a wood-handled .44 caliber Colt Army Model, a spyglass, a bag of gunpowder, and several lead balls.

The revolver was a bartered item for some major stagecoach work Papa had done. As far as she knew, Papa had never used it in the months he had owned it. He preferred his trusty muzzle-loaded Tennessee rifle for his fall hunting expeditions.

She picked up the spyglass and rotated it in her hand, admiring its polished mahogany and knurled brass flanges. The spyglass had been a gift from Papa's brother, who'd used it as a crew member on cargo ships working England's coast. Uncle Douglas had even had the wooden tube engraved with a gold calligraphic rendering of Papa's initials: JMW.

Yee Sim will love this, she thought as she slipped the spyglass into her haversack alongside the carrots. She swung the strap onto her shoulder, closed the chest, and ran outside to the cart.

———

The west bank of the Fraser swarmed with activity. Merchants, traders, and miners gathered in small groups as they awaited the sternwheeler's arrival. A loosely organized collection of wagons, wheelbarrows, rowboats, and canoes lined the riverbank. The usually vacant and peaceful area was filled with men calling out to each other and women directing their children away from the chaos of wagon wheels and hooves. Horses shook their manes and whinnied at the commotion. Nikaia sucked in a breath, thrilling at the bustle, and scanned the crowd for familiar faces.

A clatter of horseshoes sounded behind them on the winding roadway to the river. She looked back to see a large freight wagon closing in on them.

"Ho, Rooster," Papa called, and he steered the mule toward a level spot in the gravel.

The wagon driver was a fresh-faced boy in a button-up black vest. He perched nimbly on his bench as he worked the reins. A dashing figure, Nikaia thought, with his rolled-up sleeves revealing sturdy arms. He looked at Nikaia, gave her a toothy smile, and touched his cap. Nikaia averted her eyes, abashed. Klima waved gaily as the freight wagon rumbled past them.

Papa pulled on Rooster's reins. He stepped off the cart and brought his face close to the mule's head. Nikaia could hear him speaking in conversational tones. Papa had a habit of explaining the plans of the day to Rooster, addressing the beast as if it were a slow-minded brother. It was Papa's way of organizing his thoughts,

Nikaia assumed. He wrapped the mule's lead rope around a large rock on the beach.

Nikaia swung her legs over the side of the cart and hopped to the gravel. Papa leaned against the cart and drew out his pipe and smoking pouch from his jacket's inner pocket. The rich scent of tobacco leaves emerged as he unfolded the pouch and layered the tobacco into the burled cob of his pipe.

"Papa," Klima said, "tell us about what happened to the *Fort Yale*."

"Again?" Papa cocked an eyebrow and smiled. "Well, the *Fort Yale* was one of the finest sternwheelers on the river. It could carry three hundred people, plus cargo. And when it blasted its steam whistle, you could hear it from a mile away. It was the pride of the Fraser, and—so I'm told—had one of the best riverboat captains anywhere."

Papa looked to the river and blew out a gray cloud of tobacco as if to illustrate the puffing of the steamboat's smokestack. "There were several boats working the river then, and they would compete to see which could push its way upstream the quickest. Whichever boat got here first would take on most of the downstream customers. So there was considerable money to be made, and it was a high-stakes race."

Nikaia turned to Klima. "They'd stoke the fire under the boilers to go faster."

"That's right," Papa said. "They'd throw in wood and coal to get the boiler piping hot. The hotter the steam, the faster they could turn the paddlewheels."

"And that's what made the *Fort Yale* explode?" Klima asked.

"It shouldn't have. There's a valve in the boiler that keeps the steam pressure at a safe level. The captain must have tied off the pressure valve, so he could run the boat faster."

"And the boiler blew up!" Klima said.

"It did. From what I hear, a lot of captains tie off the valves and over-run their boilers. It must have been a frightful scene, men being scalded by water as the boiler split apart or crushed by flying pieces of metal. And the other poor souls on board were strewn into the river as the boat disintegrated, where the currents pulled them down."

Nikaia tried to imagine the suffering of the passengers as they fought to stay afloat in the deadly folds and whirlpools of the river, all while witnessing the horror of their friends and loved ones drowning.

"It must have been a taste of hell on earth," Papa added, shaking his head. "People dying by the fury of fire or the chilling waters, or both."

Papa had told them the story before, but in a tempered-down version that glossed over the deaths—in deference, Nikaia knew, to Mama's cautionary looks. His stories improved when Mama wasn't there to protect her daughters from some of the lurid details.

"How many people died?" Nikaia asked.

"The captain and four passengers were killed. And some Indians and Chinese on board."

Papa's tone was delicate, and Nikaia knew why. *No one bothered to count the Indians or the Chinese.*

"This boat won't explode today, though," Klima said. "Will it?"

"By the time the boat reaches the eddy, the captain will have backed off on the boiler." Papa closed his eyes and pulled in a long draw on his pipe. "I certainly don't expect any disasters today."

The crowd began to stir. Nikaia looked downriver and spotted a faint rise of black smoke clearing the riverside hills. She could already hear the sputtering *ka-chug* of the boat's steam engine.

Before long, the shallow bow of the *Umatilla* broke into Nikaia's view. She winced as its steam whistle screamed. The onlookers released a chorus of shouts, and some of the more boisterous in the crowd discharged pistols and rifles in celebration. The gunfire startled her and caused Rooster to shuffle anxiously.

Nikaia thrilled to see the white boards of the paddlewheel digging into the Fraser. They shed their water noisily as they rotated up from the river. The wheel, over twenty feet in diameter, towered over the men on deck.

Papa shielded his eyes from the sunlight reflecting off the water. "See how the paddles are in the stern? That allows the captain to run the boat close to the canyon walls. Closer than he could with a sidewheeler."

The great boat approached the shore. Its main level—or hurricane deck, as Papa called it—was crowded with freight and passengers. Nikaia watched a huddled group of miners arising from blankets near the smokestack. Other travelers emerged from openings that led to inner berths and staterooms. From their layered clothing, top hats, and bonnets, Nikaia assumed they were from some higher station in life than the hurricane-deckers and could afford to travel in relative comfort. She noted one young woman whose petite face and blond ringlets were framed with a bonnet of blue silk, its lacy fringe fluttering in the breeze. She wondered how such a headpiece might look around her black-as-night hair and the copper skin of her face.

The captain waved from the pilothouse, which triggered another round of cheering and rifle shots from the crowd. The steam engine quietened marginally, and the paddles slowed. The assembly on shore congregated nearer to the riverline.

"Can we get closer?" Klima asked.

Papa led them to the fringe of the crowd. Nikaia watched with amusement as Klima hopped up repeatedly to see over the heads of the people in front of them.

He nudged Nikaia and pointed at the boat. "See how flat-bottomed that hull is? That lets the captain navigate right over sand bars and shallows. Mr. Haggen from Barnard's tells me that, fully loaded, these boats draw only two feet of water. One pilot bragged that, unloaded, his boat could 'sail on a heavy dew.'"

Nikaia pictured the boat drifting across the morning bunchgrass, its massive bulk afloat as though suspended by fairies. In the large back-eddy, no dock existed for the sternwheelers. The *Umatilla* pushed its bow into the gravel riverbank. Deckhands tossed out lines to men on shore, who ran the ropes up to metal rings hammered into the beach above the highwater line. His boat safely tethered, the pilot disengaged the steam engine from the paddles, and the massive wheel slowed to a halt.

Immediately, merchants and townspeople rowed out in small boats. A few paddled out in canoes, and a gangplank was extended for the departing passengers. A string of men with rolled-up sleeves passed bundles, barrels, and crates hand-to-hand from the cargo holds out to the smaller boats.

The captain appeared in the pilothouse doorway. "Wood up!" That was the signal for the crew and the on-boarding passengers to gather firewood to stoke the boiler.

"Time to get our rowboat and lend a hand," Papa said.

They walked the short distance upriver to the *Anybody Boat*. Klima held the branches aloft while Papa slid oars into the oarlocks. He hooked the bowline over his shoulder and towed the boat along the bank, his boots splashing in the shallows.

"Can I row out with you, Papa?" Nikaia asked.

"Not this time, Mischief," Papa said. "This boat'll be gunwales to the water once the iron gets loaded. You stay on shore. And out of trouble. Yes?" He looked directly at her.

"Yes, Papa." She watched the passengers disembark. One group of young men who looked not five years older than Nikaia raised raucous voices as they neared the shore. Knapsacks on their shoulders, they linked arms and sang lustily.

"Soon our banners will be streaming,
Soon the eagle will be screaming,
And the lion—see it cower!
Hurrah, boys, the river's ours!"

Nikaia watched as they progressed unsteadily up the bank toward town. She guessed that some bottles of spirits—or maybe homemade mountain howitzer—had been consumed on the journey upriver. "Bully for us!" one cried as he passed.

Nikaia backed away from the young singers and almost got bumped by two weary-looking men walking toward the river. She sidestepped and felt the haversack swing against her ribs. *Ah, the spyglass.* She tried to locate Yee Sim in the crowd but couldn't. *Maybe there's no shipment for Yee-wa today.*

She looked back at the two men. The older one wore a miner's thick checkered shirt, his trousers tucked inside his worn boots.

A slouched hat concealed his features down to his gray beard. His younger partner's chin was darkened with a fortnight worth of stubble stained with tobacco juice. A generous wad tucked into his cheek gave his face a lopsided look.

Checkered Shirt set his tattered rucksack on the gravel and looked toward the distant homes and storefronts of Fort Yale. "I'll be pleased to get the stench of this place out of my nostrils. Fraser River gold—humbug! We should never have left San Francisco."

A vacator, Nikaia thought, one of many to abandon the quest for gold.

The stubbly one turned to face the boat. "Well. When a man stops trying, he starts dying, I suppose."

"I swear to you, the only gold here is in the commissioner's storehouse. Or the colony banks. Not a flake in the river banks."

Stubbly squirted some brown spittle into the rocks and let out a wan chuckle. "The gold in the colony banks didn't grow there. Somebody found it. Just weren't us."

"And here I am, dead broke. Is the boarding begun?" Checkered Shirt peered down to the line queuing near the *Umatilla*.

"Looks it."

"You change your thinking yet? Last chance."

"There's a claim opening up in Emory Creek, or so I hear. It's been claim-jumped a few times. Most likely it's been played out." He aimed another stream of tobacco juice at the rocks and surveyed the unloading scene. "But, perhaps not."

"Good luck to you, then. I'm leaving a wake out of this scurvy-ridden town." With a heavy exhalation, he hoisted the rucksack onto his shoulders.

Nikaia had noticed the stark contrast between the men arriving and the men leaving Fort Yale. They came with shiny eyes and hearts full of aspiration. Sometimes they leapt out of the sternwheeler a few yards from shore, splashing toward the riverbank in their zeal for the goldfields. Many arrived in the spring—a misguided timing as the Fraser was in high flood then and wouldn't reveal its sandbars until months later.

Often, they returned to town before the first snow fell. Worn out from scraping unproductive dredgings from the Fraser River silt, they were changed men, their high hopes replaced with despair and disgust.

Nikaia watched the activity around the sternwheeler and her father's repeated trips rowing out to the *Umatilla*. After a time, the scene became monotonous. Papa and the others had a long day of loading and unloading ahead. Klima had found two school friends, Gregor and Eleanora, and they stood on the bank, skipping rocks into the churned-up water.

Nikaia decided to seek out Yee Sim. The day was perfect for playing Hunt.

CHAPTER SEVEN

"**D**EER TRACKS! LOTS OF THEM." Nikaia laid down her haversack and dropped to all fours. She brushed aside the Douglas fir needles to fully reveal the prints and lowered her face close to the ground.

She suddenly remembered the tender moment she and Yee Sim had shared. She considered ways she could make her pigtail fall again without making the ploy too obvious.

But Yee Sim was absorbed in the hunt. "Look at how the bunchgrass has been flattened. They must have bedded down here."

They were in Riverside Flats, a bench of forestland that lay a half-hour's walk upstream from the eddy. They could still hear the faint calls and whistles from the unloading of the *Umatilla*.

"Let's follow the tracks," Yee Sim said. "Here." He reached into the front pocket of his trousers and pulled out three throwing rocks the size of small eggs.

Nikaia laughed. "You think we can bring a deer down with those?"

"No, but maybe we can flush them out of the bushes."

"Oh, I see. Yes, good idea. Oh! Wait. I want to show you this." She opened her sack and pulled out the spyglass.

Yee Sim gave her the rocks and took the spyglass. He examined it from end to end, his fingers lingering along the smooth wood. He unscrewed the end cap and extended the inner brass tube. The instrument was almost as long as his forearm. He brought the lens to his eye and pivoted in a slow circle. A smile built on his face. "It's absolutely brilliant."

"Avast, ye swabs," Nikaia deadpanned, putting the rocks in her pocket.

"'Tis a fine instrument, matey!" Yee Sim slapped his hand over his face like an eye patch.

Nikaia snorted as he returned the spyglass. She slid the brass extension back into its wooden outer tube and laid the spyglass in her haversack alongside the carrots.

They followed the tracks, the salmonberry bushes closing in on them as the path narrowed. Nikaia pushed the branches aside, taking care not to let them spring back into Yee Sim's face. The tracks lightened in depth and soon disappeared. She reworked her past few steps in tight circles, looking for any prints that might lead to side trails.

"Here's one, I think," Yee Sim said, dropping to the ground for a closer inspection.

Nikaia leaned closer. "That's not a hoof." She drew back in surprise. "It's part of a boot print. Fresh."

Nikaia looked around cautiously. Papa always said that people were more dangerous than wildlife, at least in Fort Yale. Seeing no one, Nikaia signaled silence to Yee Sim. They followed the boot prints into the bushes. Nikaia stopped when they came upon a small clearing where the bunchgrass had been trampled. Heel and toe marks pocked the ground in random patterns.

Where the prints went from there was unclear. Nikaia took in her surroundings to regain the trail. She rotated in a full circle, taking her time to observe anything out of the ordinary. As she pivoted, Yee Sim studied her. She hoped she didn't have dirt on her nose.

A mat of alder branches caught her eye. "These have been cut." She ran her finger along the white inner flesh that dotted the ends of the branches.

Yee Sim came to her side. She reached into the branches with both arms and easily pulled them to the side, revealing a distinct mound of freshly overturned clay.

Nikaia started pulling at the soil. "What do you suppose this is? I think something's buried here!"

Yee Sim looked around and shrugged. "Maybe someone's dog died."

"Oh!" Nikaia pulled back from the dirt, horrified.

Yee Sim laughed. "Slide over, let me help." He peeled some loose bark from a weathered alder, exposing its glossy inner surface. He rolled it into a scoop shape. Kneeling beside Nikaia, he troweled out the clay, while she continued with her hands.

The loose soil made for easy digging. They were less than six inches down when Nikaia's fingers caught on something hard. She pushed the dirt away to reveal a brass buckle attached to a leather backing. It glinted softly in the afternoon sun.

They both turned back to the soil and shoved more dirt away to reveal a leather satchel. The top flap was folded over and secured with buckles. She recognized the design. There were many like it in Fort Yale, used by men to carry documents and light supplies. She had even seen some similar ones on the shelves of Yee-wa.

Yee Sim pulled on the edges of the bag to release it from the clay. "Whoa. It's heavy."

Nikaia pulled up on the handle and was surprised by its heft. "I'm thankful it's not a dog carcass." She unbuckled the fasteners. She bent open the stiff flap. The smell of fresh leather reached her nostrils.

What greeted her eyes could not have been more unexpected. The satchel was more than half-filled with gold pokes. Nikaia picked one of them up and tugged on the drawstring with trembling fingers. She spread open the mouth of the bag and gasped. Gold filled the poke to the brim. She tilted the bag to show Yee Sim, and sparkles jumped and danced across the flakes, some the size of buttercup petals. The contents seemed alive, as though the poke revealed the shimmering scales of a trapped fish.

She reached in and pulled out a nugget as large as the tooth she'd lost on her ninth birthday.

"Oh, Yee Sim! Oh, no." She had heard many tales of bloody conflicts in the mining areas near Fort Yale. Many lives had been lost in murderous rages over the madness of a few ounces of gold. The glittering display represented danger as much as it did wealth.

Yee Sim's face had equal measures of astonishment and dread. Nikaia had never seen such riches. She knew that a handful of that gold would change a family's station in life in all kinds of ways. And the entire satchel—surely it contained a lifetime's worth of treasure.

"What do we do?" she whispered.

"Put it back." He jabbed a finger toward the shallow hole. "We bury it, and we get out of here!"

Nikaia was quick to see the sense in that. Hands flying, she drew up the poke string, refastened the flap buckles, and returned the satchel to the shallow depression. They leaned into the surrounding dirt and pushed it back into place. She sat back on her haunches.

Yee Sim stood. "Nikaia…"

She looked up to see Yee Sim with his head cocked.

"I hear someone," he hissed, his eyes wide. "And he's near." He ducked into a crouch and peered through the leaves.

She heard the muffled sound of male voices and froze. Yee Sim brought a clay-covered finger across his lips. They crept forward through the trees, keeping cover and listening.

"I see them," Yee Sim whispered. He pointed toward the woods behind her.

She followed his gaze to see two dark figures in the bushes no more than a long toss of a stone away. She crawled over to hide behind the thick leaves of a salmonberry bush, and Yee Sim pressed into place beside her. She tilted her upper body to slide the haversack strap from her shoulder. She pulled out the spyglass and brought it to her eye, propping both elbows on her knees to steady her hands.

Her arms trembled slightly, causing the far end of the spyglass to spill the men out of her view. She surveyed the nearby trees and spied one with a forked notch at about eye level. Looking at Yee Sim, she pointed to it.

Yee Sim batted the air with his palms, as if to tamp down Nikaia's recklessness. "Careful," he mouthed.

Nikaia crept to the tree and settled the spyglass in the notch. The tree stabilized the lens well, giving her a clearer image of the men. The one in the large-brimmed hat had his back to her. A small gray adornment carved into some indiscernible shape was attached flat to the side of the hat. The other man, dark-haired with a black beard, was taller and thicker and wore a brown leather long coat. He gestured with his arms, but she couldn't catch any of the words.

Nikaia debated what to do. A quiet retreat homeward would surely be the safest action. And the wisest. At the same time, she was curious as to what, if anything, the men had to do with the gold.

Yee Sim touched her arm. "Let's go."

She hesitated.

Yee Sim drew nearer and hissed, "We need to leave!"

His insistence pushed Nikaia's intentions the opposite way. "No, let's get closer. I can't hear them."

"If you hear them, they hear us."

"Nobody hears me in the woods." She wanted to show Yee Sim her confidence, her daring.

"We should go, Nikaia." He shook her shoulder to pull her attention from the spyglass.

"*You* go." Using the thicker bushes for cover, Nikaia advanced toward the men.

Their voices became clearer, and soon she could decipher their discussion. She set her haversack behind a large boulder and looked back at Yee Sim. He was barely visible from his place beside the salmonberry bush. Nikaia crouched next to her bag and peered cautiously over the rock's rounded top.

"Fool!" the man with the broad hat said. "You think I'm mad enough to carry it about in open daylight? I credit more value to my life than that." He had a clipped British accent.

"It ain't so well-hidden where it lies," the taller one said.

"It's temporary. Until the crowd thins out." Broad Hat gestured toward the eddy, a half mile downstream.

"You know I'll need to bring him into this." The tall man sounded stressed.

"Tell him as you wish."

"Equal partners is the deal. There's no change there."

"No change there."

Tall Man stood a little straighter. "Split three ways."

Broad Hat nodded. "Three ways."

"So let's settle on when we fetch it."

"I'll do it alone. No sense drawing attention. I'll stash it well. Don't worry yourself."

"The hell you will." Tall Man raised his voice a notch. "We return together, or he'll suspect a double-cross. And I swear, that would not be so good for you."

Broad Hat closed the distance between them. "Keep your voice low before I cut out your tongue."

Nikaia drew her head down and looked behind her to Yee Sim. The men's threatening exchange made her want to run back, but she feared that any movement would attract attention.

Broad Hat continued in a more measured tone. "Tell him this. It'll be safe..." He dropped his voice lower, and Nikaia strained to hear.

What had he said? It had sounded like "In the garden of..." *What?* "Imperial stones?" She couldn't be sure.

Tall Man took a step back. "Do I look to be in a gaming mood? You play at riddles!"

"That's all you—and he—need to know at this time."

Tall Man's agitation was evident. "Tell me straight, or I swear he'll be after both of us!"

The broad hat shook from side to side. "We're too long gone. Back to the boats. You lead."

Cursing, the tall man turned in his boots and started walking. *Right toward me*, Nikaia realized with alarm. She pressed against the boulder. Willing herself to lie as still as the stone itself, she tried to even out her breathing. She feared her thundering heart would give her away as surely as a dancer's drum.

The bootsteps stopped a few paces from the boulder. They turned and hesitated. Nikaia pulled her haversack closer to her body and froze. He was but a step from having her in sight. Nikaia closed her eyes and thought of her guardian spirit. *Help me, Brother Owl. Shield me from this man.*

A sudden rustling of leaves came from nearby. The men spoke in urgent, hushed voices then trotted off toward the sound.

Seizing her chance, Nikaia slipped away in the opposite direction, taking care to plant her feet between the dry twigs. She passed the salmonberry bush, and Yee Sim fell into step behind her.

"Was anyone else there?" Nikaia asked. "Something distracted those men away from me."

Without breaking his stride, Yee Sim held out two egg-shaped rocks. "I'm glad it worked. The stone I threw was one of my favorites."

When they made it back to Front Street, the sternwheeler crowd was spilling back into the town's streets. Nikaia hoped she could provoke fewer questions if she subtly rejoined Papa and Klima down at the *Umatilla.*

In the distance, a gunshot rang out, and then another. The echoes ricocheted from the canyon walls. *More celebrating. The Umatilla must be pulling from shore.* The gunshots reminded her of the violence that happened almost every week in Fort Yale during disputes over gold and money. *I was such a fool to get so close to those men.*

"We mustn't speak of what happened today," Nikaia said.

Yee Sim nodded.

CHAPTER EIGHT

A PAIR OF BROWN HORSES HARNESSED to an empty stagecoach was secured to the hitching post outside the woodshop. Nikaia leaned against the carriage doors of the shop and listened. Papa was speaking to the driver about an order for wagon wheels to outfit the postal stagecoaches that carried mail from Fort Yale to Barkerville.

Nikaia thought about her pact with Yee Sim. She had never kept secrets—*well, not significant secrets, anyway*—from either of her parents. Papa would be distressed that she had ventured off without asking, but it wasn't the first time she had done that. However, he would be sorely vexed to learn that she had meddled with the gold and gotten so dangerously close to the two men in the woods. *More mischief-making. It's a good thing Mama's not here.*

She told herself she would tell Papa everything once the postal driver rode away. She leaned over the washbucket and rubbed clay from under her fingernails. Toweling off, she peered into the room she shared with Klima. Her sister was lying on the bed, lost in a book. Klima glanced up as Nikaia walked in to place the haversack on the clothes chest then returned to her reading.

Apparently, her family hadn't been too concerned about Nikaia's absence. Nikaia picked up *Voices of the Night*, by Longfellow. She flipped through its central pages, but images of the gold and the two men in the woods made it impossible to focus on the words. She reshelved the book. *I suppose I'll go stack the kitchen woodpile.* The repetitive motion seemed to help organize her thoughts. She mentally played through how she would describe to Papa all that had happened after she left the eddy.

At last, she heard the men's voices outside. The coach groaned mightily as the horses pulled it into the gravel.

Papa didn't enter the cabin right away, and Nikaia soon heard the gritty scraping of a metal edge being held to his whetstone. She decided to wait until she had his full attention. *When he comes inside, I'll tell him everything.*

She heard a chipping sound from the bedroom. Klima was striking a flint. Darkness descended early in the autumn days once the canyon walls curtained off the lowering sun. The yellow glow of Klima's oil lantern lent a soft light to the kitchen. Nikaia picked up a flat-bottomed tin scoop to clear ash from the woodstove.

She heard the carriage doors of the woodshop being pulled closed and then a sharp knock on the door. *That's odd. Maybe Papa has his hands full and can't work the latch.*

She walked over and opened the door. Two men stood on their porch. The nearer of the two was tall and finely dressed, his imposing nose buttressed by a crisp orange mustache. Under his arm, he held a large leather carry-all. The second man, as lean and wiry as a bird, stood back and smoothed his outsized muttonchops.

The taller man removed his bowler to reveal a thicket of hair. Were it not for its pumpkin hue, it would have resembled the bunchgrass that grew among the firs. His mustache swept upward, terminating in fine waxed points. She wondered if the mustache was designed to deflect attention from his mutilated left eye. A thin scar intersected his eye socket, leaving his lid permanently at half-mast. Still, it was not an unkind face.

"Good evening, Miss. Is Mr. Wales home?"

Nikaia tried to place his accent. *British?* The man took a step inside. "Your father."

"He's here... in his shop." Nikaia attempted to steady her voice. "I'll go fetch him."

"Thank you. You can tell him it's Constable Whittock. On a matter of some urgency." *Definitely British.*

Nikaia looked over his shoulder to see her father already approaching the cabin.

Papa looked inquisitively at the visitors. "I thought I heard voices. Good evening, gentlemen."

"Mr. Wales, I'm Constable Charles Whittock of the Fort Yale police force. And this is one of my deputies, Thomas Quigg."

"Good to meet you, Constable. Deputy." Papa nodded to each of them.

Quigg pulled off his satin hat and pressed flat his carefully combed and oiled black hair.

"We have a matter of some concern to discuss." Constable Whittock looked past Papa into the kitchen. "May we gather inside?"

"Of course." Papa led them to the kitchen. Wooden chair legs scraped against the floor as the men settled around the cabin's only table. Papa lit a lantern and hung it from a ceiling hook. The light swung and threw wild shadows across the floor. Constable Whittock rested his carry-all against a table leg.

Nikaia returned to the woodstove and scraped the ashes, still warm from the previous fire, into a tin pail. She positioned herself so she could watch the men, the angles of their faces alit at random intervals by the flickering lamp.

"I work for the gold commissioner, Mr. Thomas Elwyn," Constable Whittock said. His voice carried a sonorous weight of authority. "He's responsible for the safety and security of our settlement and the entire gold district."

Papa surveyed the two men. "I see. Actually, I thought that was the mandate of the Royal Engineers."

"The sappers are still here, of course. In addition to their road building, they continue to serve as our military police force to quell uprisings and Indian conflicts and the like.

"Mr. Elwyn has been commissioned by Governor Douglas to maintain law and order in this area. Which brings us to the matter at hand."

Papa leaned forward. "I'm certainly curious."

Constable Whittock paused and seemed to organize his thoughts. Nikaia shifted to better see his face, not wanting to draw attention to herself. The constable's expression was severe.

"Two troubling incidents took place earlier today," Whittock said. "In all likelihood, they're related. First, a chest of gold—dust and nuggets—was stolen from the gold commissioner's escort. It was part of a shipment from the Cariboo, due to be loaded on the *Umatilla* today."

The gold escort was a security measure in which the commissioner assigned guards to oversee the transport of gold from the northern mining operations to Fort Yale. Nikaia felt a wave of dizziness. Her hands suddenly numbed, and she dropped the tin trowel. It clanged on the stove's open door. The men went silent, and she looked over to see them staring at her. She hoped they wouldn't notice her flushing cheeks. She bent forward to pick up the scoop, hiding her face behind her hanging pigtails.

Whittock cleared his throat. "Naturally, the commissioner is in a state of uproar over this loss. The value of the gold amounts to several thousand British pounds." He lowered his voice, and Nikaia stopped scraping and strained to hear his words. "Secondly, Mr. Wales, a body was discovered earlier today in Riverside Flats. A fresh corpse, murdered. Two lead balls to the back, one through each lung. The victim was Matthew Doyle."

Papa lurched forward in his chair. "God's teeth! Who would look to do him away? Not that the Doyles aren't top-drawer scoundrels."

The Doyle brothers had a well-earned reputation in Fort Yale. Failing to secure their fortune in the sandbars, Elias Doyle and his younger siblings, Bart and Matthew, had long ago abandoned mining for more lucrative ventures in thievery and blackmail. If rumors were to be believed, many a miner had suffered a beating and lost his winnings to the Doyles, although Elias had the cunning to stay out of reach of the local police. Nikaia felt that his son Joshua probably pleased his father by carrying on the family's traditions of torment.

Papa stared at the center of the table for a moment. "May I ask why you're bringing word of this here?"

"I was hoping you'd tell me." Constable Whittock reached for his carry-all and set it on the table. He unbuckled its overflap and pulled out a long brown tube. "Perhaps you recognize this." He laid the spyglass between them on the table. "It was found today in Riverside Flats." He scrutinized Papa's face.

Papa's eyes widened, and he glanced at Nikaia. She remained still. *Didn't I put the spyglass back in my haversack?* She was sure she had felt it nudging her side through the swinging pack as she rushed home. *Wait. No, that must have been the carrots.* Then clarity struck when she remembered the notched tree.

She started to speak, but then stopped, paralyzed with uncertainty. She looked at Papa for guidance, but his eyes had settled back on the constable.

"We may be the biggest settlement north of San Francisco," Whittock said, "but there are only so many men carrying those initials. I think some answers are in order, Mr. Wales. James. Michael. Wales." He tapped the gold letters of the monogram with each word.

Papa nodded. "No question about it, that's my spyglass, Constable. I can tell you I have no idea how it got to Riverside Flats."

Deputy Quigg shifted in his chair, squaring off to Papa. He propped his hands in his vest pockets. The action propelled his elbows out to the side like stunted wings. "Perhaps you can describe your whereabouts this afternoon." His clipped words and English inflections contrasted with the gentleness of Papa's Welsh accent. The undercurrent of accusation was very clear.

"Certainly. Not just this afternoon, but most of the day," Papa said. "I was with half the town at the eddy. Picking up a supply of iron from the *Umatilla*."

"And afterwards?"

"Back to here with my load of iron plates."

"Any stops along the way?"

"None. Straight to my shop. And, gentlemen, I have no cause to tangle with the Doyles."

Constable Whittock smiled, but his eyes were hard, humorless. Nikaia thought she saw the scar across his eye darken and flare.

"Well, that's the damnedest thing about gold, isn't it? A chestful of it turns the most unlikely into villains."

"Were you with anyone on the way home?" Deputy Quigg asked. "Anyone see you?" His head bobbed forward with each question.

"I can't say anyone did, sir."

Deputy Quigg and Constable Whittock exchanged looks.

"I don't imagine you have any journeying plans?" Constable Whittock asked. "I'd appreciate it if you remained in Fort Yale. Until our investigation concludes."

"Of course. We have no plans to travel."

Nikaia heard the unsaid overtones. She felt indignant, even outraged, on Papa's behalf. She looked at her father, who was partially turned away from her, showing the crisscross of braces across his broad back. The X-shaped pattern brought to mind the image of a marked target. *Time to speak up.*

She set down the scoop, and the metal made a sharp click against the firebox floor. Papa looked over at her. Nikaia stood, wiped her hands on the front of her dress, and drew in a shaky breath. She opened her mouth to speak then stopped when Papa subtly lifted his open palm.

"Nikaia, please get the fire lit so we can put on some tea for our guests."

"Thank you, but that won't be necessary, Mr. Wales," the constable said. "I think we're done for now."

Shaking, Nikaia settled back to her knees in front of the stove.

Papa gestured toward the spyglass. "You'll be keeping this, then?"

"Indeed," Whittock said. "For a time."

"If I may say, I'd appreciate it being cared for until returned. It has some significance to me."

"Rest easy on that, Mr. Wales. It has some import to me as well, in regards to this case. And to Judge Begbie, I suspect." Whittock returned the spyglass to his carry-all. "It'll be locked in our evidentiary cabinet until this matter is settled." He rose from his chair. "I must also tell you this, Mr. Wales. The spyglass was found by one of my deputies. And I would have preferred that its discovery was handled more discreetly."

Deputy Quigg's cheeks reddened slightly beneath their furry coverings.

"I'm not sure of your meaning," Papa said.

"The fact is, word is out. About the spyglass being found near the body. And the detail of its monogram." Whittock dropped his voice as he leaned nearer to Papa. "Mr. Wales, I have concern that the Doyle brothers may take matters into their own hands. I recommend you keep your family close and your eyes watchful. It would be prudent."

The two men donned their bowlers and walked out into the night.

CHAPTER NINE

PAPA LATCHED THE DOOR BEHIND the men. Klima had emerged from her room, open-mouthed. She had evidently heard the whole conversation.

Nikaia bit her lip and looked up at her father. "Oh, Papa." Her voice quavered.

Papa held up his hand. He walked over and knelt at the stove. "Hold a moment." He took his time placing layers of kindling onto the remaining ashes. The fire coughed, spit, and came to life.

He returned to his seat at the table. For a moment, he sat there in silence, his hands connected by each fingertip, forming a steeple. Nikaia imagined he was turning over everything that had been said in the strange discussion. Outside, a horse whinnied, followed by the sound of receding hooves.

Papa brought his hands down to the table. "All right. Let's hear it."

Nikaia's voice trembled as she told him how she had taken the spyglass from his drawer that morning. "Oh, Papa. I'm so sorry. I know I should never have touched it."

Papa kept his face impassive. "Go on."

Nikaia related how she and Yee Sim had walked off from the *Umatilla* landing.

"You two left alone?" Papa said.

Nikaia nodded and instantly felt shame. *Was that so improper?*

Papa's face was serious, his mouth set in a tight line. He pulled in a long breath. "Go on."

Nikaia sensed that a discussion about Yee Sim would come another day. She told of how she and Yee Sim had come across the gold. Papa's eyes widened as she described the contents of the satchel.

"Did either of you touch the gold?" he asked.

Nikaia thought for a moment. "Yes. I picked up a nugget but then put it back."

"And Yee Sim?"

"He didn't touch it. We were scared. We buried it again."

She told him about the two men in the woods. "So we followed, and I... I used the spyglass to get a look at them. They were arguing—about the gold, I'm sure. And then they started walking in our direction and almost found me."

"Daughter, in the name of all that is good and holy..." Papa put his face in his hands. "Playing about is one thing, but you know better. Putting yourself into that kind of situation."

"I know. I know. I'm sorry." Her throat tightened, and tears began to spill from her eyes. *How stupid I was to forget the spyglass. Stupid to even leave the back-eddy. If I had only stayed with Papa and Klima.*

"Describe the men to me," Papa said.

Nikaia's recounting faltered as she struggled to remember. "One was taller. A big man. He wore a leather longcoat, brown. He had thick black hair. And a beard."

"And the other?"

"The other... I'm not sure. His back was to me." She closed her eyes. "His hat. It was a big hat, gray with a wide brim."

Papa looked thoughtful. "The tall one sounds like it might have been Matthew Doyle. The description fits."

Nikaia's mind reeled at the idea that the man she had seen was murdered. His body probably lay mutilated somewhere at that moment. *Where? In the tiny town hospital? In the police barracks somewhere?* She shook her head, trying to dispel the imagery of the man's corpse.

Klima slid onto the seat beside Nikaia. In a small voice, she asked, "What are we going to do?"

Papa rose and paced around the table. "Well, there's only one thing to do."

Nikaia and Klima exchanged looks. "Tell the constable?" Nikaia asked.

"Yes. We need to tell him everything, the complete truth."

"Will he put you in jail?" Klima asked.

Nikaia shook her head. *Silly girl. Papa's done nothing wrong.* But her thoughts leapt to the reality of it. *He's the main suspect, in both the gold robbery and the murder.*

Papa seemed to read her thoughts. "No, no, there's no cause for that. Constable Whittock strikes me as a reasonable man, a fair man. And I think he and Deputy Quigg are more concerned about the whereabouts of the gold." Papa stopped. "Nikaia, do you think you can find that spot again, where the gold's stashed?"

"Oh yes. I know how to find it." She pictured the path and the pattern of bushes that led to the covering of alder branches.

"Good. We'll show Constable Whittock where it's buried." Papa looked toward the window and stroked the growth of stubble on his chin. "But I don't think we should venture out tonight."

"I can find it, Papa!" Nikaia said. "Even in the dark, I think I could find it."

"I imagine you could. But I believe we're best staying together tonight, here in the cabin."

Nikaia caught the apprehension in Papa's voice. She recalled Constable Whittock's warning about the Doyle brothers. *Is it possible the Doyles think Papa killed Matthew?* Suddenly, the thought of going into the night with the ruthless Doyles out there somewhere seemed most unappealing.

Papa settled back into his chair at the kitchen table. He was quiet for some time. It was unusual for the cabin to be so silent.

Nikaia sat in the rocker across the room, sensing that her father needed time to reflect. He pulled out his pipe and thumbed some tobacco into it. He picked up a thin splinter of wood from the kindling pile and reached up to light it from the oil lantern hanging overhead.

Holding the flickering splinter to the bowl of his pipe, he drew air in until the tobacco glowed. "First thing in the morning, then. The three of us will pay a visit to Constable Whittock."

Nikaia pulled on her nightgown and slid into bed beside Klima. She lay still, her eyes open and ears alert. *Would there be more unexpected visitors this night?*

Klima plied her with questions for a time, wanting to understand more about the gold and the men. When Klima finally blew out the lantern, the room seemed to close in around Nikaia with unspoken questions and dread. If she and Papa led Constable Whittock to the satchel, wouldn't that raise suspicions that Papa had known about it and had stolen it? Maybe his leading the police to the stash would even add weight to the murder charge. Her stomach churned at the thought.

Her parents had taught her that the truth, the full and open truth, was always the best approach. But it seemed to her that Papa would be taking a terrible risk in the morning. She wasn't sure how such things worked.

She tried to sort through the little that she *did* know. The powerful gold commissioner wanted his gold back. The whole might of the colonial government would be intent on retrieving it. And there would surely be an expectation of punishment. Someone had to pay. With imprisonment or—she let out a small gasp—even a hanging.

Her stirring must have awakened Klima, or perhaps her sister was never asleep. Nikaia felt the warmth of Klima's hand as it brushed its way up her forearm and came to rest on the shoulder of her nightgown.

"I think tomorrow will help to settle things. Don't you?" Klima whispered.

Nikaia rubbed the back of Klima's hand. "I hope so."

We need hope, and maybe some luck. Her father was the main person, probably the sole person, under suspicion. Would the police even try to look elsewhere? Or would they just focus on Papa, seeking to snare him like a marmot?

Even worse was the killing of Matthew Doyle. Papa was implicated in that, and as much as Nikaia feared the police, the thought of the Doyle brothers seeking revenge sickened her with fear.

And the entire situation stemmed from *her* poor judgment. She silently cursed herself for her meddling, for not keeping to her own business.

And what of her family? What would become of them if they were to lose Papa to the jailhouse? As resourceful as Mama was, she would have few options to support the family. They would be destitute, relying on the favors of relatives to harbor them from poverty and ruin.

All those disturbing thoughts intertwined, leaving her stomach in knots. The stakes could not be higher for her family, for all that she loved. She lay under her blanket, rubbing Klima's hand. A bleak resolve took hold of her.

I must make this right. I don't know how, exactly. But please. Let it be so. And I swear a holy oath: I'll never make mischief again.

CHAPTER TEN

NIKAIA AWOKE EARLY TO THE aroma of bannock and bacon. The bed was empty beside her. For an instant, she imagined Mama and Klima fixing breakfast in the kitchen, then she recalled Mama's absence. She pulled the coarse blanket up to her chin and closed her eyes. *I wonder what Mama is doing right at this moment. Is Auntie Tsaht-koo suffering?*

She longed to hear Mama's voice and to tell her mother what had happened at Riverside Flats. The memory of that—*was it just yesterday afternoon?*—made Nikaia's stomach twist. Mama usually had some wisdom or practical advice that helped to settle her worries.

I wonder what she would say about the gold. Oh! The gold! Nikaia suddenly remembered the plan to retrieve it that morning with the constable. She pushed down the blanket and swung her legs to the floor.

She pulled off her nightgown and stepped into a deerskin skirt. She held up a light cotton blouse. Draping it over her chest, she looked out the window at the low gray clouds hanging over the canyon. Smaller branches of the fir trees bent and sprang back as gusts whipped the forest. She threw the blouse back in her clothes chest and wiggled her shoulders into a long-sleeved blue flannel shirt. Tightening her braids, she headed down to the kitchen.

Papa stood before the stove. One frying pan contained fatty bacon strips, and a second displayed the toasty brown surface of Papa's flatbread, or bannock. Wrapping a towel around the handle of the pan, he flipped the bannock onto a wood board and cut it into scones. Then he portioned out the bacon and the scones onto enamel plates.

"Eat well, girls," he said. "We have a good hike in store. And it looks like a chilly day out there."

Surprised Papa was not in a more somber mood, Nikaia exchanged a look with Klima. Her sister's bright expression reflected Papa's cheeriness.

After breakfast, Papa built up the fire, layering cross-hatches of knotty fir until the wood neared the top of the firebox. "This ought to give us some warmth to come home to," he said as he latched the door of the stove, silencing the low whistles howling from the stovepipe.

They left the cabin and walked into town, pulling their overcoats close as the wind swept the boardwalks of Front Street. Evidence of the prior night's revelry lay strewn everywhere: empty whisky bottles, a solitary leather glove, and the curled form of a bearded miner snoring peacefully in the dirt.

Past the schoolhouse, the barracks rose into view. The yellow logs of the structure were stripped clean of bark, and vertical lines of mortar ran smooth and gray between them. Nikaia and her schoolmates had watched the construction activity in the past year, the work being an interesting distraction viewable from the schoolyard. Papa said the barracks had been designed and built by the Royal Engineers, and its single level housed sleeping quarters for the military police, a jailhouse, and a small office. Nikaia had never entered a building of such official importance, and her pulse jumped as Papa pushed open the office door.

Deputy Quigg sat at a small wooden desk, attending to paperwork. A long black overcoat and a bowler hung from a corner hatstand. Across from the desk, six empty stools were aligned in a neat row against the wall. A dusty miner's rucksack with a wooden frame leaned in a far corner.

Deputy Quigg's black eyebrows jumped as he spotted Papa. He shook his quill pen over the white ceramic inkwell and capped the ink with a cork. "Mr. Wales." He nodded but remained in his chair.

"Deputy Quigg." Papa pulled off his hat and rubbed his hands together. "I think we may have some information for you, sir. And Constable Whittock. Is he in?"

"He is not." He waved Papa to a stool. "It regards Matthew Doyle, I presume?"

Papa gestured for Nikaia and Klima to take seats near the rucksack. Then, he slid a stool closer to the desk and sat. "I have no knowledge of Matthew Doyle's killing beyond what I learned from you and Constable Whittock last night. But I can tell of the spyglass and the location of the stolen gold."

Deputy Quigg gave a start. "Tell me all you know, Mr. Wales."

"May I ask, is the constable expected shortly? I'd like to address some of the questions he put to me last night."

"There's no need for that. He'll be out much of the morning. He's having tea at Bennett's and making plans for the Yale Ball. Evidently, there are some security concerns, given last year's fracas."

The Yale Ball was a fancy gathering held by Fort Yale's high society each fall. Last year, Nikaia had seen the partygoers assembling on Front Street, dressed in their bell-shaped hoop skirts and fur-trimmed gloves. Later, she had heard Mama and Papa discussing a disruption at the affair. A gin-soaked miner had crashed the party, hurling insults and brandishing a revolver. A flurry of men surrounded him, and in seconds, he was disarmed and dis-invited, landing in a heap on the boardwalk outside the hotel. Inside the hall, gaiety resumed, and the ball was the social event of the year, at least for the town's upper crust.

Deputy Quigg leaned his compact body toward Papa. "Tell me, then, how is it that you know where the gold is?"

Papa blew out a breath. "Sir, I'd prefer to leave my children out of this as much as we can. The fact is, my oldest daughter found the gold, quite by accident. It's buried in Riverside Flats."

Deputy Quigg leveled a piercing look at Nikaia. "Is that so?" He stroked his muttonchops. "Buried, you say. And how is it that one just happens to come across a cache of gold buried under the earth?"

"We followed tracks to it, sir," Nikaia said. "Then we saw the loose clay, and... well, it wasn't buried very deeply."

"And where is the gold now?"

"Still buried. We left it where we found it."

Deputy Quigg stood and moved around to stand beside his desk. "That's the second time you've said 'we.' Who was with you? Your father?"

Papa broke in. "No, she was with a friend. Yee Ah's boy."

"You can find this gold, this hiding place, again?" The words came rapid-fire from Deputy Quigg.

"Yes."

"And you left it precisely where you found it?"

"Yes, sir." Nikaia felt an itchy warmth spread from her neck up to her cheeks. She looked to Papa for reassurance.

But Deputy Quigg kept the questions coming. "Who have you told as to its whereabouts?"

"Just Papa. Um, and Klima, too."

"No one else?"

"No, just them."

Deputy Quigg leaned one hand on the desk and tapped his fingers against the papers. When he spoke again, his voice was louder and pitched higher. "This is far too important a matter to pursue without Constable Whittock. I expect he'll want to deal with this firsthand on behalf of the gold commissioner." He tugged on the chain attached to his pants loop and withdrew a silver timepiece from his watch pocket. He pressed the crown and the engraved cover plate sprang open. He studied the watch face. "He'll be another few hours. Come back here precisely at noon. He's best equipped to handle this matter."

"There's more to tell, sir," Papa said.

"Save it for the constable!" He sat back down, picked up the fountain pen, and waved them to the door. "And in the meantime, speak not a word of this. We'll retrieve the gold when you return."

Papa picked up his hat and stood. "As you wish."

Nikaia followed Papa and Klima out the door. The exchange with Deputy Quigg had rattled Nikaia. Coming to the police station seemed like a mistake. Their visit and subsequent revelations *had* only served to raise the deputy's suspicions. And make the police aware of Yee Sim's involvement.

"Will Yee Sim be in trouble?" Nikaia asked Papa.

He hesitated. "As far as I can see, he's done no wrong."

She noted Papa's carefully worded response. She dreaded the thought of Yee Sim's family being pulled into the mire. The sooner the gold was returned to the commissioner, the better. Then perhaps all would be settled.

Outside Bennett's Hall, a man was picking up discarded bottles and dropping them into a sack.

"Good morning, Alfred," Papa said.

"Morning to you, John," the man said, straightening. He waved at the debris. "Another night in Fort Yale."

"A bigger night coming up next week, though."

"Indeed. The well-heeled will be well hooched-up that night." Alfred laughed and shook his head. "If it's anything like last year, it'll be a lively evening."

Lively or deadly, Nikaia thought. Every Monday, schoolyard chatter would abound with fresh stories of the past weekend's mayhem from the Front Street saloons and gaming houses. The boys delighted in embellishing the gory details to shock the younger girls.

Nikaia thought it strange how a miner, having found good fortune with gold in a sand bar, would then risk it at the gaming tables. Many a miner's winnings slipped away with a roll of dice or the turn of a card. The frustration of that created brawls and havoc in the streets. Even when the cards fell in the gambler's favor, danger often ensued. Thugs walked the boardwalks at night, ready to beat and rob the lucky winners. Win or lose, the saloons were nightly producers of money, greed, and blood.

Nikaia and Klima walked ahead of Papa and Alfred through the silent early morning streets. Nikaia slowed her pace each time they passed the fine clothes and trinkets in the shop windows. She stopped in front of Meg's Dress Shoppe and welcomed the distraction of the displayed finery for both herself and for Klima, who had sunk into silence.

"Which one would you wear?" Nikaia asked.

Klima took in the display of three mannequins, their arms hanging downward at unnatural angles. Two were draped in morning dresses of heavy green silk with wide pagoda sleeves and high necklines topped by a tatted collar. The third was a full dress of white satin, its lower panels puffed out by crinolines.

Klima waved her hand as if stroking the pearly material. "I'd say that one."

"I like that one, too. I think it's a wedding gown."

"Oh." Klima giggled. "Well, if I had it, I'd wear it every day."

They walked on, gazing into the adjacent store windows. Nikaia stopped in surprise as they reached an alcove in which a man and boy stood. The man was lean and compact, his hard face staring down the street. The boy turned and glared at Nikaia. *Joshua Doyle.*

Nikaia took Klima's hand and hurried past, eyes averted. Joshua hawked on the boardwalk as they passed, the spittle splattering on the leather laces of Nikaia's deerskin shoes. The man appeared not to notice them, his eyes fixed on Papa.

When they were beyond earshot, Klima asked, "Who was that with Joshua?"

"It must be his father." Though she had never seen him, Elias Doyle was notorious for his devilry and misdeeds about town. Nikaia recalled one story whispered to her in a schoolyard hush from Agnes Druthers, who had overheard her father telling of a wicked episode in downtown Fort Yale. Elias Doyle had been playing poker in the York Saloon. With him at the table were Wilson DeLong and his two mining partners. Wilson was a fresh arrival in Fort Yale from San Francisco and was building a sluice upriver, near Spuzzum.

An argument over rules of play led to a drunken brawl. Wilson had the advantage, having at least thirty pounds and six inches over Doyle. He punched Doyle in the teeth and pitched him into the street. Apparently feeling self-conscious for stirring things up in the saloon, Wilson soon left for his tent by the river.

After a time, Elias Doyle returned to the saloon, hands bloodied. With a defiant expression, he strode to the wet bar and splashed his hands in the sink. Then he pulled a dagger from his belt sheath and dragged it through the washwater. Drying the knife on the side of his pants, he glared at the crowd in the saloon, daring anyone to speak a word.

When Wilson DeLong was next seen, the poor man was being carried aboard the next sternwheeler to New Westminster by his two companions. Dr. Polk later confirmed the rumor. DeLong's ankle tendons had been sliced, hobbling him for life. Doyle may as well have cut the man's feet completely off.

Nikaia glanced back at Joshua. Despite his meanness, she felt a pang of sympathy for him. His mother, a frail and desperate woman, had died of consumption the previous spring. Joshua lived with his father in a grim shack on Douglas Hill. Given his father's affinity for violence and drink, Nikaia imagined that life was tumultuous and dismal for Joshua.

I wonder if the man in the woods with Matthew was Elias Doyle. Would he kill his own brother? Stranger things had happened. Elias certainly had the temper for it. She tried to picture him wearing the broad-rimmed gray hat but couldn't be certain.

They returned home without incident and headed into the cabin.

"Devil take me, it's hot in here!" Papa said. "Nikaia, bring down the fire, would you?"

Nikaia selected a piece of cedar from the kindling pile. She opened the woodstove door and jabbed through the flames at the black and red stack. The squared-off logs broke into smaller lengths, and she wielded the stick to control the collapse of the fire. She tossed in the cedar and drew the door closed. Then she pulled out the coil-handled rod below the firebox to shut the stove's vents.

They ate an early lunch and talked lightly of inconsequential matters: the brisk weather that seemed to herald autumn, the readings Klima and Nikaia had to do before school on Monday, the outraged braying of Rooster as he sought shelter from the wind.

Nikaia was in no spirit to discuss their trek to the cache of gold. She didn't want to put a bugaboo on the outcome, and Papa and Klima seemed to agree.

They restocked their packs with apples, carrots, and the rest of the bannock then made their way back into town.

Inside the police office, Constable Whittock was seated behind the desk. Deputy Quigg hovered behind him, gesturing at a document on the desk.

"Good afternoon, Mr. Wales," Constable Whittock said, rising from his chair and extending his hand. "I understand we're leaving on a gold-seeking expedition."

"Yes, sir." Papa shook his hand. "Nikaia can lead us to it."

Constable Whittock strapped on a belt, pulled on leather gloves with gauntlet cuffs, and settled a revolver into a holster on his hip. Seeing Klima's eyes widen, he gave her a reassuring look. "Just a precaution, my dear. Always safer to have a firearm when gold is being transported." He looked at Deputy Quigg. "Better bring yours as well, Thomas. Oh, and the rucksack." He gestured at the miner's pack in the corner.

Deputy Quigg had changed into grimy trousers and scuffed boots, appearing well-prepared for the hike to Riverside Flats. "Sir?" he inquired.

"We need something to haul the gold back in. Unless your pockets are deeper than mine." Whittock's left eye remained clouded, but his good eye contained a sparkle of good nature.

He must be delighted at the idea of retrieving the gold for the Commissioner. As they walked, Papa told Constable Whittock and Deputy Quigg about the two men in the woods. They asked many questions. Nikaia responded as well as she could but had few details to offer.

"I suppose it could be two men with some other reason for being in Riverside Flats. Unrelated?" Quigg conjectured.

"Perhaps," Whittock said.

They left the boardwalk and headed toward the eddy, then took the upstream path from the river. Nikaia led the way with Klima on her heels. The route rose up to the bench and leveled off as they approached Riverside Flats. Nikaia hesitated as the trail disintegrated into the thicket. She backed up a few steps and found the fork that she and Yee Sim had taken. The men had to bend low to clear the bushy canopy that shrouded the path.

"Here it is," Nikaia said. She pointed at the broken alder branches and the small mound of loose earth and clay, just as she and Yee Sim had left it.

Deputy Quigg lowered his packsack and extracted a trowel from it. "Let's have at it, then," he said, passing the trowel to Nikaia.

She scraped the dirt away, pulling the metal blade sideways through the soil. Klima was quick to join in, her face aglow with excitement. Constable Whittock hovered, studying the surrounding ground. Papa and Deputy Quigg hunkered down to watch the digging. As the dirt piled to the sides, Nikaia started to fret. *I should feel the satchel by now.* She could feel Deputy Quigg's bird-eyes observing her.

She scraped more deeply, hoping with each pull of the trowel's edge that she'd feel the give of leather beneath it. She and Klima built up a berm of earth on all sides. Soon her trowel hit hardened ground and unmoving rock, a layer of earth long undisturbed.

She wiped her forehead with a grimy forearm. "I don't understand. It's not here."

Papa asked, "You're sure this is the spot?"

"I know it is! It's precisely the spot. Someone's taken it."

Dirt covering her arms and hands, Nikaia threw down the trowel and tried to bring order to her tumbling thoughts. "The man in the woods—he said something about retrieving the gold. He must have come back for it already." She looked up at Papa. Constable Whittock rubbed the points of his mustache.

Deputy Quigg swung the empty rucksack over his shoulders. He looked at Constable Whittock then stared at Papa. "That's inconvenient, Mr. Wales."

CHAPTER ELEVEN

WORRY CLOUDED THE AFTERNOON, BUT chores still needed to be done. And with Mama away, there were more than enough tasks to go around. Nikaia prepared to make a water run. No plumbing system existed in Fort Yale, so water for washing, cooking, and bathing had to be pulled from the river. Hauling the water was rigorous work, but Nikaia didn't mind it. Besides, more often than not, she would meet Yee Sim along the way as he performed the same duty for his family.

The day had warmed since the hike to Riverside Flats, so Nikaia went to her room and changed into a cotton shirt and light skirt. In the kitchen, she picked up the five-gallon bucket and started for the door. Looking back at her parents' bedroom door, she paused and set down the bucket. She stepped into the bedroom and picked up a slender vase of clear glass from the windowsill. *This will go to waste with Mama not here.*

The vase was filled to its lower third with violet-colored lilac petals submerged in water. Nikaia put her palm over the mouth of the vase and shook it, then she put the container back on the sill. The delicate petals drifted downward as she dipped her index finger into the liquid. She dabbed the fragrant water behind her ears.

She stepped outside with the bucket in her arms and headed for the river. As she walked past Yee-wa, she caught her image in the store's window glass. Only a few seasons ago, her profile had been as stick-like as Klima's. She realized she had grown half a head taller, and her reflection showed the long limbs and gentle curves of her mother. In recent months, she had noticed a change in how men and older boys looked at her. Being the target of their attention was puzzling, pleasing, and frightening, all at the same time.

She trekked to the river's brink and carefully picked her way around the small boulders. She settled her container into the water, taking care to keep the brim near the surface so as not to introduce sand.

With her full bucket, she threaded her way back along the path, balancing the weighty load against her hip. Her foot slipped on a wet stone, knocking her off balance. The bucket flipped over as she went down, and she cried out when the cold water splashed her from shoulder to belt.

Annoyed and feeling foolish, Nikaia got to her feet and took a step to test her ankle. Footsteps crunched on the rocks behind her.

"Are you hurt?" Yee Sim asked. He swung an empty three-gallon waterbag in each hand.

Nikaia waited for him to laugh, but his eyes held only concern. "No! Stupid bucket."

"Here, let me help." He tossed his waterbags to the rocks and reached for the bucket handle.

Nikaia was suddenly aware of her clothes clinging to her wet form. She pulled the shirt and skirt material away from her body, feeling the blood rush to her cheeks. Yee Sim had the decency to avert his eyes as he took hold of the bucket. Nikaia covered her embarrassment with a laugh.

"Wait here." He carried the bucket to the river and soon returned, managing the weight of the watery load easily with his wiry arms. He stepped carefully between the lichen-covered rocks. "Here, follow my steps up to the bank." Yee Sim scooped up his empty waterbags and handed them to her, then led the way up the rocky incline.

A male walking ahead of a woman, or even a girl, was a breach of proper etiquette. But Nikaia recognized that Yee Sim was granting her some privacy with her wet clothes. She was grateful not to be walking in front.

Yee Sim set the bucket down in the grass when they reached the cabin. The warm breeze had pulled most of the dampness from

Nikaia's clothes. Together, they poured the contents of the bucket into the rain barrel.

"Thank you, Yee Sim," Nikaia said. "For your kindness."

He looked into the barrel. "Let's get another load."

"I'll bring a pail, and we can both carry."

On the way back to the river, she decided to tell him about the constable's visit. Yee Sim listened as they walked, his eyes widening at the news of the murder.

"And today," she said, "we went to Riverside Flats with the police to show them the gold. But it wasn't there. It's gone."

He frowned. "They think your father has it?"

"I don't know." Nikaia felt a catch in her throat. "Yes, I think so. And worse, they think he killed Matthew Doyle."

"Oh." Yee Sim sucked in his breath.

They scrambled down the trail from the bench to the river.

Yee Sim spoke as they stepped into the sand. "The two men at Riverside Flats. One was Matthew Doyle?"

"Yes, I believe so. The black-haired man."

"It must have been the other man who killed him, then."

She nodded.

"I couldn't see him from my vantage point," Yee Sim said. "Did you get a look at him?"

"Not well. His face was hidden from me. Under his hat."

"What else? Shirt? Trousers?"

Nikaia thought a moment. "A gray shirt, I think. Yes. And black trousers. Both of a common type." She stopped and closed her eyes, trying to envision what she had seen through the spyglass. "Brown boots and... wait! The hat. There was something. A brooch or adornment of some kind. In the hatband."

"What did it look like? Do you think you'd recognize it again?"

"Maybe." Nikaia played through the scene in her mind. "It was small and a good distance away. Gray, I think. And it wasn't quite round... um, more like two circles that overlapped."

"Was it like an emblem? Or a cap badge? Perhaps like a military man would wear?"

Nikaia considered that. "No, I don't think so. It looked—I don't know—decorative." She scowled at her own lack of foresight. She should have noticed more details about the men.

They reached the river and filled the containers. With a grunt, Yee Sim hoisted one up onto his shoulder. Under their burdens, it was difficult to talk until they cleared the slippery rocks of the beach and neared the cabin.

Yee Sim slowed to close the gap between them. "Anything else you remember? His belt, perhaps? Braces?"

"He may have had a belt. I didn't see that. No braces, I'm quite sure." She tried to think of other details. "I don't recall anything else distinctive."

"What about his voice?"

Nikaia shrugged. "Ordinary?"

"The hat might be important. And the brooch," he said. "It could help us find him somehow."

"I suppose we need to tell this to the police."

Yee Sim set down the bucket and stepped closer. "The police think they've got the killer already," he whispered. "And why would they believe his daughter? I think it's up to us to find the man we saw. Yes, we've got to do this ourselves, at least figure out who he is. I don't see another way."

Nikaia stared at him. His face, normally so calm, had taken on a firmness. She wasn't sure what to say. So she simply nodded in agreement.

He picked up the bucket and continued to her cabin. "What do you think the brooch was made of? A jewel? Ivory?"

"I would guess it was stone."

They made it to the cabin and took turns pouring the water into the barrel.

"Jade?" he asked. "We have some jade brooches at the store."

"No, it was dull and gray."

"Well, did it look like something that might have been made here? In Fort Yale?"

"I don't know." She thought for a moment. "Maybe... if it was soapstone." Soapstone was abundant in the area, and native

Indians carved elaborate figures, pipes, and ornaments from it. "I suppose it *could* have been soapstone. And if it was, it could very well have been made here."

The door to Yee-wa opened, and Yee Sim's mother appeared. She looked over at them, her lips drawn into a tight line.

"I need to tend to my own chores," he said. "Tomorrow, let's go to Oppenheimer's. We'll shop for some soapstone."

"Thank you." Nikaia watched him walk away. She raised her hand to wave at Yee Sun, but she had already gone back inside the store.

She had been agonizing about how to untangle the mess, feeling desperate and alone. As she turned to go into her home, she realized Yee Sim had become something more than a friend. He was an ally.

CHAPTER TWELVE

IKAIA'S HOPES WERE HIGH AS she and Yee Sim headed to Oppenheimer's. The night had been a sleepless one as she lay in bed, imagining what the day might bring that could help resolve the mess she had created. Any course of action, even with slight odds of success, was preferable to stewing in her own worries.

With two stories and covering most of the city block, Oppenheimer's was the largest store in town. Portions of the building were constructed with brick—a hedge, Papa had told her, against the fires that devastated the town every few years.

They stepped up onto the veranda covered by a wooden overhang supported by slender white columns. A pendulum clock hung on the outside wall. Businessmen in top hats and bow ties leaned on the columns, smoking cigars and pipes on the shaded decking. Store workers in dress shirts and suspenders weaved through the men, carting steel-banded kegs and boxes into the store.

A large sign read, "Oppenheimer Bros. Mercantile Store." Smaller signs in the windows touted the store's vast inventory: Wholesale and Retail Dealers in Provisions, Groceries, Hardware, Mining, and Agricultural Implements. Havana cigars, tobacco, wines and liquors, clothing, dry goods, hats, boots, shoes, drugs, and patent medicine.

They made their way to the door and stepped inside the store. Nikaia had been in Oppenheimer's occasionally, shopping with Mama, but still she pulled in her breath at the sight of shelves laden with all things imaginable. Men, women, and children crowded the aisles, picking through the food shelves stocked with honey, rice, oatmeal, pearl barley, pickles, hams, bacon, and lard.

Looking for the jewelry display, they passed an aisle of open boxes containing butter and drums of cheese. Sawdust lined the boxes and spilled out onto the floor. Nikaia saw the striped kerchief of her schoolmate, Lillian, who stood with her mother at the far end of the aisle. Nikaia skipped ahead to avoid being seen.

"Good morning, Nikaia!" Lillian called out, then "Oh!" as she saw Yee Sim.

Lillian's mother cast a long look at the two of them. Nikaia gave a small wave and kept walking, quite certain that tongues would start wagging since she'd been seen out with Yee Sim. She looked back at him, but his face showed no concern. *Things are so much simpler for boys. Why do girls have to take such care around the town gossipmongers?*

The next aisle, stacked high with kegs of vinegar, resembled a makeshift fort. Smaller shelves held cocoa, coffee beans, cayenne pepper, and other spices. The variety of colors and smells were almost overwhelming. Her family's simple existence seemed far removed from the plentitude displayed throughout the store.

At the tills, two men in identical mustaches tended to customers bearing boxes of candles, matches, tobacco, brandy, and soap. The clerks laboriously scratched out each item on paper receipt pads.

"This way, I think," Yee Sim said, gesturing toward the far end of the store. They navigated through the miners' outfitting section, which offered the essentials for a newly arrived gold seeker: mackinaw suits, knitted sleeping caps, top shirts, buckskin mitts and moccasins, heavy woolen socks, sleeping bags, Wellington boots, tents, and compasses.

Yee Sim stopped at the end of one aisle where sheath knives, rifles, pistols, and kegs of gunpowder were displayed. "There it is." He pointed at a countertop display.

A young woman, her light brown hair pulled back into a neat bun, looked over at them from under the fringe of hair that curtained her forehead. She wore a white silk scarf around her neck, and its tassels hung down over her blue cotton blouse. Before her were several rows of wooden racks that showcased rings, bracelets, and other trinkets.

"Good morning," the woman said as they approached. She looked barely older than Nikaia.

"May we look?" Nikaia asked.

"Of course."

The racks held a small selection of brooches with different designs in maple, ivory, and jade. Nothing looked at all similar to what Nikaia had seen in the woods.

"Are any of these of interest?" the woman asked. She ran her tiny fingers along the top rack. She lowered her voice and looked at Yee Sim. "Lots of young men buy these for their special girls."

Nikaia hoped that Lillian hadn't wandered into earshot. She wanted to look at Yee Sim's face but didn't dare. Instead, she kept her eyes on the woman. "Do you have any brooches made of soapstone?" she asked, her words coming out rushed.

The woman scanned the racks, then reached under the counter. "We do." She brought up a wooden box and opened its hinged lid. "Yes, here are a few." She swiveled the box around and put it on the counter.

Nikaia sifted through the small pile. She pulled up a few and held them to the light. Her fingers latched on to one of the larger gray pieces. "Yee Sim," she said quietly, "I think this is it."

She held it up between finger and thumb. The brooch sported an intricate design of two owls. The birds were carved side by side, wings touching. Their outline gave the stone a double-oval shape. She handed it to Yee Sim, who flipped it over in his palm. On the backside of the brooch, a short pin extended, capped with a silver backing.

"This could be used in a hat," Yee Sim observed. "The pin is long enough."

Nikaia turned back to the counter. "Do you sell many of these?"

"Of that design? No, I've never sold a single one. Pretty, though, don't you think?"

Yee Sim spoke up. "Do you know who the supplier of these is? The soapstone brooches?"

"That one's been in the box since I started here. Let me think, though." The girl's demeanor changed as two men walked by the counter. One was a portly fellow with a brown beard and wire spectacles. Speaking in a thick German accent and carrying himself with courtly authority, he directed the second man toward the weapons section.

"I'm not sure I should say," the girl said, lowering her eyes to the counter.

The bearded man pivoted and approached. "Anything I can help with, Celeste?"

"No, sir," she said. "Thank you, Mr. Oppenheimer."

He studied Nikaia then turned to Yee Sim. "Looking for something for your sweetheart?"

Yee Sim looked over at Nikaia and then looked away. He shook his head. "Maybe someday."

Nikaia felt a rush of blood to her ears. *Is everyone in the store conspiring to embarrass me?* She stared at her deerskin shoes. Mr. Oppenheimer gave them a bemused look and walked away.

Yee Sim leaned over the counter. "Can you tell us who makes these?" he said, holding up the soapstone brooch.

Celeste sent a nervous glance toward Mr. Oppenheimer, who remained within earshot. "I really don't know where they come from."

After thanking Celeste, Nikaia and Yee Sim left the store. They walked past the chatting businessmen to one end of the veranda and sat on a bench.

"I think she knows who makes them," Nikaia said.

"We'll have to find another way. How many people can carve soapstone like that?"

"I'm sure there are many, not just here but all through the canyon." She had seen several soapstone carvings from relatives in Lytton.

She looked up to see Celeste coming toward them.

The clerk approached and leaned toward them as if to tell a secret. "Most of the soapstone comes from an Indian woman named Kalalse. She's local to the area. That's all I know."

"Celeste!" someone called from inside the store. "Customers."

"Thank you," Nikaia whispered.

The girl turned, and with lively steps, she hurried back into the store.

"*Kalalse.* How do you suppose we find her?" Yee Sim asked.

Nikaia swung her feet off the veranda. "Let's start at the reserve."

Yee Sim looked up at the ornate numbers of the clock face. "I'm sorry, Nikaia, but I can't. I'm due back to help with unboxing and restocking new items. I'll meet you later. I promise I won't be long."

"I'll find you."

They separated and Nikaia headed toward the reserve on the north end of town. As she walked, she wondered what her friend had meant when he'd told Mr. Oppenheimer, "Maybe someday."

She passed the first of the small homesteads on the reserve and shook those thoughts from her head. She had to concentrate on solving the mystery and saving her father.

CHAPTER THIRTEEN

NIKAIA WALKED TO A SMALL cabin on the reserve. Leading up to its doorway was a neat row of upright supports, fashioned from bundles of fir branches. Tied together at the top, the lower ends of the branches splayed out into the dirt. The conical shapes of the supports resembled a miniature encampment, as if tiny forest beings had hastily assembled them as overnight shelters. Weathered gill-nets had been draped over the supports, ready to be repaired once they dried in the sun. The webbing shimmered and glistened in the breeze.

She waved at a young girl playing with a stuffed doll on the steps leading up to the porch. "Hello, Lizzie. Is your brother home?"

Lizzie George waved back with her chubby hand and nodded. She disappeared behind the cabin then returned with Albert, who carried a long-handled axe.

He stopped when he saw Nikaia, his mouth opening in surprise. He dragged his fingers through his long black hair. "Your father need me?"

Nikaia attempted to be casual in her reply. "Oh! No. I saw a nice soapstone brooch at Oppenheimer's. I'm trying to find out who made it. I thought you might know."

Albert put the axe head on the ground and let the handle fall against the side of the cabin. He straightened his rolled-up shirt cuffs, studying them intently. "Not sure I would know that," he said, keeping his eyes on his sleeves.

Nikaia caught the stiffness of his words and sensed some tension, but she couldn't place why. "The shop girl said it came from someone called Kalalse. Do you know that name?"

"Kalalse?" He looked up and squinted at the clouds. "Kalalse. Yes. It's a name that an old woman on the reserve uses to label her basketwork. No one calls her that, though. She goes by her baptized name: Annie Adams."

"Oh, that's wonderful!" Nikaia brought her hands up to her chest, delighted.

Albert's face relaxed into a smile. "Annie weaves baskets mostly. But it wouldn't surprise me if she also carved soapstone. She's very good at handiwork, although she's getting on in years. It's been a long time since I've seen her."

"Could you tell me how to find her?"

"She lives alone, up on Chokecherry Flats."

Nikaia looked at him blankly.

He chuckled. "Hard to give directions, but I can take you there if you want. Some of my cousins live nearby."

"Oh, thank you, Albert." Her heart quickened with anticipation. She reached out and squeezed his forearm.

He looked at her warmly and gestured for her to follow him down. As they climbed a wide horse trail that rose into the hills above town, he asked about her family and Papa's work projects. She could feel his demeanor softening as they progressed.

Albert had been a familiar presence in her life for several years because of his work with Papa. She had long suspected that he was attracted to her. He often gave her soft lingering looks, and he would always find reasons to work late at his wheel-building tasks if she was there in the shop. But if he had a desire to be closer to her, he had never spoken of it or acted upon it.

She had ignored his apparent interest and dismissed it as an amusement. *I probably offended him,* she realized. She looked over at his powerful strides and his sinewy brown arms, lean and lined with narrow ridges that rose and fell as he moved his hands. *He's not unattractive, with his straight nose and dark hair dropping to his shoulders.*

"So what's so special about the brooch?" he asked.

"Oh, it's very beautiful." She tried to paste on a nonchalant smile but knew she probably sounded senseless with such a vague response.

She wondered how he would react if she made herself open to his attentions. He had a seriousness about him that made him hard to decipher. It was difficult to imagine him making her laugh the way Yee Sim could, but he was a hard worker and a gentle soul, and that counted for something.

And what of their families? Albert's parents had always been affectionate toward her. Nikaia guessed that they would be pleased to see their son come courting to the Wales' cabin. And Mama? Why she might even be thrilled to see her daughter connected to a respected native family like the Georges. As for Papa, she found it hard to predict what his reaction might be.

She tried to envision what might come about if the currents of her life flowed in such a direction. *Nikaia George.* She mouthed the name. It rested easily on her lips, not nearly so strange a name as *Yee Nikaia.*

She knew she was running ahead of herself, thinking of twists and bends far downstream when she didn't even have an oar in the water yet. But being with Albert would, in so many ways, give her the clearest path, the easiest route, to marriage and motherhood. *It would probably be the best arrangement for all concerned.*

Before long, the trail opened up to reveal a cabin nestled amidst a stand of ancient fir trees. Smoke curled from the stone chimney.

"Well, at least she's home," Albert said. He knocked and bellowed, "Annie! Annie, it's Albert George!" He turned to Nikaia. "She's nearly deaf."

When there was no response, Albert knocked and called again, and they heard the scrape of a chair on a wood floor.

The door was opened by a weathered old woman, her tiny frame evident even with several blankets layered over her shoulders. Nikaia was struck by her eyes, which were the darkest of browns, almost black.

"Alby, my goodness. It's you." The folds of skin around Annie's eyes deepened as she gifted him with a warm smile.

"How are you, Annie?"

"Oh, I'm well. Busy, as always." She waved her hand toward the interior of the cabin. "Are you here for tea?"

"Thank you, no. My friend here is curious to see some of your carvings."

She set her gaze on Nikaia. "Ah. Well, come in, and let's have a visit then." She stepped to the side of the doorway.

Nikaia was unprepared for the sight inside the cabin. The walls of the one room were lined from floor to ceiling with baskets of intricate designs hanging from nails and hooks. A black pot of water gurgled in the fireplace, cedar cuttings extending above its mouth. The warming cedar lent a sweet smell to the cabin. Woven containers at different stages of completion were laid out on the floor. The room reminded Nikaia of Papa's woodshop with its different work areas and specialized tools.

"The old woman needs to sit," Annie said as she settled into a rocking chair, the only seat in the room. "Please, find a spot on the floor."

Albert moved a small pile of cedar strips to clear an area and sat cross-legged on the plankboards. Nikaia followed suit.

"These baskets, they're so beautiful," Nikaia said. The tight weaving and even coils testified to Annie's workmanship.

Annie nodded and smiled.

"However did you learn to make them?"

"Oh, my mother taught me. Beginning when I was a young girl, even younger than you are now. My mother grew up in Spuzzum, where the best baskets are made." Annie's expression softened, and her eyes glistened with the reflected light from the fire. "She would select roots from the red cedars, pulling them out of the soil. Most of the roots were long, as long as she was tall. She'd stack them outside our cabin, letting them dry for many months."

The old woman started her chair to rocking. "Then we'd bring them to the creek and weigh them down with rocks in the cold water. A few days later, they'd be ready to split. Mother would carve an X-shape into the end of the root and split it all the way down, dividing it into quarters. Some roots were hard to split. She'd hold the end in her mouth and pull the split section away with both hands. The shorter roots and cut-offs, she'd leave for me to practice with. We spent many hours working until our fingers ached."

Annie studied Nikaia's face. "Say, are you Kate Wales' daughter?"

"Why yes. I'm Nikaia."

"You carry the look of your mother. She's a handsome woman and a kind one, too." Annie's cheekbones stood out as a warm smile settled on her face. Her features reminded Nikaia of the peeled apple heads that she and Klima would carve in the fall. With short knives, they carved out deep eyes, prominent noses, and toothless mouths into apples, then set the fruit by the woodstove until they shrunk into tiny faces, brown and wrinkled.

"How do you happen to know her?"

"Oh, it's been a long while. It was shortly after she moved here... from Lytton, no? She bought one of my smaller pieces." Annie reached to the floor and picked up a partially made weaving.

"One like this," she continued. "A berry basket. They've always been my favorites. I recall each one I've made. See here, child." She gestured for Nikaia to come closer. "This one's complete except for its tumpline. Some weavers use cedar slats for that. But my mother always took the time to weave a bundled coil as a carry handle. To match the rest of the material."

Nikaia knew the container well. In the spring, her mother would sling the tumpline over her forehead or chest to support the load of berries.

"My mother made larger burden baskets in the same way." Annie fingered the lip of the berry basket. She handed it to Nikaia, who admired the tiny stitches that locked the coils together.

"Weaving is part of our lives. Especially for the Nlaka'pamux people. Beginning from our earliest moments, when mothers twist and fold to shape our sleeping cradles." She touched various baskets near her chair as she spoke of each variety. "We weave containers to carry salmon from the river, to collect berries, nuts, roots. We store our food in them in the winter then serve that food in woven trays. You can even cook from some of the watertight ones by placing hot rocks into the water."

Nikaia was anxious to ask about the brooch. "Do you carve as well? Soapstone?"

Annie appeared not to hear. She got up and walked over to a large basket near the fireplace. The heavy piece was adorned with a fine-tiled checkerboard pattern. "See the weave on this market carrier? It's woven on the diagonal, so it can be flexed and folded." She demonstrated, pressing in the center of the material and bending over the upper half.

Albert George sidled up near Nikaia and whispered, "I think we should listen some more about the baskets first."

Annie took her seat again. "In time, our babies leave their cradles. Our sons and daughters marry, and we cloak them in woven ceremonial blankets. Those are made in a special way. Would you like to see one?"

Nikaia recognized the depth of meaning that the craft held for Annie. Her work was more than a skill, more than a livelihood. It was part of the fabric of her being. "Yes, I would."

The elderly woman pushed back on the rocker and let its rebound lift her to her feet. She walked back to the small room in the rear of the cabin.

Albert shrugged and leaned toward Nikaia. "Best to let her go on for a bit."

"I'm happy to visit with her," Nikaia said.

Albert seemed to appraise her anew. Nikaia thought of Albert helping her father in the shop. Annie's care in the basket work reminded her of how Papa approached his woodwork with a loving attention to detail. She recalled the day Albert had assembled eight arc-shaped pieces to form a wagon wheel, the peg of each piece fitting precisely into the round notch of its neighbor. Eight hardwood spokes converged from each section into a solid hub. As the final step in the construction, Albert hammered a thin cylinder of steel into the hub to serve as a bearing.

Before he had it fully seated, Papa noticed a minute line, the width of a mule hair, snaking along the outer surface of the metal. He stopped Albert's hammering and brought his eyes close to the center of the wheel. "This hub lining has a flaw."

Albert crouched alongside Papa and peered at the hub. Then he stepped back, eyeing the nearly completed wagon wheel.

"What do you think, son?" Papa asked him.

"I'll disassemble the wheel. Start over with a new bearing."

Papa laid a hand on Albert's shoulder. "I was hoping you'd say that."

Albert picked up a mallet to knock apart the outer wheel. He gave Papa a half-smile and said a phrase that Papa often used in the shop. "It's what can't be seen that makes for a wheel that lasts."

Annie emerged with a cloth bundle. She sat back down, and with slow and tender motions, she unfolded it across her lap.

Nikaia had never seen a blanket like it. The warp threads were invisible, completely enveloped by the weft strands. An intricate pattern of tan and dark brown stripes covered the material. The design was duplicated on the underside of the blanket.

"It's called twined weaving," Annie said. She drew in a quaking breath. "I buried my oldest son, David, in a blanket much like this. He was so beautiful in it. I had to make another one just like it." Her deep-set eyes pooled with tears as her long fingers fluttered across the blanket. "Just like it. To keep near me."

Nikaia was moved by the old woman's grief. "I'm so sorry, Annie."

Annie rocked in her chair, her moccasined feet tilting up on her toes as she leaned back.

Finally, she spoke. "Well, now. You asked about soapstone. These days, I prefer the silence of weaving, but I occasionally try my hand at carving. Or I did for a time."

"May we see some of your carvings?" Nikaia asked.

"I'm afraid I haven't any left. I sold most of them to various people in town. They come by here from time to time to see my work. And the rest, I've sold to the supply stores."

Nikaia considered that for a moment. "Annie, at Oppenheimer's, we saw a carving of two owls sitting wing to wing. It was a soapstone brooch. Was it one of yours?"

"Oh, yes. I do remember that one. A nice design for a small brooch. I've made several of those."

"Did they all go to Oppenheimer's?"

"Oh, they went to different supply stores. And I did sell one from here just this past summer."

"Can you tell me who you sold it to?"

"What curious questions. You really want that brooch, it seems." Annie peered at Nikaia. "Not right to ask an old woman to recall who bought a brooch two months ago."

Nikaia held her hopes in check as Annie sat and rocked.

"But that one... yes, that one I do remember. It was not one of my usual customers. How could I forget? I sold it to a lady of the night."

On the walk back from Annie's, Albert George paused at a fork in the horse trail. "I'm going to head up the hill and see my cousins, Mary and Eugene George. You know them?" He turned to look at Nikaia. "I'd be pleased if you joined me."

"Oh. I don't think I've met them." Nikaia wanted to find Yee Sim and tell him what she'd learned. "I think I should head home. But thank you so much, Albert. I'm very glad to have met Annie."

Albert nodded. His gaze lingered on her for several seconds, and he looked as if he wanted to say something important. At last, he said, "I hope I see you soon, then." He smiled and turned toward the higher trail.

Nikaia figured she was at a dead end with the brooch clue. Annie had no recollection of the name of the lady who had purchased the brooch and hadn't been able to offer a meaningful description. She would have to find another way.

As she approached town, Nikaia saw a small cluster of dark-dressed people walking down from Regent Street. She watched them cross the street and recognized Joshua Doyle among them. She looked to find a doorway to slip into, but to her alarm, Joshua Doyle spotted her and marched in her direction.

"You got some gall to be walking about on this day," he said.

"I don't know what you mean."

"They just buried my Uncle Matthew. Don't play dumb. I know all about your father." Joshua glowered at her, his eyes blazing.

Nikaia's outrage overcame her fear. "My papa had nothing to do with that!"

"That's not what the police think. And that's not what my father thinks, either."

Nikaia couldn't think of how to answer that. "I have to go." She spun on her heel and walked away.

Joshua cried, "My uncle Matt! He'll be remembered. His killing will be answered for. You'll see!"

Nikaia tried to keep her pace steady, but after a few steps, she couldn't help but break into a run. She crossed the street and made her way up the incline into the higher properties, not slowing until only a stand of high bushes separated her from Joshua's line of sight.

"Nikaia! What is it?"

She wheeled around and saw Yee Sim. He trotted toward her, his eyebrows lowered in concern. She started to speak, but the words caught in her throat and all that came out was a choked sob.

Yee Sim wrapped his warm hand around hers. "Come. I'll walk you home."

She felt that tragedy in some unknowable form was looming over her and her family. He seemed to sense her distress and gave her hand a series of squeezes as they walked. She told him about the encounter with Joshua and the fruitless visit with Annie. He listened, saying nothing but giving her sympathetic looks.

A thought occurred to Nikaia. "What about the satchel? The one we dug up? That might be another clue to identifying the man in the woods. I've seen bags like that in Yee-wa."

Yee Sim nodded. "Yes, we do have those."

"Maybe he purchased it there?"

"Every supply store in Fort Yale sells those same satchels, including the Hudson's Bay trading post and Oppenheimer's. And that bag is standard issue for the Royal Engineers. It's a common item."

"So it could have been purchased anywhere."

"Yes."

She tried to fight off a sense of defeat. Unless they were lucky enough to stumble across a man wearing the same hat, their search seemed hopeless.

"Time to take stock," Yee Sim said.

"Take stock?"

"Yes. Figure where we are in all of this." He slowed his pace. "The hat brooch seems to be a dead end. And the satchel that held the gold is too common to be a useful clue. Is there anything else you remember? What the men wore? What they said?"

She thought back to the encounter in the woods. "There was something. The man with the hat said something about the gold being buried with the imperial stones. It was odd."

"Imperial stones? It doesn't mean anything to me."

"Nor to me."

Since their walk had slowed, Nikaia began to feel self-conscious. She released her hand from Yee Sim's grip.

"Is there someone who might know?" Yee Sim seemed to be asking himself.

She considered the roster of people who might be able to help. Papa? Maybe. Or Mama. *Imperial stones.* The phrase seemed strange. She wondered if it was perhaps biblical. That brought to mind the most learned man she knew.

"Reverend Poole," she said. "He may know. If anyone knows, he would know. I'll find a way to ask him on Sunday!"

CHAPTER FOURTEEN

"O Trinity of love and power!
Our brethren shield in danger's hour;
From rock and tempest, fire and foe,
Protect them wheresoe'er they go;
Thus evermore shall rise to Thee
Glad hymns of praise from land and sea."

FOR A QUIET-SPEAKING MAN, PAPA had a singing voice that was full and rich. His deep tones joined with the other congregants to fill the tent. Behind them, Mrs. Hampton fingered the melody on the harmonium, her plump face glistening as she worked her legs furiously on the foot pedals.

Nikaia was pleased that the services were held in the makeshift tent. Sometimes in colder weather, the more well-to-do parishioners would offer up a house as a worship place. Those services were more comfortable, with padded chairs and heated rooms, but Nikaia preferred the familiar canvas walls and wooden seats of the ministry tent. She would miss the tent when the Royal Engineers finished their work on the new Anglican church.

Papa had been quiet in the two days since the unfruitful trip to Riverside Flats. He spent long hours in the woodshop, and when he returned to the cabin in the evenings, he seemed tired and lost in thought. His silence made Mama's absence even more noticeable. It was reassuring to hear his voice strong and unwavering.

And Klima, cueing off of Papa as always, trilled out the melody with gusto. Nikaia was relieved to see her sister's spirits lifted. Klima, usually so quick to sass and laugh, had withdrawn the past few days. She had spent the last two evenings working quietly on her schoolwork in the bedroom.

As the final chords of the hymn faded, the rotund Mr. Dawes, wearing a black frockcoat, walked to the front of the tent. He welcomed the congregants and announced that Reverend Poole was in Lytton. The reverend's presence had been requested by the native Indians in that area, who were hoping to establish a church and have the full-time presence of a minister. Murmurs of approval arose from the churchgoers.

Nikaia bit her lip in frustration. Reverend Poole would be away for the next two Sundays. Another dead end. It seemed that she had few courses to follow to help her father. With each angle she pursued, the route disintegrated like an abandoned deer trail.

The thin walls of the tent billowed in and out as chilling breezes found their way through the canvas seams. A wave of shivers rippled through her body. She clenched her forearm muscles and wondered if her shuddering was from the cold or from the sense of despair that shrouded her thoughts. As the service progressed, she was grateful for the Anglican traditions that prompted the congregation to repeatedly stand, sit, and kneel. The movements helped to fend off a coolness that seemed to be working its way into her bones.

Mrs. Hampton pumped out the final strains of the closing hymn, "Lo! He Comes with Clouds Descending." Three women rose from the seats in front of Nikaia.

One lady with a cameo pin of carved shell attached to the collar of her dress turned and laid a glove of soft black goatskin over the chair in front of Klima. She gave the girls a pleasant smile as she pulled on her overcoat. "I wondered where those sweet voices behind me were coming from."

The heavyset woman beside her lowered her pleated fan and examined Nikaia and Klima. She wore a brown dress fringed with white lace, her gray hair pulled back from her forehead in a practical bun. "It's a refreshment to listen to the sound of Christian worship, especially in this godless country."

The third lady, who wore a high-brimmed bonnet and whose frame was of equally large proportions, nodded emphatically, causing the folds of skin below her chin to waggle. "Indeed. And speaking of which, why is *she* here again?" She glared with disapproval across the tent.

Nikiaia turned to see a woman sitting alone with her curly red hair barely contained under a loose bonnet. She held a handkerchief to her eyes and was crying openly. Hard days had cut deep lines into her face. Her dress of green gingham was faded and threadbare at the elbows, but not of poor quality. Nikaia was sure she had seen the woman on previous Sundays.

"I suppose the York is closed on Sunday mornings," the lady in the brown dress added.

Her friend gave her a scandalized look and covered her tittering with the hat she held in her hand.

As they walked from the church, Nikaia asked Papa about the heavy woman's disdain for the red-haired lady.

"Oh, that's Mrs. O'Hare. The ladies at church don't approve of her because she makes her livelihood from the companionship of men. Certainly what she does goes against the teachings of the Bible. But it wasn't so long ago she lived in town with her husband, a miner. He got mixed up in some money borrowing. Things got out of hand, and there was a fight in the Galloway saloon. Police came to settle things, and... well, I'm not sure what happened. There was gunfire, and Stanley O'Hare was shot dead."

Nikaia and Klima listened, wide-eyed.

"Mrs. O'Hare was left destitute and without a home. So she does what she has to do. I expect one day she'll have to answer for it." He looked at the behatted ladies exiting the tent's canvas door. "But it's not for us to judge."

A lady of the evening. The thought occurred to Nikaia to ask Mrs. O'Hare about the twin owl brooch. But she felt it would be wrong at that moment to intrude on the poor woman's private sorrow.

CHAPTER FIFTEEN

THE CABIN DOOR CREAKED AS Nikaia eased it closed. She paused, tilting an ear against the surface. All was silent inside her home. She hesitated, then she pulled her overcoat close against the chilly air and stepped into the darkness.

She knew full well she was risking the worst scolding from Papa. It was *never* safe for a young woman to be out alone at night. *Desperate times call for desperate measures*, she told herself. She hurried and kept to the shadows as she neared the lights of Front Street.

Even from outside the thick double doors of the York, she could hear muffled laughter, yelling, and music. She pulled in a deep breath to embolden herself and swung open the door, recoiling at the dank odors of tobacco, beer, and spirits so heavy she could almost taste them on her tongue.

The room was astir with activity. On low tables, quartets of men faced each other over tin tankards and decks of cards. Along one wall, dealers worked a bank of faro tables, their sleeves rolled back and banded with elastic at the elbows. Serving girls bobbed and weaved among the men, carrying platters with bottles of spirits and beer. Nikaia blinked in surprise at their necklines, which were cut low and revealed much skin as the girls bent to top off the tankards. In the corner, a bald man pummeled the keys of a tuneless piano in a valiant effort to be heard above the din. Overhead, the low ceiling was partially obscured by a muddy brew of cigar and pipe smoke.

Nikaia ducked into the crowd, hoping to be inconspicuous. Her heart drummed in her ears. A cluster of six young men linked arms near the piano and burst into song in a chorus that had few notes in common with the bald man's efforts.

> *He's hitching at Yale for a night on the town,*
> *There's whisky in the bottle, there's blood upon the ground,*
> *The cards are on the table, his poke is on the line,*
> *Will he keep the ladies waiting? Come on, seven! Come on, nine!*

> *Hand upon the holster, his luck could not prevail,*
> *A debtor's got no better lot than sleeping in the jail,*
> *His wife is home a-waitin', the source of all his fears,*
> *He'd rather take a beating with the Royal Engineers!*

A third verse was attempted but dissolved into drunken laughter as the men stumbled over the words.

A lean young man barely old enough to shave shuffled up to Nikaia. He leered, taking an indiscreet survey of her from head to toe. "I'm Lloyd," he said, his voice booming.

Nikaia winced at the cloud of beer that carried his words. "I'm leaving," she replied and escaped through the swinging door back into the night air.

She leaned against the wood paneling of the saloon, her head tilted back to face the sky. *This was a terrible mistake.* She closed her eyes, clearing her head of dizziness from the smoke.

A click-clack of boot heels sounded nearby. Two miners stumbled toward the saloon. It was apparent that the York was not their first stop of the evening. They slowed and eyed Nikaia.

The one with his cheeks covered in wolflike tufts of hair walked right up to her. "Well, well," he said, his face rearranging into an uneven grin.

She felt exposed, and the York's crowds suddenly seemed a desirable refuge. She jerked away from the wall and fled back into the saloon.

The miner called from behind her, "I'm just being friendly!"

His partner hooted in laughter. Nikaia twisted into the room, past the barmaids and the poker tables.

Oh my gosh, there she is. Seated at a low table was the lady from church, dressed in vivid mulberry purple. She smoked a thin cigarette. Two other women sat with her, as well as a fair-haired girl no older than Nikaia.

Unlike others of her profession, Mrs. O'Hare wore little rouge or foundation. With her straight nose and tumbling red hair, she must have been considered very pretty in her younger days. The advance of time, as well as the habits of tobacco and saloon spirits, had not completely undermined her attractiveness.

Nikaia drew in a deep breath, pulled back her shoulders, and walked up to the table.

All of the women looked up at her. Mrs. O'Hare showed no signs of recognition.

"Mrs. O'Hare, my name is Nikaia Wales. I'm... I'm sorry to disturb you, but I wonder if I might have a moment with you."

The woman's eyes hardened. "What is it, child?" She glanced at the men seated at nearby tables. "And call me Frannie, for God's sake. I'm not my mother-in-law."

One of the other women snorted. Her large head and protruding lower teeth lent her a horse-like appearance.

"Sorry. Frannie." Nikaia looked at her shoes, unsure where to begin.

"Out with it, then," Frannie said. Then her tone softened marginally. "What's troubling you, and what has it to do with me?"

"Likely, nothing, ma'am," Nikaia said. "But I have a question. I've seen a brooch, a pretty brooch of soapstone. And I thought... well, I thought you might know of it." Blood rushed to her ears.

Frannie pulled her head back. "A brooch? Why on God's earth would you think I might know of it? Was it stolen? And why would you even care, girl?"

I'm a ridiculous fool for even being here. But I've come this far, I can't stop now. "It's quite peculiar, and I'm trying to find its owner. It's carved in the shape of two owls, one beside the other."

Frannie shrugged. "I haven't the slightest notion. And frankly, I'm puzzled as to how you come to be asking me about it."

Nikaia couldn't very well tell her about Annie's remembrance of selling the brooch to a lady of the evening. At least, not without further offense. "I just... I saw you at church, and I thought you might know."

"Sorry. Now you'd best be getting home. Besides"—she made a sweeping gesture with one hand—"you're not helping with our business here."

The other women snickered.

Nikaia put her hand to her face and took a step back. "I'm so sorry."

The young girl at the table briefly raised her pale blue eyes, then returned to studying her empty hands folded in her lap. Her expression had been a plaintive look, and it suddenly dawned on Nikaia that the girl was in York Saloon for the same reason those women were.

Nikaia took a long route home, steering clear of the clamor of Front Street. As she neared the cabin, she took in the comforting aroma of smoke from the woodstove consuming its nightly load of green wood. Inside, she went straight to her room, undressed, and eased into bed beside Klima, hoping the odors of beer and cigar smoke would dissipate from her clothing by morning.

Her mind flashed back to the blue-eyed girl in the saloon. Her chest ached, and a horrific thought struck her. *If Papa is jailed, I could find myself in that circumstance, doing the unthinkable just to survive.* She shivered. *It will never come to that. Not for me. Or Klima or Mama. Surely.* She wrapped her arms around her torso and forced her thoughts to other things until sleep finally came.

CHAPTER SIXTEEN

"YOU GIRLS WAIT IN THE cart. I'll be right back." Papa handed Rooster's reins to Nikaia, jumped from the wagon, and walked into the post office.

A row of mules and horses were tied to the hitching rail in front of the post office. Rooster eyed them with disinterest. While Nikaia and Klima waited, a driver navigated a stagecoach up from Albert Street. The coach was painted in bright red and yellow and labeled Barnard's Express Services. The driver pulled his four-horse team up beside their small cart and flipped the horses' lead over the rail.

Another man emerged from the covered cargo area and passed a mailbag onto the shoulders of the driver. The two of them began hustling parcels and bags into the post office.

A few minutes later, Papa emerged and took a meandering route back to the cart. His eyes were cast down, and he carried an opened envelope in his hand. He came over and passed the letter up to Nikaia. "It's from your mother."

She scanned the letter, with Klima looking over her shoulder. The word from Lytton was not good. Auntie Tsaht-koo was worsening, and Mama feared her sister had little time left.

"I need to get to Lytton to be with your mother," Papa said. "And with Aunt Tsaht-koo." His brow wrinkled as he scratched his fingers through his hair. A lungful of air fluttered past his lips. "I hesitate to bring you girls."

Nikaia thought of her Mama and her suffering aunt. "I want to go, Papa."

"I do, too," Klima said, her face stricken.

"You girls are about as stubborn as your mother," he said, shaking his head. He took back the letter. "Mama wants you there. But we're going to need to talk about how to stay safe in the midst of the disease."

Nikaia nodded solemnly.

"We'll be careful," Klima said.

Papa looked at them for a moment. He turned and walked back into the post office. When he came out, he was with the driver from the postal stage.

"I aim to reach Cook's Ferry by tonight," the driver said. "I expect I can get you to Lytton by late afternoon."

"Much appreciated," Papa said. "We'll be at the Express Office in one hour."

Papa leapt into the cart and took the reins from Nikaia. "I need to get you and Klima home so you can pack some clothes and food. I'll make arrangements for Rooster. We'll be gone for a few days, I expect."

He eased the reins on Rooster, and the mule cart jerked forward.

The freight wagon was a covered stage, its brown canvas canopy pulled tight with ropes across the hoop frame. The driver, a young man with a goatee and springy brown hair that escaped his cap at all angles, brought the last of four fresh horses into position. Nikaia watched with interest as he adjusted the elaborate harnesses.

The cargo area was filled with crates, kegs, and several postal sacks. She saw no place to sit.

Papa came up beside her. "We'll make it comfortable. The next passenger stage doesn't leave until tomorrow morning, so we'll have to ride with the freight."

With Klima's help, Nikaia rearranged the boxes to provide a sitting area. They unloaded their blankets and some of their clothes and spread them on the floor for cushioning. The front bench of the wagon was exposed to the elements, barely wide enough for two people to sit side by side. Papa took a seat on one end of it.

The driver leapt into the wagon and sat to Papa's left. "All set?"

Papa nodded. "Girls, this is Mr. Lagner. Mr. Lagner, my daughters: Nikaia and Klima."

Mr. Lagner raised a hand to his cap. "Ladies. Sorry to hear about your auntie. We'll get you to Lytton as fast as can be done." He released the brake and whipped the reins free.

Partway through town, Mr. Lagner stopped the horses outside the police barracks. Papa got down, trotted up to the door, and knocked. He waited a time and knocked again. There being no answer, he returned to the cart.

"Do you have a paper and pencil?" he asked Mr. Lagner.

The driver leaned back to the wooden toolbox. Flipping the latches, he pulled up its hinged top and removed a sheath of receipts and a stubby graphite pencil.

Papa penciled out a note then looked up at Nikaia. "With the Matthew Doyle matter in question, I'm letting Constable Whittock know of our trip. No sense raising suspicions."

The need to inform the police hadn't occurred to Nikaia. *Thank goodness he didn't overlook that in the rush to get to Lytton.* It reminded her that Papa was probably fretting about the Matthew Doyle murder as much as she was, although he had said little of it since they'd returned from Riverside Flats.

Papa stuffed the note into a crack in the barracks door then climbed back onto the wagon. The cart swayed as they left Albert Street and entered the grooves and ruts of the Cariboo Wagon Road.

The trip to Lytton would take a full day. Nikaia and Klima had made the trip only once, and in the reverse direction, four years before when the family had moved from there to Fort Yale.

Once they got on their way, Klima's spirits were revived, her face flushed with excitement. From the cargo hold, she called out questions to Papa and Mr. Lagner about the horses, the road, and the cargo. Mr. Lagner was an agreeable sort and seemed to enjoy sharing his knowledge of the canyon roads.

Papa appeared pleased to have Klima distracted from the unpleasant circumstances awaiting them in Lytton. As for Nikaia, her thoughts were elsewhere. *Lytton. It looks like I'll get to see Reverend Poole after all.*

CHAPTER SEVENTEEN

"THERE IT IS, LADIES," Mr. Lagner said, turning back to the girls with a grin.

Nikaia and Klima scrambled toward the open front of the freight wagon. Ahead, the double towers of the newly built Alexandra Bridge soared into view. Matching towers on the far side of the river became visible as the freight coach descended from the west side of the river.

The cart passed the anchorages, where the bridge cables terminated in a bed of rock and mortar. Nikaia marveled at the bundled wires, each the girth of a gallon cider keg.

"Those are the main cables," Mr. Lagner said. "And the smaller ones dropping down from them to hold the deck up, those are the suspenders." He pointed at the bridge. Its wooden decking arched upward toward the midsection of the span.

The coach tilted and creaked as the wagon advanced. Nikaia appreciated Mr. Lagner's gentle way with the four horses. He was light on the lash and encouraged them with whistles and by calling out their names as they labored up the steep inclines. "Go, Black! That-a-boy! Come on, Star, keep it going! Oats ahead!"

Mr. Lagner explained that the four horses would be changed every twenty miles or so at the hostling stations, which purchased unbroken horses and trained them for staging. The hostlers took jealous pride in their care, giving each horse its own name and harness. The experienced horses were cooperative in their pulling work, knowing that a good meal and a warm stable awaited at the next station.

Earlier in the day, Mr. Lagner had pointed out the many ditches dug into the earth along the riverbanks. They were sluice operations. The creation of them required considerable labor, but Mr. Lagner said they yielded more gold than the more common pail, pan, and rocker operations.

The river had been in view for much of the journey. He told them the names of the sand bars that lay between Fort Yale and Spuzzum: Wellington, Sailor, Pike, Madison, Steamboat, Humbug, Surprise, Washington, and Kelly bars.

"The bridge is named after Princess Alexandra, of Wales," Papa said, a touch of pride showing. "Queen Victoria's daughter-in-law. It's quite a sight, isn't it?"

"Oh, yes!" Klima exclaimed.

Nikaia agreed. The bridge truly was a wonder. When her family had moved downriver to Fort Yale, they had crossed the river there on a simple ferry boat.

Nikaia noticed some movement down toward the river. "Look at the dip-netters, Klima!"

A dozen men and women worked along the far side of the river narrows. Salmon meat hung from fish-drying racks like a collection of scarlet flags.

On the far side of the bridge, a tollhouse had been erected. Beside it, a squat man with a close-cropped beard stood by the bridge decking. Another man, tall and red-shirted, sat in a wooden stall. He looked up from his writing papers and watched the cart approach.

Papa turned to Mr. Lagner. "How do you plan to handle the toll at the bridge? I can cover the fee."

"Much obliged, John, but no need. It's taken care of," Mr. Lagner said. "Courtesy of BX."

"What troll at the bridge?" Klima asked.

Mr. Lagner and Papa laughed.

"I think someone's been reading too much Grimm," Papa said.

Mr. Lagner pulled up on the reins, and the wagon came to a stop at the tollhouse. The squat fellow's boots came nearly to his knees, and his oversized topcoat gave him a squarish outline. Nikaia thought with a private smile that he did bear something of a resemblance to a troll.

"Good morning, gentlemen," the tollman said. "Freight conveyance, four horses: eight shillings and fourpence sterling. Good to see you, Lagner."

Mr. Lagner returned the greeting. "Any word on the state of the road between here and Lytton?" He held out the money.

"Nothing unusual," the tollman replied. "Some rain last night, causing some minor slides. Nothing you can't steer the team around." He accepted Mr. Lagner's payment.

The man in the red shirt set aside his writings and walked over. Nikaia could see a holstered revolver strapped to his belt.

"Good day, gentlemen." Red Shirt peered into the covered part of the wagon. "May I ask the purpose of your travels this morning?"

Mr. Lagner responded, "The usual supply run, up to Barkerville. My friend here and his family will be going as far as Lytton."

The man studied Nikaia and Klima in turn. Nikaia recognized his tunic as one of the Royal Engineers. He turned to Papa. "Your name?"

"John Wales."

Red Shirt tilted his head to view further into the freight area. "A bit unusual, Mr. Wales, that you wouldn't take the passenger coach up to Lytton?"

"It is. This is the earliest ride we could arrange."

The man raised his thick eyebrows.

Papa added, "We're tending to some pressing family concerns in Lytton. My wife's sister is ill, struggling with the pox."

"Ah. A lot of that going on up there, I'm afraid." He looked at Nikaia. "Particularly with the natives." He scanned the contents of the cart. "I'm loath to delay your journey, but I'll need to take an accounting of your cargo. It may take an hour."

Mr. Lagner frowned. "I was hoping to make Cook's Ferry by tonight. I hadn't factored in an inspection." When Red Shirt's eyes hardened, Mr. Lagner was quick to add, "Not that it's my place to question the government's business, of course."

"Of course." Red Shirt folded his arms across his burly chest. "It seems there's been some misplaced gold from the commissioner's office. So we're on the watch."

"Could we do it at the lodge? I can switch out my horses there at the same time."

The man looked over at the high-walled building beyond the tollhouse and nodded. "Let's get it started then."

Papa waved the girls out of the coach. "You have one hour, girls."

"Can we go down to the river and watch the dip-netting?" Nikaia asked.

"That'd be fine, but I want you within earshot of my whistle. I don't want Mr. Lagner to be delayed any longer than he already is."

Nikaia and Klima found a well-used route leading down the steep bank toward the fishermen. The river was choked into a narrows there, the bank thick with red cedar and Douglas firs. The sides of the river ran red with spawning salmon struggling to make their way upstream through the gorge.

Mama had warned the girls to respect native fishing sites, and they slowed as they approached the fishermen. Nikaia sat on a boulder and motioned for Klima to join her. Klima shinnied to the top of the rock and stood up to get a better view. The smooth rock reflected the warmth of the noonday sun.

Below, a woman hung salmon on a drying rack, and beyond her, a young Indian worked his net from a rocky outcropping. Shirtless, he was tethered to the bank by a leather cord around his waist. He held a long pole of maple wood and moved the net at its lower end in fluid motions through the churning water. The pole was tied to the shore with a smaller line.

The fisherman swept his arms downstream. The pole jerked.

"He got one!" Klima exclaimed.

The man hefted up a sockeye salmon, its head and tail flashing red in the cedar strands of the net. With a twist of his arms, he sent the fish onto the rocks, where another man captured it and brought a rock down upon its head. The second man then threw the fish into a basket, its tail fins still thrashing. The first man returned the pole to the water, feeling for the next fish. His expert motions, fluid and repetitive, had a mesmerizing effect.

The woman near the drying rack looked up at the girls and lifted her hand. "You came on the freight wagon?"

"Yes," Nikaia answered. She hopped off the boulder and walked over to the woman. She told her of their trip to Lytton and her aunt's sickness. The woman nodded as she listened, looking from Nikaia to Klima with kindly eyes. She looked to be about Mama's age.

"May we go closer to watch?" Klima asked, pointing at the men below.

"Better yet, you can help me," the woman said. She had already cut off the head and fins from the salmon piled beside her. The fish had been gutted and drained. She knelt and adjusted a cedar plank on the rocks, its surface scratched with knife marks and tinged red with blood. She moved a fish knife and a small bundle of vine maple sticks closer to the board. "Here, pass me one of those fish."

Nikaia used both hands to hoist up a red sockeye and set it on the plank. The woman ran her knife deep along the backbone and split apart the fish, exposing the pink meat. The belly skin of the fish served as a hinge as she rapidly drew her knife crosswise into the meat in a series of strokes a finger's width apart.

She reached to her side to select three of the sticks and skewered the meat to hold open the flesh. "In a week, this will dry into *st'wen*," she said, holding the fish up for them to see.

Nikaia had tasted dried salmon and enjoyed the chewy toughness of the meat.

The woman dropped the knife to the plank. "I'll go hang this. Would you cut open the next one?"

Nikaia picked up the knife. It rested lightly in her palm, a fraction of the weight of Mama's adze. Pleased to be trusted with handling the food, she felt that the woman had bestowed a small honor to her. She carefully sawed into the back of the salmon, plunging the knife deep alongside the spine. She unfolded the two sides as if opening a heavy book bound with scales.

Klima knelt beside her, and Nikaia knew her sister was eager to participate. Klima already had three maple vine twigs in her hand, and she poked them into the flesh as Nikaia held open the fish.

With the second time, their skills improved, and by the fifth fish, they were processing the sockeye almost as quickly as the woman.

"Your mother has taught you well," the woman said, casting an approving eye over their work.

Nikaia heard a whistle from the road. "That's our Papa. The wagon must be ready to leave."

"Ah. Thank you for the helping hands. Here, before you go, let me call for a blessing." The woman clasped their hands in hers. Her fingers were rough and smelled strongly of fish guts. "The same one my mother would give," she said, her head tilted back, eyes closed in the sunlight.

"Creator, hear my cry for your daughters. May their way be lit by Brother Sun, and in night, by Sister Moon. Let the wind clear their path of stones and their souls of troubles. And may they always have choices as wide as the sky."

After the prayer, Nikaia thanked the woman then led Klima up the uneven slope to the Alexandra Lodge. The sprawling roadhouse was used for meals and overnight stays of canyon travelers. According to Mr. Lagner, the lodge was the finest along the entire route to the goldfields.

Alongside the main building were the hostling stables, where they found Mr. Lagner harnessing fresh horses to the wagon. Smoke puffed from a portable forge, and the girls watched an aproned blacksmith strike his hammer against an anvil. Using tongs, he lifted a horseshoe, its tips still glowing red, and dropped it into a water bucket. Clouds of steam hissed from the water. Behind him, a farrier worked a rasp against the hoof of a white mare.

Papa helped the Royal Engineer return the last of the boxes to the wagon. Apparently satisfied with his search, the man waved them off.

Mr. Lagner pushed the fresh horses more determinedly, seeking to make up the time he had lost. He resumed his commentary as the wagon labored northward. "Look there! Way down the canyon. That's Hell's Gate."

Far below, the river waters jammed into a choke point where the canyon walls closed in. The cliffs soared straight up from the river level towards the sky. The constriction confused the waters into a gigantic cauldron of swirls and whirlpools. Mr. Lagner related how the river's namesake, Simon Fraser, had struggled to bypass the gorge on his pioneering expedition some fifty years before.

The wagon rose and fell as it traced the road's contours through the canyon. They passed a string of colorfully named sandbars, including China Bar, where sluices and rockers had been worked by Chinese immigrants. Further along was Boston Bar, named by the Indians for the American miners working alongside Anderson Creek.

The jarring and tilting of the freight wagon became mind-lulling. Nikaia watched the rocks and gravel and the few sage shrubs as the wagon rolled past. Her mind turned to Yee Sim. She felt a growing closeness to him. In the midst of her cares, it was a comfort to have him as a confidant and a friend. She thought of his wry comments and mimicry. She closed her eyes and felt her face relax.

Her musings were interrupted by Klima. "I know who you're thinking about," she said in singsong fashion.

"And who might that be?"

"Your beau, Yee Sim."

Nikaia flushed furiously. "He's my friend, you gourd-head. Not my beau." She punched Klima's upper arm.

"But he's your best friend."

Best friend? *Probably my only friend.* "Yes, I suppose he is that."

"Next to me," Klima added.

Nikaia cringed as the horses climbed a precarious uphill stretch. The wagon shook with violent tremors as it passed over the uneven crossbeams of trestles that connected the patches of road. Surely the shaking would pull the wagon wheels from their bearings. She hoped Papa had been the one who had constructed the wheels. The river resembled a thin brown vein, hundreds of feet below.

"This is Jackass Mountain," Mr. Lagner said. "Not long ago, when this was just a mule trail, a pack donkey panicked and lost its footing here. It was crushed to death as it fell." He leaned over the side of the trestle and beamed. "Who could have imagined the day would come when we'd have a magnificent road like this? What a marvelous modern time we live in!"

Nikaia eyed the trembling trestle and exchanged a fretful look with Klima.

Mr. Lagner caught their expressions. "Only two more hours to Lytton," he said cheerfully.

Feeling queasy, Nikaia decided to lie down in the cargo hold and get some sleep. She settled into the blankets, but the unpredictable shaking of the wagon soon dismissed any notion of getting some rest. Her throat dry from the flying dust, she willed the time to go by faster.

Papa swung his legs over the driver bench and joined them in the cargo area. He sat on a crate, displacing Klima, who moved to nestle in beside Nikaia in the blankets at Papa's feet.

Klima said, "Tell us about your courting days with Mama."

Papa chuckled and tapped out his pipe against the wagon siding. "What would you like to know?"

"You know. The old stories."

Papa smiled. "Well. Let me think. Your mama, she was a very quiet girl. Much quieter than the two of you."

"Mmm-hmm." Klima rolled a shirt into a makeshift pillow.

"I remember, in our early days in Lytton—before you girls came along—I'd spend long afternoons visiting with your mama's parents, getting to know them. And they wanted to know me. It wasn't common then that a white man would come courting an Indian family's daughter."

"Not common now, either," Nikaia said. When Papa turned to her, she winked.

"I suppose not. Mama would be in the kitchen, and soon there'd be the smell of coffee beans being crushed in the mortar. Her family never drank coffee, but your mama always had some there for me. She'd get the water steaming while I tried to make conversation with her father. I think part of her intent was to get the kettle whistling to ease the silences."

He laughed lightly. "Your grandfather was not the easiest man to talk to. Soon I'd smell the coffee brewing, and she'd bring a steaming mug out to me. That seemed to be the signal for her parents to tend to other matters, and she and I would sit and talk about many things."

He studied the passing canyon walls as he spoke in a soft voice. "After we were married, she'd bring coffee beans home and carefully sort out the green ones. She'd crush those later and spread them among the carrots and beets. The good beans, she'd grind in the mortar. Then she'd pour the grounds in the coffee pot and stir the fire to bring the water to a boil."

Papa's voice was soothing, and Nikaia had heard the tale many times. Her eyes became heavy, and she laid her head on the end of the bunched-up blanket.

"She still does that, Papa," Klima said. "Every morning."

He sat in silence for a moment. He patted the bump in the blanket made by Nikaia's knee. "You know the humorous part?"

Eyes closed, Nikaia nodded her head slightly. "She has no liking for coffee."

"She thinks it smells like boot silt. I suppose it's just one of the ways I know your Mama cares for me."

He sat quietly as the wagon wheels rolled on. Nikaia finally drifted off to sleep.

"Nikaia." Papa's soft voice stirred Nikaia from her slumber. "There's your mountain."

Nikaia looked out the open front end of the wagon. Mount Nikaia cut a striking profile against the canyon's blue skies. Its neckline held masses of ice and snow melting into a lake rich with mountain trout. The lower reaches were adorned with small falls and the twisting currents of Nikaia Creek tumbling toward the silty flow of the Fraser. The mountain was one of the beloved places of her mother's people.

They reached Lytton in the late afternoon. When they left four years before, the town had about fifty houses and tent-dwellings.

To Nikaia's astonishment, small homes now filled the riverside benches in neat rows.

Like Fort Yale, the town had originally been a fur trade fort but had turned into a gold rush town. Mr. Lagner remarked to Papa that the town held five thousand people, still a fraction of the size of Fort Yale. But given its geographic prominence, the ancient town was rumored to be in the running for capital of the mainland colony, once that was inevitably established. Lytton seemed destined for a bright future.

The most striking feature of the town was the one that had been there for all time—the meeting point of two great rivers. Below, she could see where the aqua-colored waters of the Thompson River met the brown flow of the Fraser. For a short distance, the two ran in adjacent lanes, the Thompson a blue fringe of ribbon aside the dark vastness of the Fraser. Downriver, the combined flow melded to a light ochre hue, draining the mainland territory of its waters in an endless pull to the sea.

The sight of the great confluence brought a flood of childhood memories: exploring the creeks with Klima, playing at the water's edge with Auntie Tsaht-koo, running barefoot in the hot gravel from their family cabin to Nana Klat-su's home. She stared at the mingling rivers. *I'm home.*

The wagon dropped down the road into town, toward Mama and Auntie Tsaht-koo.

CHAPTER EIGHTEEN

THE FREIGHT WAGON CLATTERED ACROSS the rocky ground in front of Nana Klat-su's cabin. Gusts of wind swept up from the river and whipped at the wagon's canvas covering, bending its hooped frame from side to side. Nikaia leaned toward the front of the wagon, shielding her eyes from the grit that rose in dusty coils from the wheel tracks.

Two young faces stared out from the cabin's front window. They disappeared, and Nikaia heard shouts of excitement. The planked cabin door sprang open and a half-dozen children spilled out. They gathered about the slowing wagon like chickens to a hen.

Mama peered through the open doorway, a folded brown sheet draped over her arm. She threw the sheet aside and stepped out into the wind. Black strands of hair fell across her face, and she hurriedly pulled them back into the wrapping of her braid.

Even before the horses came to a stop, Nikaia saw deep tiredness—or perhaps worry—in the lines of her mother's face. *Has she even slept since she left Fort Yale?*

Klima cried out in joy and hopped from the wagon. She ran to Mama, arms held high.

Nikaia climbed from the wagon and walked toward them, wishing to come across as more adult-like than Klima. But as she neared, her mind flooded with all that had happened since the last time she had seen her mother's face. She galloped the last few yards and fell into shuddering sobs as Mama's arms wrapped tightly around her.

"Goodness, love! What's gotten into you?" Mama cupped Nikaia's face with her hands.

Nikaia swiped her cheeks. "I'm just... just so happy to be with you again, Mama."

Papa pulled their bags and blankets from the wagon and exchanged a handshake with Mr. Lagner. He walked to Mama and pulled her into his arms.

Nikaia and Klima hugged their younger cousins. They were taller versions of the toddlers she and Klima had said tearful good-byes to four years earlier. Then Nikaia picked up the bags and started for the cabin.

Mama called after her, "Leave them outside the cabin, Nikaia."

Nana Klat-su stood in the doorway, beaming. Her grandmother was smaller than Nikaia remembered, and she had to bend a little to hug her.

"You've stretched!" Nana Klat-su exclaimed, giving her a strong squeeze. "Oh, and you, too, Klima!"

Mama and Papa laughed. They all followed Nana into the cabin.

Mama's two brothers were in the front room. Like Mama, they went by their baptized names, Raymond and Lawrence. Of Nana Klat-su's children, only Auntie Tsaht-koo had never taken to her baptized name, Tess, and so was always called by the name given to her at birth by Nana Klat-su and Grandfather.

In whispers, the adults discussed Auntie Tsaht-koo. Many others on the reserve were also showing symptoms of the strange illness, and some had died.

Klima went to Mama's side. "Can we see Auntie Tsaht-koo?"

Mama shook her head. "No, not now. Soon."

Klima skipped off, happy to play with the cousins. Before long, Mama and Papa went into Auntie Tsaht-koo's room, where they remained for a long time. Nikaia stayed with the other adults, listening to their soft exchanges. She sensed that a form of code was being used, with their indirect references to the disease and its devastating effects on so many. Eventually, Mama and Papa returned.

Papa sat across from Uncle Lawrence. "What is the doctor saying?"

Uncle Lawrence raised his shoulders. "To give her much water. Keep her warm. Let her sleep."

"When was he last here?"

"Four days have passed."

Papa looked alarmed. "Four days!"

Mama laid a finger on his knee. "The sickness is all over the west side. Dr. McLeod is only one man. He's being pulled like a leaf in the wind."

"Tsaht-koo needs to be seen," Papa said quietly.

Uncle Lawrence responded, "There's little he can do, except give pain medicine. And we have that."

Raymond rose from his chair, his face stretched taut. "Understand this, John. White men brought this upon us. But can they help us now? No! They have no power over this." His hands shook as he spoke.

Nikaia sat in the corner, her knees drawn up to her chest. The room seemed to grow sticky and warm.

Papa's face did not change. "I fear you may be right, Raymond. But whatever help we—any of us—can offer your sister... I'm just saying we have to try."

"We'll beat the hand drum for Tsaht-koo tonight and sing the healing songs. We'll call to all the great spirits."

Papa started to speak, but Mama silenced him with her upheld hand. "We're all tired. Let's not speak of this."

Nana Klat-su spoke. "Yes. Let us turn our words now to brighter things." She directed the conversation to how much Nikaia and Klima had grown and how much Nikaia resembled her mother. Then she turned to reminiscences of the younger days of Tsaht-koo and her siblings. The adults followed her lead respectfully and took part in the gentle sharing of old memories.

During the conversation, Papa left the cabin for a time. When he returned, he was accompanied by a silver-haired white woman. She was tall and thin. Her movements were graceful as she stepped lightly up to the cabin, carrying a small purse.

Papa led her over to where Mama sat. "Kate, this is Caroline McLeod, Dr. McLeod's wife."

Mrs. McLeod smiled at Mama, showing her small straight teeth.

Mama took her hand. "It's good of you to come. How is the doctor?"

"Oh, he's doing fine. His days are long and wearying, of course. He needs rest. But that could be said for many in these times." Her lyrical voice reflected an advanced education. *Cultured* was the word that came to mind.

"Is he back from the west side? My sister is worse, I'm afraid," Mama said.

"So Mr. Wales told me. I am so sorry." Mrs. McLeod gave Mama a sisterly look and reached out to clasp her palm. "Jonah will be here before long. In the meantime, I told your husband I'd come by and see what I might do."

"I appreciate that very much. Please, do come in." Mama's words were warm, but Nikaia wondered if her uncles would resent the presence of the white doctor's wife.

Mama led Mrs. McLeod to the rear bedroom. In a few moments, Mama returned to speak quietly with Papa. Then she nodded at Nikaia. "It's time to see your auntie. Go get your sister."

Nikaia found Klima outside, and they followed Mama into the darkened bedroom. Auntie Tsaht-koo was in bed, covered in wool blankets up to her chest. Her sleeved arms lay lightly atop the covers. Nikaia's eyes adjusted to the light, and she drew in a short breath. Auntie Tsaht-koo's face, once as smooth and evenly brown as Mama's, was pitted with rose-colored blisters and pocks.

Under Mrs. McLeod's direction, Mama and Nana Klat-su laid cold compresses on Auntie Tsaht-koo's forehead. Mama used a dry towel to wipe the water as it drained from the compress and ran down her sister's forehead and cheeks. She patted her face gently, taking care not to aggravate the weeping sores that beaded her skin.

Mrs. McLeod pulled a small timepiece from her purse and studied it as she held Auntie's wrist. Then she laid her hand, palm down, on Tsaht-koo's chest.

Mrs. McLeod turned to Mama. "Kate, can you find some sticks of balsam fir? Not from a living tree, but fallen on the ground."

"Yes." Mama looked at her with curiosity. Then she turned to Klima. "Come with me, girl."

"We'll need only a handful of it," Mrs. McLeod said. "Nikaia, please go heat some water. Not to boiling, just warm."

Mama and Klima left the cabin. Nikaia went to the kitchen and added pine logs to the woodstove, positioning them along the side of the firebox below the kettle of water. She recognized in Mrs. McLeod the instinct to keep the family members busy. Activity gave them a sense of purpose, and it overcame the helplessness of watching and waiting.

Mama returned shortly with a handful of small branches.

Mrs. McLeod met her in the kitchen and inspected the flat needles that spiraled along each shoot. "Thank you, Kate. Klima, please scrape off the needles and add them to a mug. Fill it halfway. Then have your sister pour the warm water into it."

Mama looked at Mrs. McLeod. "Balsam wood. I've seen that used, long ago, for healing."

"Yes. It strengthens the blood."

"I've never seen it used by a white doctor," Mama observed.

Mrs. McLeod leaned over and spoke in a conspiratorial voice. "This one's not from my husband's bag of tricks. Some of the teachings from the elders are worth more than what our husbands learned in school."

The two women shared a smile as Klima brought the mug to the stove. Nikaia tipped the kettle, both hands on the coils of its large handle. A small cloud of steam erupted from the mixture, carrying with it the pleasant fragrances of pitch and fir.

Mama stared at the steam. "My husband, Lord love him, he thinks that every problem can be fixed, as if every situation we encounter is solvable somehow. Like a broken wagon wheel that can be spliced and repaired." She looked at the half-closed bedroom door and covered her mouth with a quivering hand. "But I fear that some things, once broken, cannot be made whole again." Tears pooled in her eyes and tumbled onto her cheeks. Her face contorted as she sobbed.

Mrs. McLeod put her arms around her. "I know, I know." She patted Mama's back.

Nikaia instinctively reached for Klima, and the two of them held each other and wept at the sight and sounds of their mother's sorrow.

After a moment, Mama pulled out of Mrs. McLeod's embrace and dabbed her eyes with the backs of her hands. She crossed the kitchen toward her daughters and pulled their heads against her chest, kissing them lightly on top of their heads. "Let's get that drink to your auntie."

Nikaia took the warm mug into the bedroom, taking small steps to avoid a spill. She handed it to Mama then helped tilt Auntie Tsaht-koo's birdlike frame into an upright position. Mama brought the balsam infusion to her sister's lips.

The clap of horseshoes signaled Dr. McLeod's arrival. Nikaia left the bedroom with Mrs. McLeod and, through the front window, saw the doctor tie his laden pack horse to a post near the cabin. She felt a surge of renewed hope for Auntie Tsaht-koo.

The doctor trudged up to the cabin, swinging a heavy black bag. He doffed his top hat, revealing thin white hair. His forehead and clean-shaven cheeks were lined so heavily that they might have served as a roadmap for his recent travels.

He greeted his wife in a gentle voice and walked inside. Nikaia noticed that he moved about the cabin with familiarity. Mrs. McLeod followed him into Tsaht-koo's bedroom. In a few moments, Mama came out and sat beside Papa. They held hands, and Mama stared toward the bedroom door with an unfocused gaze.

A half-hour passed before the physician emerged. Papa and Mama rose from their seats. Dr. McLeod gave a slight shake of his head and raked his fingers through the sparse straggles of his hair.

"Can this be eased for her?" Papa said.

The doctor nodded. "I've given her opium. It will lighten her discomfort." He placed his hand on Mama's shoulder. "Be with your sister, Kate. I fear she hasn't many breaths remaining. I'm sorry."

Mama closed her eyes, nodded, and returned to the darkened room.

Dr. McLeod looked with grim kindness at Nikaia and Klima. He opened his mouth, but seemed barren of words. "Ladies," he said at last, fingering the brim of his hat in his hands. He donned the hat, picked up his black bag, and left the cabin. Nikaia followed.

The doctor helped his wife into the saddle of the pack horse. He walked beside the animal, loosely holding a lead. The man carried the weary countenance of someone who had seen too much suffering. *To the doctor*, Nikaia thought, *we must be one more sad family of so many.*

As the day fell into twilight, more relatives and family friends gathered at Nana Klat-su's cabin. Some had traveled from the west side of the Fraser, tying their horses to wooden rafts. Nikaia remembered the sight of that from her younger days in Lytton. The horses would face upstream and swim furiously, while the men paddled against the current to move the raft from one bank to the other. A missed stroke—or worse, a broken paddle—would mean a long and potentially perilous trip downstream. It was not a crossing for the faint of heart.

Nikaia oscillated between the adult conversations and the playful children, caught between both worlds. Mama spent a long time in the back room with her sister. Gradually, more of the adults joined her there, and Mama finally beckoned Papa, Nikaia, and Klima to enter as well.

Relatives and family friends lined the walls of the room. Everyone was a step or two back from the bed, which had been pulled into the center of the room.

Auntie Tsaht-koo's slitted eyes flashed with recognition as Nikaia approached the bed with Klima. Papa laid a hand on the shoulder of each girl, stopping them a few feet from the bed.

Klima looked at Mama. "Is she getting well?" she whispered.

"No, my girl," Mama said.

Auntie Tsaht-koo closed her eyes and began to murmur, the words coming in short breaths. She and Mama spoke gentle words to each other in their native tongue. Somehow, the glottal stops and cluckings of the Nlaka'pamux language always sounded as soft as a brook from Mama's lips. Soon, Auntie Tsaht-koo lay quiet again, and her birdlike frame sank a little lower beneath the blankets.

More people entered the room, most of them unfamiliar to Nikaia. She recognized Mr. Sam, an aging, longtime neighbor of Nana Klat-su. A young man entered, his black hair dropping straight down past his shoulders. He carried a hand drum. Prayers went up in the old language. Nikaia knew enough of the words to understand some of it.

"Brother Bear, we summon you. Bring our sister strength and wellness. Brother Eagle, hear our words now. Help Tsaht-koo rise above this illness. Carry her and fly her high away from this suffering. Father Creator, hear our cries. Her time with us must not be over. She has many tasks on this earth to complete."

The prayers continued from Nana Klat-su, Mama, and others. Most of the words eluded Nikaia, but the anguish in the room needed no translation.

Mama left the room with Uncle Raymond. When they returned, Mama carried a small soapstone bowl and placed it beside Auntie Tsaht-koo's bed. Mama dropped some dried sage and juniper tied into delicate bundles into the container. Her brother struck a flint into the bowl, and the contents began to glow faintly in the shadowed room. Uncle Raymond blew gently into it. A thin wisp of smoke curled up from the burning herbs.

The fragrance was powerful, even stronger than the incense Reverend Poole would sometimes burn in the church tent back home. The elders began to chant ancient prayers in the Nlaka'pamux tongue. Uncle Raymond held the bowl near the head of the bed. Mama moved her hands in graceful arcs, scooping the smoke over her sister's face. Tsaht-koo's chest rose and fell as she inhaled.

Uncle Raymond moved the bowl in a tight perimeter around Tsaht-koo's body, while Mama continued to waft the aromatic scents over her sister, her thin fingers undulating rhythmically as she bathed her sister in the healing vapors.

The chanting subsided, and the boy with the long hair raised the hand drum to his shoulder. With a small arm motion, he struck it with a stick topped with a padded leather head. The drumbeat repeated in a slow, steady cadence and grew in volume. The motion of the white tip drew an arc in the dim room as the boy swung it against the stretched leather skin.

Eyes closed, the boy threw his head back and, in a full-throated cry, sang the opening tones of the Healing Song. From the corner, Nana Klat-su joined in, and then others did as well, until the room filled with their mournful voices. Auntie Tsaht-koo's lips moved, and Nikaia could hear her singing, a low and quavering garble.

As the drumming continued, Uncle Lawrence brought forward a long soapstone pipe. The tobacco glowed orange in the shaded room. He offered the pipe to Nana Klat-su. She pulled in quick breaths on the stem. With each puff, the tobacco in the cob pulsated with light. Its sweet aroma came to Nikaia, enveloping her like a salve.

Nana Klat-su exhaled a stream of smoke toward the bed and passed the pipe to Uncle Raymond. He brought it to his lips and smoked, then passed it to Mr. Sam. The pipe moved hand to hand around the room, and the bed became encircled with floating ribbons of gray.

Nikaia closed her eyes, overcome by the richness of the emotion in the room. The drumbeats reverberated in her chest. Her ears were filled with her family's cries lifting up their despair in prayerful appeals. The air was saturated not only with the aromas of sage, juniper, and tobacco, but with love, grief, and hope.

Nikaia didn't know if Auntie Tsaht-koo would live or die. Or if she did die, when that time might come. But she knew the moment would live on within her for the rest of her days.

As the evening turned to darkness, only the closest older relatives remained: Nana Klat-su, Mama, her brothers, Papa, Nikaia, and Klima. The family held vigil in silence. The short breaths from the bed grew more shallow and uneven. Auntie Tsaht-koo's spirit slipped from the earth, and she was gone.

CHAPTER NINETEEN

I N HER DREAM THAT NIGHT, Nikaia found herself walking along a wide, sunlit path in the woods. The trail grew progressively more difficult, with snagging thorns and muddy pools to sidestep. She reached a fork, and hoping for better traction, she chose the left path. For a time, that route was pleasant. Then it deteriorated, the branches closing in. She encountered more forks, more decision points.

After one juncture, she chose a path that began narrowing rapidly. The awful realization struck her that there would be no more junctions. The blackberry bushes pulled in close, and the canopy overhead lowered, darkening the trail. Her footfalls, once sure and hopeful, were tentative, her toes stretching out to test the uncertain ground. The way of the path was devoid of hope, overcome by shadows of black and gray.

She awoke with a sense of despair.

Nana Klat-su and Mama quickly arranged the funeral for Auntie Tsaht-koo. Nikaia assumed that the haste was out of fear that her aunt's body would spread the disease.

Relatives and neighbors once again descended upon the tiny cabin. Under clouded skies, they arrived from the reserve and from the west side of the river, bearing baskets of salmon, root vegetables, and berries. Mr. Sam brought generous cuts of deer, elk, and black bear. Nikaia helped with the salmon preparation, slicing fish steaks and fillets and absorbing the murmured comments about her practiced hand from women neighbors. She glanced up at Mama, who was arranging berries in serving baskets. Mama met her eyes and allowed a small smile. It was good to see Mama's face relaxed, if even for a moment.

Throughout the day, Papa had Nikaia and Klima wash their hands in piping hot water, scraping with a hard soap that produced few suds. Nikaia knew he was trying to protect them with the hope of washing away the threat of the strange disease that had taken Auntie Tsaht-koo. He scrubbed his hands along with them as they made ready to leave for the funeral.

In the church tent, Reverend Poole began the service by leading the small congregation through the melodies of old hymns. No organ or musical instruments were in place.

"Lord God, Heavenly Father," Reverend Poole prayed, "we do not presume to understand thy ways. We can only trust in thy will and lay down our lives into thy hands. We are a people bound together by our oppression. Oppressed by disease. By sinfulness. By all the wicked ways of our earthly world. Today, we say our tearful good-byes to Tsaht-koo, our sister, daughter, aunt, and friend. We despair for her suffering. And we send our thanks that her hard journey, her time of trial, is at its end. In our faith, we rejoice that she now dances in the house of the Lord."

He raised his voice. "Surely, trumpets are sounding in thy gardens! Surely, all the company of heaven celebrates as angels take Tsaht-koo into their arms. From this day forward, there is naught but joy for Tsaht-koo. Father, let it be so with us. Here on this good earth, we look to thee. We look to each other. And we remind ourselves that, with thy grace, we carry on. Whatsoever comes, we shall endure."

Papa stood up for the reading. In his hands, he held not the Holy Bible but a book of poetry.

> "But now, alas! the place seems changed;
> Thou art no longer here:
> Part of the sunshine of the scene
> With thee did disappear.
> Though thoughts, deep-rooted in my heart,
> Like pine-trees dark and high,

Subdue the light of noon, and breathe
A low and ceaseless sigh;
This memory brightens o'er the past,
As when the sun, concealed
Behind some cloud that near us hangs
Shines on a distant field."

Nikaia and Klima knew the poem well: "A Gleam of Sunshine," from Longfellow.

Reverend Poole invited the village elders forward and turned the service over to the Nlaka'paxum. An elderly woman, loose skin hanging below her hollow cheeks, led the recitation of long prayers, some in English and some in the native language. The words flowed in their ancient rhythms. Many in the congregation spoke the words with her.

"*Axscas, axscas,*" the old woman said.

"*Axscas,*" the congregation replied.

The prayers ended. The woman looked down, and all was quiet.

Then a wail arose from Nana Klat-su, who stood beside Nikaia with her hands to her heart. Her cries stabbed through the silence, released from the deepest stretches of her soul. Others did likewise, from all rows of the tent, creating a haunting chorus of shared grief. Shivers passed through Nikaia's body.

Reverend Poole was an eloquent speaker, but his words seemed trite next to the searing calls from Nana Klat-su and the elders. Nikaia closed her eyes and took in the awful rendering, the exposing of the most tender reaches of the elders' hearts. She imagined the souls of those about her, dancing in their nakedness, stripped raw of all artifice and howling in their anguish.

This is who I am. She pressed her trembling lips together.

The wailing rose to crescendos then fell. Rose and fell. Rose again and fell, like waves washing into shore.

Axscas. Axscas.

So be it. Amen.

Auntie Tsaht-koo was buried in the cemetery above the triangular stretch of sand where the Thompson waters merged with the Fraser. Scattered around her gravesite were rows of freshly dug earth. The wave of disease had found its way to Lytton, and Auntie Tsaht-koo was not the first to be swept under by it.

Afterward, Mama sat with Nikaia and Klima in the sand. The clouds had lifted, and the day was warming. Nikaia looked at Klima, who appeared so quiet and full of thoughts. Such a contrast from her usual confident manner and uncomplicated approach to life. Nikaia faced the upstream wind, her cheeks wet with tears.

Mama laid an arm across her shoulders. "Child of mine, it's a joy to see the tenderness of your heart. You're a loving girl."

Nikaia sniffed and rubbed the heels of her palms into her eyes. "Poor Auntie Tsaht-koo. It's awful how she suffered. How horrid she looked." The aunt she remembered, with her girlish smile and carefree manner, seemed impossible to reconcile with the image of the ravaged and shrunken body.

"I know. It troubles me, too," Mama said. "But she's no longer in pain. She's in heaven, jingle-dancing in joy. Or maybe playing chase with the other angels."

Klima looked up. "Oh, do you think so?"

"Why not?"

"I never thought of heaven like that."

"That's how I like to think of it." Mama turned back to Nikaia. "Do you know that it is possible to feel joy and sorrow at the same time? The things that bring happiness bring sorrow when they leave. Then they offer joy again when you remember them. We should let our memories of Tsaht-koo bring us joy. It honors her."

Nikaia wrapped her arms around her mother.

When they returned to Nana Klat-su's cabin, Nikaia spent time with her cousins and uncles, uncertain when she would see them again. And if she did, would it be because of someone else's sickness? She worked in the kitchen with Uncle Raymond, arranging the uneaten surplus of food into covered baskets.

He threw a light towel in her direction, startling her. "Here, wrap these berries, niece." His face wore a tired smile.

She scooped blueberries into the towel from the serving plates.

Uncle Raymond asked, "Have you had your spirit training, Nikaia?"

Spirit training was a grueling ritual carried out by native youth at the time of their coming of age. When Nikaia had experienced her first monthly cycle—or *moon time,* as Mama called it—she began her preparations. She recalled with humor the day her mother had spoken to her of the upcoming ceremony.

One morning, Mama shooed Klima out of the girls' bedroom and sat on the bed beside Nikaia. "This is where you will find yourself, Nikaia," Mama said. "As I did, and Nana Klat-su, and all the women, the ancient line of mothers, who came before us."

Papa eased his head through the bedroom doorway. "May I enter?"

Mama hesitated. "Yes...?"

He stepped in, carrying his small bush kettle. He set it on Nikaia's clothes chest. "This might come in handy when you're in the woods."

Mama looked pointedly at Papa. "Ah. I did not realize you possessed experience with spirit training."

"Well, I've spent many a night out in the bush. Under the stars."

"Not quite the same, love." Mama stole a look at Nikaia and rolled her eyes playfully.

Taken aback, Papa opened his mouth to speak then apparently thought better of it and exited the room. Mama described the ceremonial gear that Nikaia would take on her mountain quest.

A tentative tapping came at the door a few minutes later, and Papa entered with a length of gray hemp cord neatly coiled in a figure-eight pattern. He held it up, and Nikaia suppressed a smile at the boyish pride written on his features.

"Papa?" Mama said, a trace of annoyance evident in her tone.

"This is useful for many things," Papa said. "Snares. Fishing. Lashing things to your pack. And in a pinch, it can be unraveled and lit to make the startings of a fire." He looked at Mama and placed the rope on the chest.

"Papa," Mama said, "tell your daughter about your own spirit training. Back across the ocean in Britain, was it? With all the other Welsh Indians? Really, I had no inkling." She folded her arms across her chest.

Papa looked at Mama with his mouth hanging open. Nikaia started to fret at the tension. Then both her parents broke into laughter. Mama stood and took hold of Papa's forearm with both hands.

She pivoted him to face the bedroom door. "Out. This is for women only."

Mama had then finished her instruction. Nikaia listened, moved by her mother's sisterly tone as she described the passage from childhood to womanhood.

Not sure her uncle would understand the interplay between her parents, she responded, "Yes. Last spring."

"Tell me about it," Uncle Raymond said.

Nikaia thought back to that day and related the story to her uncle.

Mama had awakened her the first morning and said, "Today is a day of fasting."

Other than that, the day was a normal one until dusk. At that time, Mama gathered a bundle of materials into a rolled-up blanket and walked with Nikaia to the base of the mountains that rose steeply on the east edge of town.

Her mother opened the bundle and pulled out a square sheet of white cloth. After folding it into a triangle, she wrapped it around Nikaia's forehead and tied the ends behind her head. She shook out the finely woven blanket, its black background decorated with diagonal patterns of white and red. Mama draped it over Nikaia's shoulders and secured it in place over her breastbone, passing a sewn-in peg through a reinforced slit in the blanket.

Mama then gathered light fir branches and intertwined them into a headpiece. She positioned them over the bandana. The branches cascaded down past Nikaia's shoulders. In other circumstances, Niakaia might have felt ridiculous, but her mother's serious demeanor brought a sense of solemnity to the moment.

Mama stepped back and examined Nikaia from crown to foot. She pressed her lips together and nodded. "I suppose that will do."

Nikaia looked down at the elaborate costume. The blanket was already weighing down upon her, and the fir branches atop her head were starting to itch. But despite those discomforts, she felt proud to be in that moment, in that place.

Mama cradled Nikaia's face in both hands and kissed her lightly on the lips. "Time to go, my daughter."

"No kettle?" Nikaia asked innocently.

The corner lines around Mama's eyes deepened as she let out a short laugh. "No kettle."

Mama handed her a flint and turned away.

Nikaia walked upward alone, sweating under the heavy blanket. The firs and cedars, so dense at the base of the canyon, thinned as the craggy bones of the mountain showed themselves in its higher reaches. She spotted a small ledge above the river and started to traverse a slope of scree to get to it.

The blanket restricted her leg movements and made the crossing an awkward venture. The loose rocks gave way under each footstep, creating tiny landslides. She feared that she'd be carried downward toward the canyon cliffs, but the clattering black rocks slowed and settled into new patterns of repose. She aimed her line of travel to a point above the ledge in order to offset the collapsing terrain at her feet. The effect reminded her of ferrying the *Anybody Boat* across a downstream current.

The ledge was small and flat, about the size of a large quilt. It jutted out like a lower lip on the mountain's face. She walked to the edge. The vast emptiness below dizzied her, and she swayed before catching herself. The fir headpiece tipped forward, its thin branches covering her eyes. Dropping to sit cross-legged on the ground, she straightened the headgear and pulled the scratchy needles back from her cheeks.

Nikaia took in the profile of the eastside canyon, its upper edges pushing skyward in uneven bursts of granite and ice. Below the white crowns of snow, the mountainside rocks and trees took on a deep blue sheen. Nikaia had always puzzled at the phenomenon, as the blue always dissolved into the familiar green, brown, and black colors of the forest as one neared.

Below lay the gaping maw of the canyon lowlands. The lights of town sparkled as the shopkeepers and saloon owners brought flints to their lanterns. The settlement resembled a bowl of jewels, as if the Creator cupped it in the flat of his palm and guarded it with craggy, upstretched fingers.

Small patches of irrigated benchland sprang green amidst the duller stretches of rocks and gravel. Splitting the canyon, east to west, was the Fraser River, a dark brown rope dropped from the heavens. Nikaia imagined that if she beheld the scene in an oil painting, she would dismiss it as impossibly beautiful, an inspired rendering from some fanciful artist.

As darkness fell, she made repeated trips into the trees above the ledge to gather dried moss and bundles of dead twigs. She lit a small fire, its base barely bigger than a dinner plate. Enough to offer warmth, but not so vigorous as to have its light overwhelm her ability to see the rough peaks around her. She watched as the blue outlines faded to gray. The night was moonless, and stars crowded the black sky.

Then, as Mama had taught her, she sang ancient songs and danced around the fire, calling to the spirit of the Dawn to bring about her spirit helper. After much dancing, she tired and lay beside the dying embers. A dream came to her. In it, she was playing alone in the forest, and an old owl appeared in a nearby fir. It eyed her unblinkingly and, to her surprise, began to sing in low tones.

Its sweet song ended, the owl left the branch, pushing the air downward with its great wings, and landed on her shoulder. The bird shifted its weight from one talon to the other and leaned its feathered head against hers. "Daughter of Ke-mat-pa, granddaughter of Klat-su. Your walk ahead may be long and obscured by dark clouds, but do not lose heart. In the hour of storm, look for light. It will appear for you. When your path is lost in the night, look to the sky. It will be your guide. And you shall be known to me as Koh-tap-se: Lightning Star."

And thus, Nikaia was anointed by her nature helper, her guardian spirit. She awoke from her dream, exhilarated.

Uncle Raymond nodded gravely when she finished her tale. "I think, though, that the old owl named you wrong."

Nikaia continued working the food, suddenly self-conscious. "Why do you think that?"

Uncle Raymond hung the towel on the hook. "You have the look of a young woman, but the heart of a bear. I've heard from your mother how you stand up not only for your friends but for those who need a friend. She has told of how you protect your sister and find the courage to protest when a wrong is being done."

He pointed at her. "Nikaia, there's only one name for you: Warrior."

⸻

Too soon, it seemed, it was time to return to Fort Yale. Papa had secured transport in a stagecoach—*a passenger coach!*—that would offer a more comfortable return than their outbound journey.

Nikaia stuffed her spare clothing into her packsack and slung it over her shoulder. As she walked through the front room, she glanced into the cabin's second bedroom. Nana Klat-su was sitting on the bed, slumped over and studying her empty arms, as if holding an invisible baby. When she saw Nikaia, she straightened and tugged the sleeves of her shirt down to her wrists.

"I'll miss you, granddaughter," Nana Klat-su said. She held out her hands.

Nikaia rushed into her arms. "I love you, Nana."

After saying good-bye, Nikaia left the room, wondering if she would ever see her wise, sweet grandmother again. Before Nana Klat-su had pulled down her sleeves, Nikaia had seen the soft red spots breaking through the leathery skin of her forearms.

Their bags were ready for travel, lined up neatly against the cabin's outside walls. The morning was pleasant and bright, and the family waited outside for the coach to arrive.

"Kate, I don't want to add to your burdens," Papa said, "with your sister and all that has happened here. But I need to let you know about some happenings from the past few days in Fort Yale."

Papa told her everything. Mama said very little. Her eyes widened at the telling of the stolen gold and Matthew Doyle's murder. When Papa got to the part about the spyglass and how it implicated him in the eyes of the police, her mouth set into a grim line. Nikaia braced herself for a scolding.

When Mama finally spoke, she only gave a cool analysis. "You've done no wrong," she said in a steely voice to Papa. "And Nikaia was merely playing a childish game. Surely, the police will come to understand this. And the Doyles, too."

Papa nodded. "Yes, that's what I would think. Reason will prevail. I wanted you to know, though."

"Of course." Mama stared off into the distance. When she spoke again, it was to Nikaia and Klima. "You girls had better go say good-bye to your cousins."

At the doorway of the cabin, Nikaia looked back at her parents. Mama had reached over and was clutching Papa as if he might disappear from her very arms. Papa's narration had reminded Nikaia of the peril facing him and the jeopardy the whole family would be in if he were imprisoned. *Oh my word! How could I forget all about Reverend Poole?*

No stagecoach was in sight, yet. She gave Mama and Papa a flustered excuse, saying she wanted to say good-bye to the minister. She tore down the road toward the parish house.

CHAPTER TWENTY

NIKAIA PERCHED ON THE CHAIR opposite Reverend Poole in the study of the newly built cabin, constructed by Lytton residents as an enticement for the Anglican church. The minister leaned back in his armchair. Behind him was a shelf stocked with books and a collection of small statuettes and stones.

He turned his pale blue eyes her way. "It's been a difficult time for your family, Nikaia. I didn't know Tsaht-koo well, but since arriving in Lytton, I've heard much about her. She had an uncommon spirit."

"Yes. She did." Nikaia stared at her fingertips, wondering how to steer the conversation toward what she needed to know.

Reverend Poole leaned forward and looked out the window. In the distance, the Indian cemetery was in view, indented with rows of freshly dug graves. "Sometimes, it's easy to be angry with God." He crossed his arms and fluttered his long fingers against the coarse sleeves of his shirt. "I feel that way at times. But I must say, the faith of Klat-su's family is very strong. Like many of the people in Lytton."

His hands were slender and delicate, a scholar's hands, and his fingernails were smooth, almost flawless. Nikaia envisioned the roughness of Papa's fingers, his nails chipped and blackened from the harshness of working with wood and steel. Side by side, their hands would look as if they belonged to two completely different species.

He relaxed back into his chair. "Well, I should let you speak. What brings you here, Nikaia?"

Nikaia pulled in a breath. "Reverend Poole, I've heard an expression: the imperial stones. Is that from the Bible? Do you know what it might mean?"

"My goodness! What an odd question." He reached to a side table for his Bible, a heavy tome with gold lettering inscribed into its black cover. He flipped through the pages. "Where did you hear it?"

Nikaia crossed her fingers beneath her leg. "From school, I think. I'm not sure."

"The 'imperial stones'? Hmm... I'm not sure it's a biblical reference. The word *imperial* is a worldly term. It means 'of the empire.' Or I suppose, 'of the emperor.'"

Nikaia thought back to her books at home. "Isn't Queen Victoria called Her Imperial Majesty?"

Reverend Poole smiled. "Indeed. And her realm is the Imperial Kingdom." He stroked his chin. "I suppose one might call the Queen's crown jewels the imperial stones. But I've never heard them described that way." He put down the Bible. "Is it possible the word you heard was *empyreal*, not *imperial*?" He spelled both words for her.

Nikaia thought back. The man in the broad hat had spoken with an accent. Perhaps she had misheard. The two words certainly sounded similar enough. "Empyreal. What does it mean?"

"It means 'from the highest reaches of heaven.' Empyrean is the dwelling place of the highest beings, of souls so divine that they're said to be made of pure light. According to the old Greek legends, that is." He hummed softly as he thought. "Hmm. Empyreal stones. Heavenly stones."

"Could it have to do with the tablets? From Moses?" Nikaia asked.

"That's an interesting thought, Nikaia. Those *are* believed to have been made of stone, of course. There's some logic to calling those heavenly stones." He considered for a moment. "I've heard them called the Stone Tablets, as well as the Tablets of Law, and occasionally, the Tablets of Testimony. But the term empyreal stones would be an unusual way to refer to the tablets from Mount Sinai. No, I don't think that's it."

Nikaia felt she had reached the dead end of a cave, and her time was running out. She listened for the rattling of the passenger stagecoach.

Reverend Poole turned to the bookcase. "I wonder..." He pulled out a thin leather-clad volume and flipped through its pages.

Nikaia could see drawings of various stones: bauxite, quartz, onyx.

Reverend Poole paused on a page. "Ah, now this is intriguing. There's one ancient mineral that, for centuries, has been known as the Stone of Heaven."

He reshelved the book. Reaching for the shelf behind him, he picked up a smooth, marine-colored rock. "Nikaia, this is the Stone of Heaven. Jade."

Jade. Nikaia thought back to the conversation she'd overheard in the woods. A plan started to take shape in her mind. She knew exactly where to start looking when she got back to Fort Yale.

CHAPTER TWENTY-ONE

THE STAGECOACH WAS AN EIGHT-SEATER with two benches that faced each other. Four sleeping miners of various ages were spread out inside. Mr. Harrison, the driver, roused them and had them move to sit on the rear-facing bench. Nikaia and her family squeezed onto the other bench across from them. The men were scruffy and reeked of sweat and unwashed clothes.

"They boarded the stage in Barkerville three days ago," Mr. Harrison said to Papa in an apologetic tone.

"We'll make do, and I'm much obliged," Papa said.

The day was warm, and the air in the coach still, even with the window curtains pulled open. Aside from that, the ride was comfortable compared to their northward journey on the freight wagon. A light curtain hung over the sliding window that separated them from the driver.

Mama and Papa leaned sideways on each other, covered with a light blanket, and sought sleep. The miners were ahead of them in that regard, having tipped up their flasks before the first rotation of the coach's wheels in Lytton. The men snored softly.

Klima snuggled into their mother's side. "Mama, when will Mr. Harrison change out the horses?"

"I don't know. Probably in Boston Bar," Mama said, murmuring so as to not disturb the miners.

"Do the horses know? It's hot. They seem tired."

Mama yawned. "Maybe so. They're pretty smart."

"Mama, will Papa have to go to jail?"

"Goodness! No, of course not."

"Is Auntie Tsaht-koo in heaven yet?"

"Oh, yes," Mama said. "It's a quick trip."

"Will we see Auntie Tsaht-koo in heaven? How will we find her?"

"Oh, Klima. Some things are known only to the trees."

For a moment, the only sound was the crunch of the gravel under the coach wheels.

Klima dropped her chin to the blanket. "I thought the river knows, too."

Mama laughed softly. "Yes, the river, too."

<hr />

At midday, the coach stopped at the hostling station in Boston Bar. Papa helped the driver unharness the four horses. Mr. Harrison was a particular man and argued with the hostler for some time over the selection of fresh horses.

Nikaia and Klima sat cross-legged on the side of the wagon road and watched the whisky jacks swoop down to the hard-packed gravel in groups to pick at invisible morsels. With black bands between their snowy foreheads and throats, the birds looked like flying burglars.

A BX cargo coach clattered toward them, coming from the south side of Boston Bar. The girls scooted back from the road to give it room. The conveyance had only two horses, and the driver appeared to be a teenage boy. "Chuck-chuck," scolded a whisky jack, circling overhead as the wagon passed. A small fluttering of dust rose in the wake of the coach.

"Oh, no!" Klima cried and ran to the opposite side of the road. She reached down into the fresh wheel tracks and walked back to Nikaia with her hands cupped. "It's a bird. The wagon ran over it."

Nikaia looked into Klima's hands. Black eyes peered back at her, amid a ball of feathers as gray as soot. "Why, it's only a hatchling! Poor thing." A fully grown bird squawked angrily and flew in patterns above them. "That's probably its mother."

"I think its leg is broken." Klima cooed softly and stroked down the spiky hairs on its tiny head with her thumb. The bird shuddered and retracted its neck deeper into its body feathers.

"It'll die soon, won't it." Klima said it as a statement. "I'm going to keep it. And try to help it. What kind of bird do you think it is?"

"It's a whisky jack, silly. A baby whisky jack."

She gently brushed its mottled feathers. "It's a girl bird. It's not a Jack. I'll call you Jill," she said to the bird. "I'm going to save your little bird life."

Klima placed small grass seeds near its beak, but the bird ignored them. Nikaia walked away and sat on some dried bunchgrass, watching the river wind southward below the town. Her thoughts drifted back to Auntie Tsaht-koo and to Papa's situation. She poked at some small fir cones with a stick. She wished Yee Sim were there to make her forget things, to make her laugh.

Mama came over and knelt beside her in the grass. She put an arm across Nikaia's shoulders. "You have a lot of thoughts these days."

"Mmm."

"I hope there are some good thoughts in there. Not just the troubling ones."

"I don't know." Nikaia jabbed at the fir cones, sending one tumbling over the bank. "I'm worried for Papa. And for all of us."

"How are you and Yee Sim getting along?" It was an unexpected question. Mama had a way of sensing the thoughts of her daughters. "He seems like a nice boy."

Nikaia felt her face redden. She continued to face the river and lobbed the stick over the bank. "He is."

They sat in silence for a time. Mama patted her shoulder and started to rise.

"Mama, what did Grandfather and Nana Klat-su think when you and Papa were courting?"

Mama settled back into a kneel. Her pretty face shed years as she looked down at the distant river. "They were worried for me," she said softly. "They knew little about white people. And Papa was one of the first white trappers in Lytton. But more than that, they feared that I would be pulled away. Become something apart from my own people. And truly, they were right about that. It did create a separation. Some of my family would say I live the life of a white woman now. But white people... well, they see me as native Indian. Which of course I am. In some ways, I became an outsider to both worlds."

She looked at Nikaia. "But in the end, you need to be with the one you were meant to love. And for me, that was your father."

Nikaia considered that. Soft whistles from the whisky jacks sounded overhead. Mama sat still, seeming comfortable in the silence. As much as Nikaia tried to bring order to her thoughts, they bubbled and popped in her head like boiling coffee water. She knew of no better example of love than her parents. But what was that love, really? It was grounded, surely, in their caring, but there was something more. An ease with each other, a peacefulness, and a joyousness that rarely seemed far below the surface.

Her parents' affection for each other was subtle. It showed itself in different ways, like in their shared laughter, which created the happiest sounds of Nikaia's childhood memories. And they laughed often, even though their humors were so different—Mama with her wry comments and gentle teasing, Papa with his meandering stories punctuated by chuckles.

Then again, perhaps love was defined in sorrier times, like the adversity that they faced with Auntie's death and the suspicions of the police. Nikaia thought of Mama's reaction to the news about Papa. Her mother had projected calmness, but in her eyes, Nikaia had seen something deeper: the instinct to fight like a mountain lion for her family.

Caring, peace, joy, laughter, a fierce will to protect... did all that add up to love? Or were those things instead created by loving feelings? Perhaps her questions had no answers.

She turned to her mother. "How did you know? That Papa was the one meant for you?"

Mama chuckled. "Oh, child. Some things are not complicated. When the time comes, your heart will sing it out to you."

With fresh horse legs under harness, the passenger coach rolled out of Boston Bar. Klima sat on the end of the bench, doting over

Jill. She had pleaded with Mama to let her keep the bird, and Mama finally relented.

"Just know, Klima, that it might not survive the trip."

Nikaia sifted through her thoughts while Mama and Papa slept. Eventually, she closed her eyes and feigned sleep. The miners across from them were starting to stir, and she did not wish to be drawn into conversation with them.

Hours passed, and the sun was almost touching the mountain tops when the horses slowed their pace. Papa opened his eyes and looked out the window beside him.

Mama asked, "Are we in Fort Yale?"

Papa dipped his head to view the profile of the mountain ridges. "No. I would say we're close to Spuzzum."

The coach stopped, and Mr. Harrison poked his head through the front curtain. "Looks like an inspection stop. I'll go see what it's about." He disappeared.

Papa pressed his forehead against the window, but the road ahead was outside their view.

In a moment, the curtain moved again. The head that came through was not Mr. Harrison's.

Deputy Thomas Quigg locked his eyes onto Papa. "John Wales, step out onto the road, if you would."

"Certainly." Papa glanced at Mama, then opened the door and climbed out of the stagecoach.

Mama followed before the door could swing shut. She shot a look back at Nikaia. "Watch your sister. Both of you, stay in here."

One of the miners opened his bloodshot eyes, then closed them again. Nikaia could hear voices clearly through the open windows. From her seat, she could see Deputy Quigg at the side of the jailhouse wagon, its iron bars covering the small openings of its passenger compartment. Two other men were with him. They wore serge jackets. *Royal Engineers.*

"Mr. Wales," Deputy Quigg said, "I believe Constable Whittock requested that you stay in Fort Yale while we investigate."

"He did," Papa replied. "And that was my intent. We had a family illness, my wife's sister in Lytton. She died this week of smallpox."

"And yet, Constable Whittock specifically asked you to not leave Fort Yale." Deputy Quigg puffed out his chest and glared at Papa. "A bit of an embarrassment for the constable, you being on the loose. Especially with the judge expected to arrive soon by sternwheeler."

Mama cut in, her eyes fierce. "But look! He's returning to Fort Yale! Not leaving."

The deputy ignored her and kept his eyes trained on Papa.

"I did leave a message at the police office," Papa said.

"Is that so? This is all quite suspicious, I must say. First, the spyglass. Then the gold just up and disappeared. And you seemed to know exactly where it was buried. Now, you're slipping away upriver, despite your travels being forbidden by the police authorities." He looked toward the stagecoach. "And how, I wonder, would one pay for a family of four to travel by stage to Lytton?"

"I'm a working man, Deputy Quigg. You know my business."

"Well, it begs one's curiosity." Quigg gave a head nod to the Royal Engineers, and they closed in nearer to Papa. "We will have to take you in for questioning. It may take some time, as Constable Whittock is busy with the Yale Ball preparations. You can expect to spend the night in the jailhouse."

"What! My husband has done nothing wrong!" Mama cried and reached for Papa.

A Royal Engineer held out his arm to stop her.

Mama tried to push him away. "He's done no wrong!"

The engineer grasped her forearm and led her a few feet away.

"Then he has nothing to fear," Deputy Quigg said.

Nikaia pressed her cheek to the window of the coach.

Deputy Quigg turned to Papa. "Your Indian wife has more front than Brighton. It would do her well to know her place."

"Her place is with me," Papa said, "and mine with her."

"Not tonight, Mr. Wales."

Nikaia opened the stage door and stepped out. She brought her fingers to her face to stop her quivering lips. Papa had the appearance of a man with a noose tightening against his neck. The engineer released Mama and walked to Papa's side.

"Kate," Papa said, "I'll be all right."

Mama glared at Deputy Quigg. An engineer stood at each of Papa's elbows and prodded him toward their wagon.

He turned his head to tell Mama, "I left Rooster with the O'Briens."

Mama nodded. Nikaia saw her mother's hands shaking, her eyes brimming. Deputy Quigg and the Royal Engineers led Papa into the wagon. An engineer locked the door from the outside, and the wagon pulled away.

CHAPTER TWENTY-TWO

MAMA RUSHED INTO HER BEDROOM to put away her bag. She threw on her cape. "I'm going to the jailhouse to see your father. I'll fetch Rooster from the O'Briens' on the way back. Don't fret, girls. This will all get sorted out in time."

Klima sat with her bird, taking obsessive care of it. It seemed to give her solace.

Nikaia laid a hand on her sister's shoulder. "I'll get some water. We'll boil potatoes for dinner." She left the house and went straight to Yee-wa.

Through the store window, she saw Yee Sim and his mother counting through a pile of neatly folded work shirts draped over his arm. When he looked up and spotted her, he dropped the shirts to the floor and headed for the door. Yee Sun's lips moved, her expression sharp. Yee Sim responded without breaking his stride.

He let out a heavy breath when he met her at the store entrance, and his eyes seemed so warm and moist that, for an instant, Nikaia thought he might reach out and embrace her.

"Father told me about your papa," he said. "I'm so sorry, Nikaia."

Nikaia was relieved that she didn't have to tell him the awful news. She didn't know if her heart could stand her putting into words the anguish she felt at her father's arrest. It dawned on her how much she had missed Yee Sim and the peace she felt in his presence. *Has it been only four days since we left for Lytton?*

"Mama's gone to see him now in the jailhouse." She tried to keep her voice steady. "But the police seem set on going after him for the murder."

"I'm sorry," he repeated.

"And the judge is coming on tomorrow's sternwheeler. I fear that Papa will be taken to court and put on trial." She hadn't articulated that before, and the saying of it brought a lump to her throat.

Yee Sim blinked and frowned. "I don't know what we can do other than look for the man we saw in the woods. Maybe we should watch for him on Front Street. He might want to gamble there with some of the gold. And tomorrow, we can sit outside the Yale Ball and try to spot him. Half the town will be there. Maybe we'll see his hat. The brooch."

"Yee Sim, I think I know where the gold might be buried." She related her visit with Reverend Poole.

"Empyreal stones: the Stones of Heaven," Yee Sim repeated. "Jade. The Indian graveyard." He looked skeptical. "Why would someone dig up the gold and bury it again somewhere else? Why would he go to that trouble?"

"I can't say. The man said the hiding place was temporary. They mentioned someone else, a third man. So maybe the man with the hat wants to keep it hidden for himself until he can safely leave town." A new thought occurred to her. *The next sternwheeler gets here tomorrow and returns to the coast tomorrow night. Maybe that's his escape? If it is, I'm running out of time.* "I only know that the man said he'd rebury the gold. Before he shot Matthew Doyle. So I have to go and look for it. Will you come with me?"

"Of course I will."

"We haven't much time. I can't leave Klima for long."

The air carried a chill as they rushed up the bench to the graveyard. They had reached the first gravestones, in the white part of the cemetery, when Yee Sim grabbed her shoulder.

"Listen!" he said.

Nikaia heard voices approaching from the river side of the graveyard. They crouched behind a family headstone, a large smooth boulder inscribed with many names and dates. Yee Sim peered over the top.

"Keep low!" Nikaia hissed.

"It's the gravedigger," Yee Sim whispered.

Nikaia peeked over the top of the boulder. Mr. Collier wore a black cap and a topcoat with tails reaching down to his ankles. Following closely behind him was the wiry frame of Elias Doyle. The gravel crunched under their boots as the men walked over and stopped about ten yards from where Nikaia and Yee Sim were hiding.

"I presume the site meets with your satisfaction?" Mr. Collier asked.

Elias Doyle looked down at the newly leveled soil and the simple wooden cross. The smaller words and dates were hard to see, but Nikaia could read the name *Matthew Clyde Doyle* carved into the horizontal bar of the marker.

Elias Doyle nodded grimly. "What'll it be, then?"

The gravedigger's thin lips curled. "Well, as we like to say, lives come cheap in Fort Yale. But a gravesite will still cost you half a crown."

Doyle retrieved a small drawstring pouch from his jacket pocket. He selected a coin and handed it to Mr. Collier.

"Pleasure doing business with you, Mr. Doyle. And my condolences on the loss of your brother." Mr. Collier touched his cap and started away.

"Hold on." Doyle dug in his coin pouch and held up another half-crown.

Mr. Collier eyed him warily. "You're in a generous spirit, Mr. Doyle."

Doyle's face was hard as clay. "I expect you'll have yet another grave to fill before long."

He flipped the coin from his palm, and the undertaker snagged it out of the air. Doyle spat into the dirt. "Might as well start diggin', Mr. Collier."

Nikaia watched and waited, her stomach tumbling as the two men walked away. The bitter words of Elias Doyle, spoken with such grim conviction, alarmed her to the point of panic. Any excitement she'd held for exploring the graveyard evaporated.

When the men disappeared from view, she looked at Yee Sim. "Let's go back."

He nodded, and they returned to the path, wary of every twig snap until they reached the safety of their homes.

CHAPTER TWENTY-THREE

S ETTLED BENEATH HER HEAVY COVERS that night, Nikaia welcomed sleep. It brought with it many dreams. She found herself riverside, poking at a campfire with a fir branch. Yee Sim sat next to her on a piece of flat driftwood, watching the smoke curl into the night air. He reached for her hand. Bending toward her, he brushed his lips against her fingers.

An owl hooted. *Was it real or part of her dream?* She stirred and lay between sleep and wakefulness, not wanting to disrupt the tender scene in her mind. *I must still be in my dream. I can smell the campfire.*

Wait. Something is burning! She threw back her half of the blanket. She pushed open the bedroom door and gasped as her mother darted past her toward the kitchen.

She started to follow her. "Mama?"

"Wake your sister!" Mama's voice was filled with urgency. "Now!"

Nikaia looked past her and saw a wall of flame in the kitchen. "Klima!" She raced back to their bedroom.

Klima met her at the door, her eyes wild.

Nikaia shoved her toward the front door. "Get out! Quickly!"

They both rushed to the gravel clearing between their cabin and Front Street. Rooster, tied to the woodshop, stamped the ground and twisted in circles.

Nikaia took Klima's face in her hands. "Stay here. I need to move Rooster away from the cabin."

Klima clutched her shoulder. "No. I'll move Rooster. You help Mama."

Nikaia looked back at the cabin. Light flashed and danced at the kitchen window, and Mama's outline appeared as she struggled against the advancing fire.

Nikaia ran back inside. Her eyes stung with the smoke that already covered the walls and ceiling as she made her way to the kitchen. "Mama!"

One of the log walls was awash in flames, the dry wood crackling and throwing off cinders. Mama was leaning into the standup cupboard, inching it away from the burning wall. Overturned on the floor beside her was the wash bucket.

Mama turned to Nikaia. "Take the bucket! Go to the river."

"Mama, what about our own water?" The outside rain barrel had been partly full after yesterday's washing and cleaning.

"It's gone. I've used it!"

Nikaia snatched the bucket from the floor and fled from the cabin, her eyes watering. In a beat, Klima was beside her. Rooster was tied to a post near the road, braying in fear but safely separated from the flames.

"Get Rooster's grain bucket. We need river water," Nikaia said.

Klima hitched up her nightgown and sprinted for the bucket. She returned with it swinging from her hand, and they raced across the street to the riverbank, trying to avoid the sharper rocks with their bare feet. Nikaia sank the grain bucket deep into the eddy. Klima grabbed the handle and ran back to the cabin. Nikaia filled the kitchen bucket. She willed herself to keep the bucket from spilling as she overtook her sister.

As they approached the cabin, Nikaia's hopes fell. The outer logs facing the woodshop were nothing but a barrier of orange flames. The few gallons of water they carried would be of no significance.

Mama dragged the kitchen cabinet out the door. Her face was smudged with sweaty soot. Nikaia swung her water at the wall, but her effort had no noticeable effect. She ran back to Klima to get the grain bucket.

We need help, and lots of it. Can't the neighbors hear Rooster?

The thought had barely entered her head when she saw silhouettes of people approaching the cabin. Yee Ah and Yee Sun carried metal buckets from the store, as did the McGregor men—a father and son. The Claringtons carried shovels and pails. Others appeared through the haze: Mrs. Knight with her two teenaged daughters, Albert George and his father, and James Wesley, a shopkeeper who lived on Front Street.

The wind and the hungry flames combined to make for a bellowing roar in Nikaia's ears. James Wesley put his fingers to his mouth and whistled loudly. Once everyone gathered around him, he organized a bucket brigade. The neighbors started to pass buckets, hand to hand, from the river to the cabin.

Mrs. Knight brought blankets to Nikaia and Klima, even though they were both filmy with sweat. Nikaia stared in shock at the activity around their home. The cabinet was out on the gravel, as well as the chest from Papa's bedside.

Mama came over to where they sat. Her forehead was dripping and blackened, but she kept her voice calm. "I need you to get your blankets and clothes. And your sister's, as well. Stay clear of the flames. Don't touch anything hot. Can you do that?"

Nikaia looked over at the incinerating cabin. In the face of her mother's composure, Nikaia felt a peaceful kind of ferocity. "Yes."

"Take all you can in one trip, then don't go into the cabin again."

Nikaia knew with those words that their home was lost. It was time to salvage as much of their belongings as they could.

She ran through the door and pushed through a blanket of heat that grew thicker as she moved into the front room. The fire was limited to the walls, but smoke was collecting and filling the room. She pulled in a lungful of air and bolted toward her bedroom.

She ripped open drawers, slinging clothes and blankets over her arm. She gathered the deerskin shoes from under the bed. Sweat flowed freely down the sides of her face and soaked through her shirt. She spun and raced around the perimeter of the room, seeking anything else she should collect. Near the bed, she spotted a bundle of material. With one arm laden with clothes, she scooped up the bundle with her free hand and stuffed it into the open neckline of her nightgown.

As she stepped through the bedroom doorway, a low groan sounded from overhead. She looked up to see a log beam shuddering in the ceiling. Suddenly, it splintered and threw off a shower of sparks. She backed into the room, dropping the clothes and blankets, and covered her face with her arms. The wood joints shrieked as they ripped apart from the walls. The beam crashed to the floor, landing outside her bedroom door in a black cloud of ash.

She brought her arms down and saw a wall of fire blocking her way out of the room. Terrified, she gauged the height of the flames. *I can't leap over that. Lord help me, I'm trapped.*

She brought her hands to her mouth. "Mama!" Her words were lost in the roar of the fire.

She scanned the room and ran to the small window beside the bed. She pounded on it with the heels of her hands, but the sturdy glass held firm. The smoke thickened, and she dropped to all fours, gulping in the cleaner air near the floor. She tried to call for Mama again but could only draw in small gasps of breath.

She looked back toward the fire. The beam had fractured, and one small piece of it jutted into the room like a broken limb. Nikaia crawled to the pile of things she had dropped and pulled out a weighty wool blanket. She wrapped the blanket around one end of the broken section, thankful that it had not yet been seared by the fire. She pulled with all the strength she could muster, and a short chunk of wood separated from the main beam.

The piece was a stub, two feet long and heavy. Nikaia got on her knees and hoisted the wood to her shoulder. She slid the weight forward to balance it, wincing as the coarse wood scraped her skin through the light cloth of her nightgown. She rose and pivoted toward the window, which was barely visible through the black smoke. She let out a cry and charged toward the wall. At the last instant, she heaved the log. A vertical crack appeared in the glass as the wood dropped to the floor. She picked up the log and threw it again. The window shattered.

Instantly, cold air swept across her face. Behind her, the fire roared with new energy, a living beast devouring the stream of fresh oxygen. She darted to the pile of belongings and hurled them through the open window. She hoisted her upper body to the sill, tilted forward, and landed in a heap among the blankets.

She gathered their possessions and ran across the gravel to Klima, who looked stricken with despair. Nikaia dropped her armload into the weeds beside Rooster's post. Mama appeared beside her and added to the pile with some of hers and Papa's clothes, an oil lantern, an axe, and Papa's rifle.

Mama turned back to the cabin. "I'm going to get some more things from the kitchen."

Nikaia stared at her in horror. "Mama, no! The roof is coming down!" The words scraped in her throat, and she coughed to clear the smoke from her chest. She reached for Mama's shoulder, but another coughing spasm forced her to lean over and catch her breath.

"I'll see if I can knock the fire down from the walls. That might give me more time in there." Mama picked up the axe. "I'll be careful."

A sick grip of fear took hold of Nikaia's stomach as she watched her mama disappear into the smoke.

Klima stared at the pile on the ground. "Jill. I forgot to get Jill." She started to tear up as she looked at Nikaia.

Nikaia reached into the unbuttoned opening at the top of her nightgown. She passed a crumpled red handkerchief to her sister. Klima unwrapped the small bundle and let out a whoop of joy. She placed the bird on the blankets then wrapped her arms around Nikaia's waist. Squeezing hard, Klima burst into tears, shaking as she held Nikaia tighter and tighter.

Hearing shouts from the water brigade, Nikaia pulled away to join the line. She heard the knocks of an axe against the kitchen wall. *Mama.* The outside wall of the cabin cracked and popped as if in agony while being consumed. The wind whipped and snapped the flames into a searing frenzy.

Mama stepped out of the house, wiping her face with her sleeve. In her other hand, she dragged the axe. Her eyes held only resignation. Their home was lost.

The efforts turned to protecting the woodshop and keeping the fire from spreading to the surrounding homes and stores. The water brigade slowed, and the men picked up shovels provided by Yee Ah. They dug into the clay ground to form firebreaks and stamped the burning speargrass with their boots.

Klima nestled her bird, staring blankly at the blaze.

Nikaia drew a blanket around them. "We're safe," she rasped.

A tear rolled down Klima's cheek. "Where will we sleep?"

"I don't know. We'll talk to Mama, and..." Nikaia trailed off when she caught sight of Constable Whittock. He and a stocky red-bearded man walked to the side of the cabin. "I'll be back in a minute," Nikaia said to Klima, and she followed a few steps behind the constable.

The men spoke quietly as they surveyed the ground. Constable Whittock hunkered down with a long fir branch and prodded the soil near the smoldering cabin. Then he poked at the charred wood of the wall.

The bearded man wiped his brow with a meaty hand. "It's a curious smell, sir."

Constable Whittock moved his nose closer to the wall. He turned and looked at the other man. "Curious indeed, Mr. McRaney. It's kerosene." They turned back toward the street, and Nikaia rejoined Klima.

She took in the scene. The remains of the cabin stood blackened and scarred. Flashes of light and burning embers lit up the cabin windows. She wondered what was burning... her bed, her clothes chest? Mama's rocking chair? Papa's old trapping gear? And the books... the books would all be lost. *All our belongings are nothing more than kindling.*

Atop homes up and down the street, tiny points of light flickered in the night. Sons and daughters had been sent to the rooftops with handheld lanterns and pails of sand. The planked and cedar-shingled roofs were as dry as stove kindling, and the burning of one home could easily lead to the devastation of an entire block.

Her back to the fire, Nikaia looked out into the blackness. An ember floated past, aglow in orange and twisting in the wind like an autumn leaf reversing its descent to the forest floor. She watched it travel upward and land on a nearby rooftop. A lantern light swung as a child approached the ember to pour sand on it.

The wind regained its vigor, and with each gust, a constellation of ashy embers took to the air then rained downward. It looked like the nightscape of a mad world with its firmament collapsing and stars descending in fiery spirals down to the earth.

She caught a glimpse of Yee Sim looking out toward the cabin from the slanted roof of Yee-wa. Their eyes met. Then a spark landed behind him. He picked up his bucket of sand and retreated behind the roofline, out of sight.

Nikaia waited for him to reappear, but he did not. She turned back to watch the embers and saw something that put a cold grip on her heart. A figure, clearly a man, was half-hidden in the forested darkness behind the cabin. For an instant, the roof flames overcame the shadows and lit up his face. He retreated and disappeared into the night. But Nikaia had seen enough.

Elias Doyle.

CHAPTER TWENTY-FOUR

"NIKAIA," MAMA SAID, "YOU AND Klima will stay with Mrs. Knight tonight." She squeezed Nikaia's shoulder.

Nikaia stiffened. She wanted to be as close to safety as possible, and if she couldn't be near Papa, she certainly wanted to be with Mama.

Before she could protest, Mama pressed a finger gently on Nikaia's lips. "I'll be right here at the woodshop, and I'll come and get you both in the morning. Nikaia, you be strong for your sister."

Mama's forehead was streaked with black soot. Her long black hair had escaped the bundle of her braid, and the acrid scent of sulfur arose from its singed endings. Her cotton nightgown, soaked in sweat, was swathed in dark smears of gray and black. It occurred to Nikaia that the sight of Mama, along with the hoarseness of her smoke-ravaged voice, might have given an onlooker the impression of a wild woman. But Mama's eyes were calm, and the stains of the night's exertions couldn't hide the graceful arc of her eyebrows or the relaxed curve of her lips. Mama may have been desperate, even foolhardy, in her struggles against the fire, but Nikaia couldn't help but admire her mother's ability to summon a composed presence – even if only for the benefit of her daughters.

Nikaia glanced over at Klima, who was fussing over Jill. Mama smiled wearily and brushed Nikaia's nose with her finger. Nikaia nodded and turned to sift through their things for items they might need for an overnight stay.

She separated Mama and Papa's clothing from the pile. For herself and Klima, she had managed to salvage a handful of shirts, some underclothing, two pair of shoes, and two skirts, along with the wool sheets from their bed. The blanket she had used to wrap the ceiling beam still smoldered, and Nikaia pressed it into the soil to cool it.

"Klima, put your shoes on and let me pass you some of this." She tossed the moccasins to her sister then put on her own. She shook out the shirts and skirts and laid them over Klima's arm, taking care not to cover the bird.

The meager selection represented all that had been salvaged from the cabin. The family had always lived simply, but their worldly possessions had now been reduced to a pathetic collection that would barely cover the floor of Rooster's cart. The same thought must have come to Klima because her eyes reddened and watered as she looked at the small pile.

Nikaia gathered a chemise and stockings for each of them. She gave Klima a shoulder squeeze. "Come on. Let's carry this to the Knights'."

Mrs. Knight occasionally assisted Mrs. Trey with the younger grades at the schoolhouse. Her husband had worked as an accountant for the gold commissioner until Mr. Knight had died of influenza last year. She and her daughters, Sarah and Hannah, lived in an ornate two-story house on Albert Street.

The Knights' home loomed tall and stately as she and Klima approached. Warm lights glowed from between the tasseled curtains covering the windows. They climbed the bannistered set of steps that led to the front door.

As Nikaia lifted the brass knocker and let it fall, she felt Klima tugging at her shoulder.

"Is my nose clean?" Klima asked, tilting her head back slightly.

Nikaia suppressed a smile. Sooty tearstains covered Klima's cheeks, flecks of ash speckled her black hair, and her clothes reeked of smoke. Surely both of them looked like vagabonds. Still, she gave Klima a quick inspection. "Small cub in left cave," she whispered as the door opened.

Nikaia and Klima settled into a shared bed at the Knight home. Nikaia marveled at the large room and well-appointed furnishings. A pair of housecats, one an orange tabby and the other as white as cotton, roamed the house in regal fashion. The white one, Lily, sprang onto the bed and settled between Nikaia's shins. She reached down and stroked its head, eliciting a rumbling of pleasure from the cat.

Nikaia thought of how odd it would be if the tables were reversed and the Knight girls had to stay with the Wales. Sarah and Hannah would be tucked in with rough woolen blankets, rather than the quilted linen layers of bedspreads. And the cats... well, Rooster was the closest thing the Wales had to a pet, except perhaps for Jill, who was sleeping in a handkerchief on the nightstand. Klima had not been happy to see the cats and didn't trust them enough to leave the bird on the windowsill.

The comfortable setting at the Knight house might have been a welcome distraction. But the strong smell of smoke from her nightgown made it impossible to push back the terrible happenings of that day.

Across the room, Sarah and Hannah stood in their long white nightgowns, negotiating who would sleep on which side of the second bed. The two of them wore sleeping caps fringed with lace.

"Thank you for lending us your bed, Hannah," Nikaia said.

"You're welcome. Sarah doesn't mind sharing her bed with me for the night. Do you, Sarah?"

"No snoring," was the reply.

"You, too! And no kicking, either."

"And no humming!" they both said at the same time, then broke into good-natured laughter.

The Knight girls were a few years younger than Klima. Nikaia knew them from the schoolyard but hadn't interacted with them much. They were quieter at school than in their home setting.

Sarah walked over to the nightstand and turned down the wick on the kerosene lamp. "I'm so sorry about your home." She blew out the light.

Later, in the dark, Klima's soft sobs awoke Nikaia. Nikaia put an arm around her sister.

Klima sniffled. "I wish that Mama and Papa were here with us."

Nikaia squeezed her tightly. "I do, too. It can't be very comfortable for Mama sleeping in the woodshop." *Or for Papa locked in the jailhouse.* Nikaia thought of her mother telling her to be strong for her sister. "We'll see Mama in the morning," she said in an upbeat voice.

Klima whispered, "I know why she wants to stay there."

"What do you mean?"

"To make sure that the woodshop is safe. To make sure... that whoever burned our cabin doesn't come back again tonight."

In the dim light, Nikaia looked over at Klima. *My sister is more aware of things than I give her credit for.*

Mama knocked on Mrs. Knight's door early the next morning. Nikaia wanted to see the cabin's remains. It was somewhat like the desire to see Auntie Tsaht-koo's body before burial. At one time, she had found that custom to be gruesome and odd, but it had come to seem more understandable. Too many losses lately.

"There's not much left to see," Mama said, "but we can walk down there. I have to do some arranging in the woodshop, in any event."

It had rained in the night, and scattered drops continued to fall from the gray clouds. Nikaia squeezed her mother's hand as the path dropped toward the edge of town. She sensed Mama's hesitation as the remnants of the cabin came into view.

A handful of townspeople were standing outside and looking at the burned carcass of the cabin. The rain had stifled the smoke, although the stench of the burnt wood filled Nikaia's nose and stung her eyes as they got closer.

Their home looked as if a child had pulled ashen sticks from a cold cooking fire and assembled them carelessly into the form of a cabin. The reading corners, the floors where she and Klima had played so many games, their favorite hiding spots, their bedroom—everything was crumbled and unrecognizable. All the colors and aromas of her childhood were soaked in black and smelling of ash.

Yee Sim stepped out of his father's supply store. Nikaia walked over to him, anticipating his words of sympathy and comfort. As she approached, she noticed he had a troubled look on his face. For a moment, they stood side by side and watched the smoldering ruins.

"Nikaia, I'm sorry. For all that has happened." He pushed the toe of his boot into the wet ground. "I have to stay away from you for a while."

The words stole the air from Nikaia's lungs. All she could do was stare at him.

"My father is very upset. Mother, too. I didn't tell you yesterday, but they were questioned by the police while you were gone. Many questions, about the gold."

Nikaia put her hand over her mouth.

"I told them everything I knew. They're fearful, Nikaia, about my father's position in this town. Our family's reputation."

Her cheeks burned in shame. *How had she brought this about, to the family of her closest friend?*

"But it's not only that." Yee Sim looked over at the charred logs. "The fire. Maybe it was an accident. Or maybe it was... retribution." He looked back at Yee-wa. "And are we next? Or what if the fire had spread to our store? What would we do without that? Drive mule trains? Eat roots and berries by the light of a candle stuck in a potato? No. We'd probably go back to China."

Nikaia was heartsick. She wanted to speak but found no words.

Yee Sim went on. "My parents, they work so hard. And last night, it would have taken no more than a north breeze, a change in wind direction, to spread the fire and have it all taken away." He waved his hand at the store. "To destroy us."

"Oh, Yee Sim, I'm so sorry." Tears overflowed from her eyes. "I do understand why your parents wouldn't want anything to do with my family. With me."

"It's not my parents. It's my decision. We can't afford trouble like this." He looked at her, then away. "I have to keep my distance. I have to protect my family. I'm sorry, too."

She watched as he walked away, half-expecting him to return and take back his words. She felt her heart tighten in anguish as he disappeared into the store. She sat alone on the ground and stared at the burned-out hull of the cabin. Thoughts tumbled in her head like sticks aswirl in an eddy line. It was time to—*what was Yee Sim's way of putting it?*—to take stock.

Papa was in the jailhouse, unfairly accused, his reputation no doubt shattered. The cabin was burned to the ground, leaving her family homeless. The Doyles were out for blood—she was sure of it. Her friendship with Yee Sim was over.

And the sternwheeler would bring the judge later that day. Constable Whittock would be pressed to have answers, to have a culprit identified. Law and order would prevail, even if an innocent man was punished.

And it was her doing, her meddling, that had caused everything. Her clumsy attempts to set things right had gotten nowhere, or perhaps even made matters worse.

Nikaia wanted to cry out her pain. No sounds seemed equipped to match what had happened to her family. In that bitter rain, she wept in silence and tasted the salt of her shame and her sorrow.

CHAPTER TWENTY-FIVE

THE CELL DOOR CRASHED AS it closed. The officer twisted a key in the lock and stuffed the enormous key-ring into his vest pocket. "I'll be nearby, Mrs. Wales. Just call out when you're done." He gave them a sympathetic look and walked back into the office.

Papa stood up from his cot and stretched his arms wide to embrace all three of them. The cell contained only a tiny bed, a low stool, and a chamber pot. Papa's flannel shirt—the same one he had worn during their trip from Lytton—had folds crumpled into it. He must have slept in it, Nikaia thought. But from the dark shadows under his eyes, she would be surprised if he had slept at all.

News of the fire had reached him, of course. His voice broke as he said, "That was the hardest night of all my life, being kept in here away from all of you." He swiped his eyes. "I've sent up many thanks to heaven that you're all safe." He drew the girls closer in his embrace.

Mama sat on the stool, near enough to touch his knee. "They don't know the cause, yet." She handed over a brown paper parcel tied with twine. "Here, I brought you clean clothes."

"I wrapped it neatly," Klima said, "but the policeman opened it when we got here."

"Thank you, Klima. I suppose he wouldn't want you smuggling in a hacksaw blade from my shop." Papa gestured in a sawing motion toward the cell bars, and Klima laughed.

"Our home is gone, Papa," Nikaia blurted. "It's all gone."

Papa threw the parcel on the cot and pulled her in to him. He reached for Klima, then Mama, their arms entangling in a warm knot.

"You all listen to me now." His voice was throaty with emotion. "That fire burned our house down last night. I know that. It's a terrible thing. Honestly, I don't know how we'll rebuild it. And I can't say how long that might take."

Nikaia pulled back to look at Papa's face.

"But last night," he continued, "as I stood here smelling the smoke and fearing for your lives, the fate of that cabin was the least of my fears. I was sickened to think of any of you being hurt, or worse."

He squeezed them hard. "You feel this? *This* is our home. Wherever we are, whatever our circumstances, our home is right here." He released them and touched Klima's nose, then Nikaia's.

Nikaia surveyed the walls of the cell and thought how strange it was to be gathered with her family in such a place. But Papa's words somehow carried truth. She buried her face in the woody fragrance of his sleeves.

"Good afternoon, all," someone said from outside the cell door.

"Afternoon, Constable," Papa said.

Constable Whittock eyed the parcel of clothes. "You won't be needing that, John. I'm releasing you."

Constable Whittock apologized to Papa, saying that Deputy Quigg had acted with unwarranted zeal in arresting him. "With Judge Begbie arriving on today's sternwheeler, we certainly want to be careful to act with due process." He secured a promise from Papa that there would be no more trips outside of Fort Yale and led them out of the cell.

The family walked home, arm in arm, adjusting their strides to match Klima's somewhat shorter steps.

Papa was jovial, his steps lively as they passed over the boardwalks. "We could have used this rain while we were on the wagon road."

"It would have kept the dust down. Look at you. Your trousers are still covered in it," Mama said.

"I prefer my home laundry to that of the jailhouse," Papa said. "Although the workers there are much more friendly." He nudged Mama's side with a grin. "In fact—" He stopped as he viewed the burned cabin for the first time.

Nikaia imagined he was recalling all of the hard work that had gone into the building of it. Mama clasped Papa's hand. It was a long while before Papa spoke.

"When we build it up again, we'll make it bigger," he said quietly. "Perhaps two woodstoves—one in the kitchen and one in a sitting room. And we'll make another bedroom. Each of you girls can have your own."

"No!" Klima protested. "I like sleeping with Nikaia."

"All right!" Papa laughed. "We have a lot of time to plan it out."

His good humor gave Nikaia a sense of lightness she hadn't felt in days. Even Mama wore a slight smile as they continued walking and neared the cabin.

"My land, who might that be?" Mama was looking toward the woodshop carriage doors.

A bonneted woman in an evening gown waited there. Beside her were two large covered baskets.

"Why, it's Frannie!" Nikaia exclaimed. "I mean, Mrs. O'Hare."

As the family approached, Frannie smoothed her dress. She addressed herself to Mama. "Mrs. Wales, my name is Frannie O'Hare. I don't believe we've met."

"Why, it's very nice to meet you. I've seen you at the church services. Welcome to our humble abode," Mama said wryly, waving at the blackened cabin.

"It's a dreadful happening. Such a neat home, I've seen it many times from the road. I'm so sorry for you all."

"Thank you. My husband's a resourceful man, and we'll rebuild as soon as we're able. For now, we'll be comfortable enough in his woodshop. Can you come in? I'll steep some tea."

"Dear me, no, but thank you so much. I just came to drop off some things." She reached for the baskets and opened them to reveal tidy layers of sweaters and blankets. "Some of my friends contributed as well. You seem like a good, decent family, and our thoughts go out to you for your troubles."

Mama pressed her hand to her heart. "I don't know what to—"

Frannie cut in. "Now, we've offered something like this a time or two before—not often, mind you—and some folks won't take it. I understand if you don't feel comfortable accepting this. But I do hope you will." Her voice wavered, and she looked at the ground. "You don't have to tell anyone it came from us."

Mama took a step closer to her. "Frannie, I'm pleased to accept it. You show us great kindness." She threw her arms around Frannie's neck.

The woman stiffened, then gradually gave in to the hug and reciprocated. After a few pleasantries, Frannie said she needed to go. She looked at Nikaia. "Child, could you remove the clothes and bring the empty baskets? I'll wait out near the street."

Nikaia rushed to do so, dumping the basket's contents onto the sleeping mats Mama had laid out at the back of the woodshop. She ran back out and down to the street.

Frannie stooped to take the baskets and brought her mouth close to Nikaia's ear. "Child, I don't pretend to know all that is happening with you. But I've been pondering about the other night when you showed up at York's. Your question about the brooch... it has something to do with your family's troubles?"

Nikaia nodded.

"Well, I *do* know about that brooch. It was purchased on the reserve by a friend of mine, Reba. She wore it for some time. She's a twin, so it was special to her. Twin owls. A beautiful piece."

"Oh." Nikaia's heart fell. She had hoped there would somehow be a connection to the man in the woods.

"She wore it a few times," Frannie said. "But then I didn't see her with it, and one night I asked her if I could borrow it. We often share our jewelry, and if she wasn't going to wear it, I thought I might. But she had given it away. To a friend, she said."

"A friend? Who?"

Frannie paused. "Child... well, I suppose you're old enough to know this. It was a gentleman caller, and in our line of work, we don't name our friends." She drew even closer and spoke in a hushed voice. "But in this case, the man is a pig, so I don't mind telling. It went to a man named Quigg. Thomas Quigg."

Nikaia drew back, her eyes wide. "The police deputy?"

"You heard nothing from me."

Nikaia's head spun as she watched Frannie walk away. She tried to picture Deputy Quigg as the man in the woods. The man under the broad-brimmed hat was slight in frame, and that fit with Deputy Quigg. But Quigg's muttonchops... wouldn't those have been noticeable? She thought back to what she had seen through the spyglass. The memory was blurred, and she could remember only that the hat brim had hung down low across the man's features.

A whistle blew from the distant back eddy. The sternwheeler was approaching with the judge on board. It occurred to Nikaia that when the sternwheeler left that evening, it could very well take the murderer, and the gold, away with it. That would make it nearly impossible to clear Papa of the charges against him. Time was running out.

Her heart pounded in her ears. She felt as if she were having an attack of nerves. Her mind flashed to Mrs. McLeod and how her assignment of purposeful actions had helped the family in its coping. *I need to calm down, I need to stop my head from spinning. What's the best action I can take?*

I need help, and quickly. Her mind turned to Yee Sim, and she recalled how cold and hard his words had been. She knew he was acting to protect his family. *Well, I have a family to protect, too.*

The day's light was already starting to fade. She found her sister in the woodshop, laying out the clothes that Frannie had delivered. "Klima, I need you to come with me."

"Where are we going?"

"To the Indian graveyard."

CHAPTER TWENTY-SIX

THE SCENT OF TURNED SOIL hung in the air. The awful disease had continued to spread through Fort Yale, and the cemetery ground, green with weeds, was pocked with the dark mounds of freshly filled graves, especially in the Indian section.

Nikaia stroked a pumpkin-sized marble stone that lay beside a simple beveled plaque of cedar with words worn beyond legibility. An overgrowth of speargrass and dandelions marked the outline of the grave.

"See this jade, Klima? It's the Stone of Heaven. Somewhere in this graveyard, the gold is hidden. I'm sure of it."

Her sister looked around doubtfully. "Where to start?"

Nikaia admitted that she didn't know. The jade stones were everywhere in that part of the graveyard. They walked past an unusually large family marker made of laminated cedar planks. It measured close to four feet and was labeled, *Peters Family*. They continued strolling among the uneven rows of graves.

"Let's split up," Nikaia said. "You walk from the far end, and I'll meet you in the middle."

"What are we looking for, exactly?" Klima asked.

"Anything unusual, I suppose." Nikaia was terrified that she had misunderstood the Empyreal Stones term, or that the man in the woods—Quigg?—had meant something different by it. Or maybe he had simply thrown it out as a ruse to put Matthew Doyle off the trail of the gold.

They separated, and Nikaia studied each wooden cross she passed. Some stood clean and upright, painted white and engraved on the crosspiece with crudely lettered names and dates. The ones from older burials lay askew like so many yellowed rows of crooked teeth.

She read the inscriptions, looking for anything that might be a clue.

IN MEMORY OF
GERALD FLEMING
BORN 1819 DIED 1861
LORD BE MERCIFUL TO ME A SINNER

IN MEMORY OF
MARY KAL'PEKA MORSE
Who Died April 14th, 1862
AGED 32 years

"Nikaia! Look!" Klima's voice carried across the cemetery.

Nikaia ran to her.

"Look!" Klima said again, gesturing at a grave with newly mounded soil. "The ground is dug up here."

Nikaia stared. "So? A lot of graves are freshly dug."

"Look at the date." Klima pointed at the headstone. "She died in 1854. Nine years ago. So why would her grave be fresh?"

Nikaia looked at the faint letters painted on the wooden marker.

Lei "Jade" Wong
Beloved Wife of Lei Lin
August 1825 - March 1854

Nikaia dropped to her knees beside the upturned soil. "Oh, Klima, you clever girl." She pulled at the dirt.

"Clever would have been bringing a shovel," Klima said dryly.

"I know! Help me."

They used their hands to pull at the loose dirt. The digging was easy, even without tools. A subtle glint of brass appeared. More scraping revealed a satchel buckle.

"It's here! It's here. We found it." Nikaia tugged the satchel from the earth. She clutched it to her chest, dirt spilling from its overfold.

Her exhilaration was interrupted by the sound of boots crunching in the distance. She looked at Klima in alarm.

"This way!" Nikaia hissed.

They crouched and weaved from headstone to headstone, scanning around for the source of the footsteps. They took refuge behind the cedar boards of the Peters marker. Nikaia laid the satchel on the ground between them.

Some of the wooden panels of the grave marker had separated, and Nikaia peered through a crack. A slight man in black trousers and dress boots came into view. He looked around nervously. *Muttonchops. It's Quigg.*

He walked over to the Lei Wong grave then stopped and stared at the strewn soil. Picking up a short fir branch, he crouched and used it to prod at the ground. Then he dropped to his knees and clawed at the soil, throwing back the dirt like a hungry dog. His head bobbed back and forth as he worked.

Eventually, he stood and wiped his hands on the sides of his trousers. Letting out a torrent of cursing, he drew a sidearm from the holster at his belt. He aimed the revolver straight up and fired.

The gunshot blast startled Nikaia. She snatched up the satchel and whispered, "Run." She sprinted toward the fringe of the graveyard, Klima on her heels.

"You scurvy! Thieving! Vermin! Get back here now, or you'll pay dearly!"

The revolver fired again. Nikaia dropped down a gully and headed for the creek. She leapt across. Klima, half a bound behind her, slipped on the wet rocks and fell backward into the water. The splashing betrayed their location. Nikaia turned back to help her sister and saw Quigg silhouetted on the ridge, a stone's throw away.

Quigg screeched against the rushing wind, "Stop! Or you'll suffer for this! Your whole family will suffer for this!" He started toward them, gun at the ready.

Nikaia yanked Klima to her feet, and they ran as if the gates of Hell had opened behind them.

CHAPTER TWENTY-SEVEN

"**W**HERE DO... WE GO? HOME?" Klima asked breathlessly as they ran up the other side of the gully.

"Yes! To Papa... then to Constable Whittock... with the gold," Nikaia said, gulping in air.

"Nikaia, my ankle. I hurt it at the creek. I can't keep up." Klima's face was strained and her strides unbalanced as she favored her right foot.

Nikaia looked behind them. Quigg had to be right on their heels. "Here, hide behind these bushes. Stay here until he's passed then run home and tell Papa!"

Nikaia ran on, deliberately stepping on dry twigs and brushing the leaves to divert attention from Klima's hiding place. Soon, she heard cursing and heavy footfalls behind her. *At least he's overlooked Klima.* She quickened her pace, but the satchel grew heavier with each step. She couldn't outrun the deputy for much longer.

Nikaia approached the lights of town. Her shoulder ached from the burden of the satchel.

Footsteps suddenly came up behind her. She looked over her shoulder, and to her relief, she saw Yee Sim. She stopped and said, "Oh, Yee Sim! It's Deputy Quigg. He stole the gold. He's following me!"

"What?"

She looked over his shoulder and saw Quigg running down the street. "Look! He's coming now. We have to run!"

She turned and sprinted toward Front Street, happy that Yee Sim ran with her and needed no further explanation. But she could hear the boots coming closer.

"He's catching up!" she gasped. "We need to split up." She switched the satchel to her left shoulder.

Yee Sim must have noticed her weariness. "I'll hide the gold," he said, not slowing his pace. "And meet you... where?"

Nikaia gratefully swung the satchel over to him. "Not at the woodshop. Not at Yee-wa." *Either place would be too obvious to Quigg.*

"Right," Yee Sim said. "We need to meet where there's a lot of people. There's safety in crowds."

Nikaia glanced over her shoulder and strained to pick up her pace. "The Yale Ball."

Yee Sim turned with the bag and raced across Regent Street and out of sight. Nikaia continued down Front Street, then zigzagged up the alleys and side roads. After a while, she realized she no longer heard Quigg behind her. *I've lost him.*

She settled behind some bushes on Douglas Street. She had a good line of sight from there to the lights and bustle of Bennett Hall.

Where is Yee Sim? Did Quigg catch him? Maybe the satchel was too heavy. Her thigh muscles were cramped from squatting, but she kept low, ears alert for Quigg. *Thank goodness Yee Sim showed up when he did.* His appearance and willingness to help confused her after the coldness of their last conversation. *And where is he now?* She dug her nails deep into her palms.

At last she spotted Yee Sim walking past Bennett's. She ran down to meet him. His sleeves were grimy with dirt and clay.

"Oh, Yee Sim! You're safe. Where'd you hide it?" Nikaia asked.

He gave her a sly grin. "Not here. Let's go inside."

"Wait." Nikaia couldn't shake the memory of Yee Sim abandoning her after the cabin fire. "I thought you were going to stay away from me." She tried but failed to keep the hurt out of her voice.

Yee Sim breathed out heavily. "I know. I meant to, for the sake of my family. But I knew you were in trouble. It seemed selfish not to try to help somehow. Or cowardly, I suppose." His voice quivered. "I couldn't stop thinking of you. And your troubles. I went to the woodshop to apologize, but you weren't home. I figured you might have gone back to the graveyard. I was worried."

That counted as a long speech coming from Yee Sim. Nikaia studied his dark eyes and lips, his fine eyebrows, and his cheek still smudged with clay. Every feature seemed to bear a glow of compassion. *Or was it something more? Fondness?* Whatever it was, she took in the warmth from his eyes and breathed it in deep. It caught in her throat. Afraid to speak lest she burst into tears, she had a sudden impulse to wrap her arms around his neck and kiss him on the lips.

Voices interrupted her thoughts. A finely dressed couple entered Bennett's through the dark wood door. Yee Sim pointed, keeping his hand movement subtle, and they slipped into the hall a half-step behind the couple.

Yale society patrons filled the large room. An orchestra of five fiddlers was assembled in one corner, playing "The Arkansas Traveler" with gusto.

All the women were dressed in their finery. Hair normally pinned into buns fell loose and long over shoulders, in the current fashion. Most wore hoop skirts or print gowns, and many sported new straw hats. The men were also decked out in bowlers, cravats, and heavy topcoats with welted flap pockets and bishop sleeves. Many carried canes, some with elaborate brass handles, others with curved ends of polished wood that the men hooked onto their forearms.

A blond woman walked past in a deep blue dress with a V-shaped bodice. Her sleeves were puffed out in an exaggerated fullness, making her waist seem impossibly small in comparison. The woman laughed gaily as her companion, an older gentleman in dashing long tails, handed her a glass of red wine. Nikaia stared admiringly as the two linked arms. Glasses of liquor clinked merrily. The babble of conversations and laughter almost drowned out the fiddlers.

Few people seemed to notice Nikaia and Yee Sim amid the bustle of the party. They walked warily along the edge of the room, twisting around the dancers, looking for somewhere to hide in case Quigg appeared.

"Are you two lost?" a woman asked. It was Mrs. Bradfield, whose husband ran a successful sluicing operation near Nicomen Creek. Her companions were standing around a table well-populated with half-full glasses of red wine.

"No," Nikaia said. "We... we're just looking for my papa."

"Isn't your father John Wales? I wouldn't expect he'd be *here*, dearie." Mrs. Bradfield sniffed and turned to reach for a fresh glass of wine.

Her friends whinnied as if she had said something wickedly clever. One of them murmured, "Try the jailhouse." The ladies tittered and closed their ring around the wine table.

Nikaia and Yee Sim pressed on through the crowd. She saw Frannie O'Hare and another lady sitting at a table containing black bottles of spirits. Frannie wore a hoop skirt of solid purple and a beige pleated blouse. Nikaia hesitated, then stepped toward her.

Yee Sim grabbed Nikaia's arm. "Oh, no." He stared toward the front door.

She turned to look. Deputy Quigg had entered the hall, his black hair pressed flat against his sweaty head. Nikaia and Yee Sim ducked behind some attendees and weaved their way to Frannie.

Quigg called out, "Police business! Where are the children? The Wales girl and a Chinese boy. Yee Ah's son."

Nikaia ran right up to Frannie and touched her arm. "Frannie, we're in trouble! Can you please help us hide?"

Frannie looked across the hall at Deputy Quigg. Nikaia followed her gaze.

Quigg was accosting a young man in a bowler near the entrance. "Answer me, man! Did you see them enter?"

The fiddlers stopped abruptly. The dancers paused then shuffled to the sides of the hall. With aggressive authority, Quigg started questioning each cluster of people, working his way up the wall toward the end bar.

Frannie hissed, "Get behind the bar."

Nikaia dove behind the counter. A strip of latticework gave her a partial view into the hall, through a forest of trousered legs and skirts. *Where's Yee Sim? I didn't give him enough time to get behind the bar.* He was nowhere in sight.

Quigg's dusty boots approached and stopped in front of Frannie. "I must declare I'm surprised to see *you* here. Slow night at the York?"

Nikaia shifted and looked up so she could see their faces.

Frannie had a smirk on her face. "Well, you're on duty tonight, so my business is slower than usual."

Her companion snorted and hid her face behind her wine glass.

Quigg glared at Frannie. "The girl. The Chinese boy. I know they ran through here. Where are they?"

Frannie shook her head. "I have no idea what you're talking about."

Quigg leaned in close. His wet forehead almost touched Frannie's. "Where are the little rats? In God's name, tell me, or I swear murder will be done."

Frannie stood as still as ice. Then she moved forward, causing Quigg to take a half-step back. "If you came here to proposition me," she said loudly, her voice cutting across the hall, "I should have hoped you had a little more steam in your boiler."

Across the room, someone giggled drunkenly. Murmuring rose throughout the crowd.

An ugly vein twitched in Quigg's forehead. "You'll pay for crossing me." He turned to continue surveying the room.

Frannie wasn't finished. "And, Mr. Quigg? I'm due a half-crown for last Saturday. Mr. Quigg!"

The crowd snickered. Snarling, Quigg retreated toward the door.

Frannie looked around the room as Yale's elite society stared at her, jaws hanging. "Pardon my coarseness, ladies. Gentlemen." She turned and adjusted her dress.

The fiddlers looked around and, with some hesitation, brought their instruments back to their chins. The music began anew.

Frannie shuffled backward to the bar. The hem of her skirt stirred like a stage curtain, and a pair of black-trousered legs emerged from the canopy of her birdcage. Yee Sim's face popped out, his ears as dark as boiled beets.

Nikaia ran out from her hiding place. "Thank you, Frannie!"

She bit her lip to keep from laughing. Surely Yee Sim would rather have faced Quigg's revolver than die of embarrassment. She clutched his hand, and they bolted out the rear door into the vacant street.

Nikaia felt a sudden lightness. *The gold is safely hidden, and we've escaped from Deputy Quigg. I'm surely close to resolving this mess.* She'd get Papa and find Constable Whittock. A sense of jubilation took hold, and her heart quickened at the thought of putting the whole sorry mess behind her.

CHAPTER TWENTY-EIGHT

"QUIGG WON'T BE LONG IN the hall," Yee Sim said as they ran up the boardwalk.

"I know. I need to run home and get Papa." A cold realization struck her. "Oh! No, I left Klima in the woods. I need to get her home."

"I'll come with you. Where in the woods?"

Nikaia tried to think and run at the same time. "Near the graveyard. But Yee Sim, I think you need to find Constable Whittock and tell him about Quigg."

Yee Sim hesitated. "I don't know if you'll be safe."

"I will be. And safer still once you find the constable."

The road sloped upward as they neared Victoria Street. "All right," Yee Sim said, gulping for air. "Oh! Nikaia. The gold. I buried the satchel near the Creaking Fir."

"Good, I'll let Papa know. Tell Constable Whittock, too. Let's split up at the next cross street."

"Wait! There's more. Before I buried the satchel, I went to Yee-wa for a spade. And I thought—"

"Stop!"

Nikaia did not need to look back to know it was Quigg. "Get the constable!" she cried.

Yee Sim darted left at the next alley, and Nikaia raced across the street. *To the woods? Or up Victoria Street hill?* She decided that going up the steep hill might give her a better chance of eluding Quigg.

Her thighs burned as she pumped her way up the incline. At the top, hearing no footsteps behind her, she slowed to a walk. Sweat dripped from her eyebrows and stung her eyes. She brushed a sleeve across her forehead and started to trot along Mary Street, a quiet roadway that paralleled Front Street. Her cabin—or at least, the woodshop—was less than a half-mile away. A five-minute run and she'd be there.

She hadn't covered fifty paces before a dark figure stepped out from the shadows and blocked her path.

"Enough games," Quigg said, nostrils flaring.

He reached out with talon-like hands and locked them onto her forearms. Even as he held her, he fought to regain his breath, his eyes bulging and his lips pulled back from his teeth. His eyebrows spasmed up and down, and a fine foam bubbled from the corner of his mouth. Nikaia thought with alarm that he might have gone quite insane.

He pulled her in close to his body. "You witch. You've caused me a great deal of trouble."

He manhandled her into the alley shadows. "This ends now. Tell me where the gold is this instant, or all that you hold dear will suffer." The words spattered like venom from his mouth. "Your father will hang. Your mother and your sister will pay for your idiocy. And you will suffer most of all. I'll see to that."

With that last phrase, he gripped her arms tighter and shook her. Nikaia cried out in pain. Releasing one arm, Quigg reached down to his side. His face seemed to relax into calmness as he raised the barrel of his revolver and aimed it at her face.

Her mind reeled in terror. Her insides pitched and rolled. A dizzying heat overtook her, and she doubled over, almost hitting the barrel with her forehead. In short heaves, she emptied the contents of her stomach onto the ground.

Quigg stepped back until her retching subsided. Wiping her mouth with the back of her hand, Nikaia prayed in desperation to the Creator and to her guardian spirit. *Help me, someone.*

She started to cry. "I know where it's buried. I'll take you to the gold."

Quigg twisted her around and shoved her forward. "Yes, you will." Nikaia led the way to the river, her legs unsteady and weak.

Quigg had her follow little-used side streets to avoid encountering anyone. Even so, he kept his revolver half-hidden in the folds of his overcoat as they walked into the gathering darkness.

They descended from the bench of land that overlooked the river, and she could see the sternwheeler resting in the eddy. It was unusual for such a boat to leave Fort Yale in the evening. The late-day departure was a sign of the rising competition among cargo-haulers. Handheld lanterns bobbed in the darkness as men loaded freight. A small group of passengers gathered around the riverbank near the gangplank.

Nikaia left the pathway and led Quigg to the Creaking Fir. She panicked when she saw no signs of digging. The limbs groaned overhead as she circled the tree. On its backside, away from the river, she spotted a patch of overturned soil.

"Get it out," Quigg growled.

Nikaia knelt and began scraping dirt from the shallow hole.

"Your meddling has surely vexed me this week," Quigg said as he waved his gun at her. "I ought to teach you a lasting lesson for it." He circled her and cackled like a crow. "But look at what you have now! In moments, I'll be aboard the sternwheeler with a fortune in gold, on my way to New Westminster and beyond. Meanwhile, your own father will be blamed, and jailed, I'm sure. Or maybe even strung up, if I know Judge Begbie. That works just fine for me! Thanks to your stupidity, you half-breed, your father certainly looks to be guilty as charged. Well done."

Nikaia's heart sank. She felt for the satchel and pulled it up out of the hole.

Quigg holstered his revolver and snatched it from her hands. He bobbed it up and down, gauging the weight of the bag. His expression turned to one of glee. "Now you listen to me. You will stay right here until the sternwheeler leaves." He patted his holster. "If I see you take so much as a footstep, I swear I'll use this and put an end to you for good."

Two whistle blasts came from the sternwheeler. Quigg looked toward the water. Ripping at the satchel buckles, he swung open the overflap. He pulled out a poke, yanked its drawstring, and glanced inside. His shrill laugh sounded manic. Then he glowered at Nikaia. "If I find you've pilfered so much as a thimble of dust from here, I swear I'll cut your ears off."

Nikaia felt the last remnants of her resolve buckling with resignation. *There's no way out of this.* Her hopes to free her family from the nightmare had disintegrated before her eyes.

Quigg refastened the bag. His eyes darted to the river. "Now, if you'll excuse me, I've a boat to catch."

CHAPTER TWENTY-NINE

N IKAIA'S STOMACH, STILL SORE FROM vomiting, coiled into knots
as she watched Quigg stride away, swinging the satchel at
his side. If the sternwheeler left with Quigg and the gold,
all would be lost. She had no ticket, no money, to board with the
passengers, and no time to get Papa, or even Constable Whittock.
Only moments remained before the sternwheeler pulled away from
its mooring.

A splash came from the eddy. To Nikaia's surprise, Klima was
pulling hard at the oars of the *Anybody Boat*.

"I saw Deputy Quigg," Klima called out as the boat scratched
into the rocky bank. "I heard what he said."

Nikaia leapt into the boat. Desperate thoughts clashed in
her head. *If we can only get to the gold and show it to the captain or
somebody, maybe we can stop this.*

Klima rowed swiftly out into the eddy. The black letters on the
side of the sternwheeler came into view: *Henrietta.*

*It's now or not to be, Brother Owl. Please, please, help us prevail this
night.*

In the dimming light, and with the clamor of the cargo loading,
the rowboat didn't draw any attention. Men were hauling the
last of the supplies on board, and passengers were walking the
gangplank up to the boat's hurricane deck.

They had rowed out in the *Anybody Boat* several times before on
sternwheeler day, but never so close to the massive vessel. Klima
steered toward the side of the boat furthest from shore. That
positioned them on the opposite side of the boat's cargo-loading
activity. They skirted alongside the paddlewheel, which towered

over them like the gear of a gigantic clock. Suddenly, the steam engine blasted, the clutch engaged with a groan, and the great wheel started spinning.

"Careful, Klima!"

Klima dug into the oars and pulled them away from the suction of the paddlewheel buckets.

A crank spun above their heads, and Nikaia recognized the grinding sound of chains pulling up the anchor. The sternwheeler vibrated and started to ease away from shore.

"We need to get on board!" Nikaia called.

Working one oar, Klima sidled the rowboat up to the midpoint of the boat, where a rope ladder was draped over the whitened hull.

"Go on up!" Klima shouted.

Nikaia reached for the lower rungs and stepped out of the boat. The rope ladder slumped and swung as she scrambled to the top. She swung her legs over the siding and looked down at the *Anybody Boat*, which sloshed and bumped against the side of the sternwheeler.

Klima struggled to tie the boat's bowline to the bottom rung of the ladder. The rope slackened and tightened with each surge of the water, undoing her half-formed knots. Finally, she secured it with a double hitch. Klima hopped to the second rung and pulled her way up, rolling neatly over the deck wall to join Nikaia in the sternwheeler.

Nikaia looked around. *Where are we? The main deck?* She had never been on board a sternwheeler, and everything looked new and foreign. They ran past the engine, ducking under the long steampipes that led to the boiler. The engine was already giving off heat, and a group of black men were laying blankets around its warm perimeter.

Nikaia was unsure of what direction to take. They climbed a metal ladder to the upper level of the boat. Nikaia assumed it was the saloon deck, with its rows of sleeping berths. Down a corridor, she could see waiters setting out food in the dining room.

A lantern swayed from the pilothouse, sending flashes of light down to the deck level. They kept to the shadows to avoid being spotted. Looking overhead, Nikaia could see the blue-capped pilot turning the steering wheel, a multi-handled device with a diameter about the size of a wagon wheel. Papa had told her that the wheel was connected to the rear of the boat with chains that ran in grooves along the hurricane deck. Running past the pilothouse, Nikaia could hear the metal links sliding in their channels as the pilot loosened the rudder. *The boat will leave soon, with Klima and me on it!*

They came to a set of large freight boxes piled four high. Nikaia suddenly stopped and gestured for Klima to stay back. Walking ten paces ahead of her was Deputy Quigg clutching the satchel. He spun around, and Nikaia ducked behind a box. She peered over the top to see Quigg cast darting glances all about him. Then he flew down a long stairwell that dropped away into the depths of the boat.

"What do we do? Follow him?" Nikaia was afraid to get too close to Quigg's revolver, or for that matter, to pull her sister in too close to the danger. Quigg's threatening words at the Creaking Fir echoed in her mind.

Klima turned her palms up and looked to Nikaia for direction.

"Let's wait a minute then go down," Nikaia said. "But we must be dead silent."

They peered down the stairwell. The crew had completed the loading, and the hold was quiet and dark, except for intermittent bands of lantern light that leaked in through the side-wall planks.

They slipped down the stairs. The cargo hold was fully laden, a maze of layered crates, chests, burlap sacks, and stacked kegs. Nikaia led the way as they ventured into the tunnel-like openings between the piles of stacked cargo.

"I see him," Nikaia whispered.

The black outline of Quigg twisted as he studied the crates. *Probably seeking a suitable hiding spot for the gold.* She watched him from behind a stack of wooden boxes. Klima found a dark spot beside a short wall of vinegar kegs.

Quigg turned back toward the stairs. He set down the satchel in a soft beam of light and opened its straps. Extracting a poke, he untangled its drawstring and rolled some small nuggets into his palm. They sparkled in the dim light.

Then something inside the bag caught his eye. He reached in and dug around, slowly at first, and then with feverish arm movements. Cursing, he overturned the bag and dumped its contents onto the floor.

And there, amid a paltry few gold pokes that had been layered on top, was Yee Sim's entire collection of throwing rocks. Nikaia stared in astonishment.

Deputy Quigg blinked rapidly at the pile then shrieked in rage. The ferocity of his cry startled Klima, who jumped back and tipped over a small keg of vinegar. The keg rumbled along the floor toward the satchel.

In a second, Quigg was upon Klima. She writhed to escape his grasp as he brought his forearm around her neck. He pulled her harshly into the light and reached for his belt line. Nikaia watched in horror as he raised his hand, the glint of a short knife visible as he held it against Klima's throat.

"Tell me where it is, you rodent," he hissed.

Klima cowered in his grip, her eyes wide and mouth trembling as she tried to form words.

Nikaia stood up from behind the crates. "Stop! She doesn't have it! Let my sister go!"

Startled, Quigg spun around to face her, Klima still in his clutches. "You!" His eyes burned in rage. "Bring it to me now, or your sister will pay the price. I'll make a sieve of her, I swear!"

Nikaia did not doubt his words. Her mind raced. She tried to shake off her astonishment and her fear for Klima. *What's happening here? Where's the gold?* She tried to recall exactly what Yee Sim had said at Bennett's.

She could remember nothing useful. But something had to be said, and she needed to be quick about it. "I can take you to it. It's back on shore but not far." She tried to sound convincing but couldn't keep the quavering from her voice.

The whistle sounded one long blast. Quigg looked to the planking overhead. "If I'm not back on board with all the gold in ten minutes, you're dead. Both of you."

Still clutching Klima, he motioned Nikaia out of the cargo hold. She led him to the rope ladder.

"You first," Quigg said. She scrambled down and readied the oars. Quigg's descent was ungainly as he jerked from one rung to another, holding Klima one-handed between him and the ladder. He kept the knife in his grip. Nikaia prayed he wouldn't slip with that edge hovering so close to Klima's throat.

Quigg unknotted the bowline from the ladder. He snatched Klima's arm again and pushed her into a seated position. He settled behind her. Putting the knife edge back to Klima's neck, he cursed at Nikaia as she rowed toward the riverbank. "Any more tricks from you, and you'll see your sister's blood."

Nikaia pulled on the oars. She had no idea what to do when they reached the bank. *Stall for time? Wander into the woods with the pretext of finding the gold there then try to slip away?* She looked at Quigg clutching her sister and despaired of any chance of escape. Quigg had let her go once at the Creaking Fir; he was unlikely to do it again.

The boat soon scraped the riverside shallows. Nikaia shipped the oars forward and stepped out with the bowline onto the slippery bank. Deputy Quigg stood in the rear of the boat, his arm tight around Klima's neck.

Sensing an opportunity, Nikaia jerked the bowline hard to the side, and the bow of the boat spun to the left. Quigg stumbled and waved his arm to regain his balance. Klima escaped his grasp and dove for the front of the boat. Quigg stood to reach for her, raising his knife hand high into the air.

A single gunshot exploded from the woods. Deputy Quigg cried out and clutched his right shoulder.

Constable Whittock emerged from the trees with several men. Nikaia recognized the red hair and beard of Mr. McRaney from the Royal Engineers. McRaney jumped into the boat, his weight causing it to tip wildly. He pressed Quigg to the floorboards. After a brief struggle, he secured Quigg's knife and revolver.

The other men pulled the *Anybody Boat* fully ashore. McRaney hauled Quigg up by his overcoat lapels and dragged him over the gunwale. Quigg stopped struggling and stood weakly as McRaney jerked open his overcoat, patting the deputy's sides in search of weapons. Nikaia saw a circle of blood expanding below Quigg's collar bone. A neat line of red lengthened from the circle and made its way into the front pocket of his shirt. Constable Whittock commanded two sappers, Mr. Broadbent and Mr. Shaw, to take Quigg to the medic at the police station. The sappers carted Quigg away, even as he groaned and cursed at them.

Constable Whittock turned to the handful of men left on shore. "Who fired that shot? You could have killed the girl!"

McRaney stepped forward. "I fired no shot, sir." He gestured toward his revolver, still strapped in its holster.

The others shook their heads with a chorus of "No, sir."

The men looked up to the bench above the river, scanning the scene in the falling light. No one was visible. Amid the hissing of the river and the wind rustling through the alder leaves, no sound could be heard save the soft triple hoot of an owl in the distance.

Nikaia reached over and clutched her sister. Klima's shoulders heaved as she buried her face into Nikaia's shirt. Nikaia closed her eyes and stroked her sister's hair.

The crunch of rapid footsteps on gravel caused Nikaia to look up. Yee Sim was pushing his way through the row of men. He ran to Nikaia and almost knocked her off balance as he wrapped his arms around her. He choked out a single sob and pressed his cheek to hers.

A shuddering nearly overtook her, and Nikaia thought she might have to push away to get a lungful of air. But she preferred to remain in his embrace, closing her eyes to shut out everything else.

Nikaia's body carried a multitude of sensations. Her stomach was tender, her mouth sour, her arm muscles aching from Quigg's grip, and her legs trembling. But with Klima safe in her arms and her tears mingling with those of Yee Sim, running warm and wet between their faces, she felt her pounding heart most of all. And it was radiant.

When she opened her eyes, she saw Constable Whittock looking her way.

"Red," he said.

"Sir?" Mr. McRaney stepped forward.

"Could you find John Wales and Yee Ah? Let them know we have their children."

McRaney tapped his forehead and strode away.

Whittock gestured at Nikaia. "And as for you three, we're going to the barracks. Where we'll have a conversation."

CHAPTER THIRTY

NIKAIA SAT BETWEEN KLIMA AND Yee Sim on the stools of the police barracks office. They waited in silence, alone except for Mr. Broadbent, who puffed on a pipe behind the desk.

The door opened.

"Papa!" Nikaia exclaimed, and she and Klima ran into his arms. His eyes brimmed with tears as he held them.

Klima was full of questions, but Papa said, "Not now." He greeted Mr. Broadbent and Yee Sim. Klima sat one seat further down so that Papa could sit between Nikaia and her. He put an arm around each of them.

It seemed a long while before Constable Whittock entered the office. Mr. Broadbent rose and settled in another chair on the side of the room.

Constable Whittock took his place at the desk. "Well, I'm going to need some straight answers." He looked at Nikaia. "From you, in particular, young lady. But first, let me offer some information. No need to fear for Deputy Quigg. The medics tell me he'll survive. We've given him some opium to lighten the pain. In his fogged-up condition, he's talking freely. And we've learned a great deal."

Nikaia hadn't been particularly concerned for Quigg, all things considered, but she decided to remain quiet while Whittock continued.

"From what we've been able to piece together, he got in with the youngest Doyle brother, conspiring to steal the gold shipment before it reached the *Umatilla*. He used his credentials at the gold commissioner's office to find out the timing and particulars of the gold envoy. For his troubles, he would get a generous cut of the loot."

Whittock shook his head. "It seems they all may well have gotten away with it. Until, that is, greed overtook Mr. Quigg, and he double-crossed his partner. He shot and killed Matthew Doyle and prepared to hide the gold until he could leave Fort Yale for the coast."

Constable Whittock opened a desk drawer and handed Papa his spyglass. "Mr. Wales, this effectively clears you of suspicions in the matter of Matthew Doyle's murder."

"I'm pleased to hear that, sir." Papa took the spyglass. "What will become of Deputy Quigg?"

"He will certainly be put to trial for the murder of Matthew Doyle, the stealing of the gold, and for kidnapping Nikaia. And, I imagine, for his threatening actions toward your younger daughter. The judge arrived in Fort Yale just hours ago on the *Henrietta*. He'll expect some quick progress. Stealing from a miner is one thing. Those disputes are hard cases to prove, and the victims often seem as guilty as the offender. But stealing from the colonial government... that's entirely another matter. And the murder... well, they don't call Judge Begbie the Hanging Judge for nothing. At a minimum, Thomas Quigg will be detained at Her Majesty's pleasure."

Whittock nodded. "You may also be interested to know that my men are picking up Elias Doyle as we speak. For the burning of your cabin. He was seen lurking in the area the night of the fire, and we'll extract a confession if one is not immediately forthcoming. My belief is that Elias had no knowledge of the robbery. Matthew was attempting this caper on his own. Perhaps with the intent of impressing his brother, I don't know. Maybe he wanted to step out of the shadow of his older brother in the Fort Yale underworld."

He unfolded a bag of tobacco from his pocket and filled his pipe. "That brings me to two questions that remain open. And both are very important." He turned to Nikaia. "Quigg said that you buried the satchel near the river before turning it over to him. From what we've found in the *Henrietta* cargo hold, that was obviously a ruse.

So let's have it. What happened to the rest of the gold, and where is it now?"

Yee Sim leaned forward in his chair. "Sir, I saw Nikaia being followed. She gave me the satchel with the gold. I ran home to get a spade, but I was worried that with us being so closely followed, we could be caught by Deputy Quigg. So I took a matching satchel from my father's store. I filled it with rocks, but before sealing the satchel, I spread a layer of the pokes on top. If you opened it, it looked as though it were full of heavy gold. I buried both satchels, in different places, and I ran back to meet Nikaia."

The constable rocked back in his chair and exchanged a look with Papa. *I'm impressed, too,* Nikaia thought, looking in admiration at Yee Sim.

"So, Yee Sim," the constable said, "you buried the original satchel... where?"

"I didn't have much time. I hid it in the loose dirt where they're building the new church. I figured it wouldn't be disturbed there, at least until morning. It was the safest place I could think of."

Constable Whittock seemed relieved. "I think we'd best get you to the St. John site and retrieve that. Mr. Broadbent, can you take the lead on that? With haste?"

"Yes, sir." The officer tapped out his pipe and reached for his overcoat.

Constable Whittock rose and approached Yee Sim. He laid a hand on Yee Sim's shoulder. "You showed some clever thinking tonight, Yee Sim. Fort Yale can be an unforgiving place, and sometimes it takes the strength of a true friend to make things come out well. Nikaia is fortunate indeed to have had your help."

"Thank you, sir." Yee Sim glanced at Nikaia and reached for her hand.

Nikaia pressed her fingers into his. She wondered what Papa was thinking, and it occurred to her that at that moment she didn't care.

Papa stood and shook hands with Yee Sim. The boy's face, still tear-stained from the time at the riverbank, relaxed into a smile as he walked out of the barracks door with Mr. Broadbent.

Constable Whittock nodded at Nikaia. "You and Yee Sim got muddled into this very deeply. You could have been hurt, or even killed. And your sister might very well have been killed. From here on, you need to leave this sort of thing to the authorities. Steer clear."

Nikaia's cheeks burned.

Constable Whittock's face softened. "That being said, without your actions, it is quite possible we wouldn't have identified Quigg as the culprit. At least, not before he'd escaped into the crowds of New Westminster. You were very brave. In all likelihood, you saved your father from having to go to trial for something he didn't do. In my opinion, there's room in this world for more goodhearted people like Nikaia Wales."

The tears rushed out, and Nikaia covered her face.

Papa pulled her into a sideways hug. "I'm grateful you and your men were at the riverbank tonight," he told the constable. "How did you happen to be there?"

"Ah. It was a busy night for us with the judge arriving by sternwheeler and the Yale Ball festivities. My men were checking in at the ball when several attendees told of Quigg's strange behavior. It struck me as curious, although I didn't view it as an urgency at that point. As a precaution, I assigned two men to cover each of the town's escape points: the Cariboo Wagon Road and the sternwheeler docking. Then Yee Sim found one of my men at the barracks and told what he knew about Quigg. Based on that, I directed more men to the riverside, knowing that the boat was soon to leave."

Papa said, "Constable, you indicated that there were *two* open questions."

"Yes. Quite." Whittock looked almost reluctant to continue. He walked back to sit in his chair behind the desk. "There is the matter of the shooting of Mr. Quigg. None of my men shot him. And there are laws, even in this territory, against that kind of violence. That kind of retribution."

Papa started to speak, but Constable Whittock abruptly pivoted and pointed the stem of his pipe at Nikaia. "Did your father shoot Thomas Quigg?"

Nikaia's thoughts whirled as madly as salmon caught in a net. Could Papa have done that? She hadn't seen him at the riverside. After everything, would she still lose her father to jail, or worse? She looked at Papa.

He said softly, "You can always speak the truth."

Nikaia looked straight at Constable Whittock. "The truth is, sir, I simply don't know."

Constable Whittock considered that for a moment. He exhaled loudly and gathered his sheaf of papers. "It seems we may never know. And most likely, the Royal Engineers have better things to do. There's talk of more troubles brewing in the Cariboo, and we've got thirty-six new sappers on their way from Victoria."

He waved dismissively. Nikaia thought it odd that he didn't directly confront Papa with his question about the shooting.

Papa asked, "So it ends there?"

"Likely so. It may be that the judge will insist on further investigation. Our medic pulled a lead ball from Quigg's shoulder. We may be able to match that with a gun. Or at least a type of gun." He paused as he stroked the points of his moustache. "Of course, even that will be immaterial if we're unable to find the gun that fired the shot."

Constable Whittock shrugged and rose from his chair. "A shot was fired at a scoundrel about to do harm to a young girl. Who knows? Perhaps one of my men took the shot after all. What I'm saying, Mr. Wales, is that I'm inclined to consider the matter settled."

Papa stood up. "I thought the colonial police were known for always getting their man."

The constable rubbed his hand along the pitted edge of the desk. "Well, as my mum might say, there's no need to over-egg the pudding. And I think we've had enough getting for one night in Fort Yale." He extended his hand. "Mr. Wales."

"Constable." Papa shook his hand.

And the Wales family walked out of the barracks and into the warm evening air.

CHAPTER THIRTY-ONE

NIKAIA WENT TO BED EARLY, exhausted with relief and content to let Papa and Klima relate the day's events to Mama. A vivid dream came to her. She was lost and alone. She stumbled down a darkened path, tripping on roots that snaked across the forest floor. One caught her foot, and she faltered. She hunched over, looking behind her, ears alert to the sounds of the woods. The reedy hoot of an owl beckoned, and she rose to follow the sound. The route broke open into a meadow, matted with clovers and adorned with wildflowers ablaze in the late-day light.

Mama was suddenly there, smiling at her with pride. Papa appeared behind Mama, his eyes fixed on Nikaia and crinkling with encouragement. And there was Klima, Yee Sim, Albert George, and even Auntie Tsaht-koo, her skin unblemished as it once had been. Uncle Lawrence and Uncle Raymond stood to one side. The small crowd behind them included Annie Adams, Reverend Poole, Mrs. Knight and her daughters, Dr. McLeod and his wife Caroline, Yee Ah and Yee Sun, Celeste from Oppenheimer's, and Frannie O'Hare. Nikaia stepped forward, awash in the warm waters of hope and community.

When Nikaia awoke, Mama let her know that Yee Sim had led Mr. Broadbent to a small scraping in the site for St. John the Divine. The gold was found buried in the clay and was soon back in the hands of the gold commissioner.

Later that morning, Elias Doyle appeared at the woodshop, restrained with handcuffs and accompanied by Red McRaney and two other stocky Royal Engineers. Papa greeted them.

"I misjudged you, Mr. Wales," Elias said, lifting his shackled hands to remove his cap. "And acted with poor judgment as a result. I regret that, and I'll likely have some time to reflect on it."

"I was sorry to hear of the loss of your brother, Elias. It was terrible."

Doyle nodded, staring down at the cap with a pained expression.

"And your boy?" Papa asked.

"Joshua will be attended to."

"He'll stay with Bart?"

Doyle shook his head. "Bart has less sense than even Matthew had. No, Joshua has an aunt in Cache Creek, and she'll care for him while I'm away."

Red McRaney covered a cough.

"Good day, Mr. Wales." Elias Doyle replaced his cap and left with his attendants for the courthouse.

After lunch, another knock came to the door. Nikaia hurried to open it, and as she had hoped, Yee Sim stood framed in the doorway. "Nikaia..."

"Wait. I'll come out." She pulled on her moccasins, and they walked around to the side of the cabin. They sat together on a large fir stump, talking about all the strange events of the past days. The peril and desperation she had felt already seemed surreal to Nikaia, as though it was something she had read about and not lived through.

Their conversation slowed, and their talk turned to everyday things.

Eventually, Yee Sim glanced over at the supply store. "I suppose I should go."

"You're something of a hero for getting the gold back." Nikaia delighted in the shy sparkle her words brought about in his eyes.

"You're something, too." He struggled for words, his face reddening.

Nikaia reflected that she could not have asked for a truer friend to help find a way through her troubles. An uneasy silence fell between them, and she looked down at her shoes. Then Yee

Sim touched her cheek with his warm hand. He leaned forward and pressed his soft lips against hers.

In that brief moment, foreign and yet so natural, all her cares were lifted to the skies, and she felt that life ahead was full of unexplored possibilities and enduring hopes. She closed her eyes and leaned into the kiss.

Yee Sim pulled back, his ears crimson. He stood and gestured awkwardly toward Yee-wa. "I should get back." He retreated to the store.

Nikaia felt blissfully numb as she stepped back into the woodshop. For the rest of the day, she relived that kiss, wondering what it meant, both to Yee Sim and herself. Occasionally, when no one was looking, she put a finger to her lips and wondered if it would happen again... if she wanted it to happen again.

As afternoon eased into evening, Papa headed for the door, carrying a small burlap sack. "Nikaia, come walk with me."

Klima asked to go, but Papa told her to stay and help Mama prepare dinner. Klima set Jill in the windowsill and pulled on an apron. The bird was weak but still surviving, nestled in a bowl of twigs and cloth.

Mama had set up a simple kitchen in the woodshop, and she was slicing up a fresh salmon.

"Clang on an empty pot to let us know when it's ready," Papa called as he and Nikaia left the house.

The cool river air felt fresh as morning dew on Nikaia's cheeks. She walked with Papa through the sand and bunchgrass. Papa slung the bag over his shoulder and walked closer to the river. Nikaia followed. He stretched open the mouth of the burlap sack. Reaching in, he eased out his Colt Army Issue revolver. Making no attempt to hide it from Nikaia, he studied it for a moment. Nikaia looked at Papa and opened her mouth to speak but stopped when he shook his head.

Gripping the gun by the barrel, he threw it overhand. It tumbled through the air, past the eddy line, and dropped into the river with a gentle cough. The waters folded over and carried the gun down into the deep.

For a moment, they stood in silence, listening to the soft whispering of the river and the distant cackle of crows high in the firs.

Nikaia heard a metallic drumming. They looked up to the bench above the waterline. Klima was rapping a stick against an empty cooking pot.

Papa reached for her hand. "Let's go home, Nikaia."

She pressed her palm into his, and they started up the sandy bank.

THE END

AUTHOR'S NOTE

While the setting of this novel is the historic town of Yale, British Columbia, and references are made to actual characters in British Columbia history, this novel is a work of fiction.

In recent years, the aboriginal peoples of British Columbia have become known as "First Nations" people, befitting their distinction as the original inhabitants of this land and correcting the geographic inaccuracy of the word "Indian." Given the historical setting of this novel, I have used the terms "Indian," "native," and "native Indian" throughout to reflect the usage common in those times. In doing so, I mean no disrespect to the First Nations people. In places, I've also used the term *Nlaka'pamux* to refer to the native people of the Thompson River and Fraser Canyon area.

Similarly, the use of the word "Chinaman" is offensive today, and I have used that term only in the context of a slur to the Chinese immigrants who contributed in so many ways to the formation of British Columbia and Canada.

While much of the story is consistent with the historical record, I have tinkered with some details to fit the narrative. The town itself was usually referred to simply as "Yale" by the 1860s, but I've chosen to use the slightly older name of Fort Yale in the story.

I also changed the timing of certain business activities in Yale. Oppenheimer's brick store was not in place until the decade following this story, although they had a smaller operation in place during the early 1860s. Barnard's Express was operational in 1863, the year of this story, although the company's storehouse was not constructed until a few years later. The sternwheeler *Umatilla* no longer operated in 1863, having made its last Fraser River trip in 1858. The Reverend William Thomas Poole is loosely modeled after Reverend John Booth Good, who served in both Yale and Lytton for the Anglican Church in the decades following this story and was an important contributor to the documentation of the native peoples of the area.

While writing this book, I learned to my delight that one of my great-uncles worked on a steam-powered sternwheeler on the lower Fraser River. It was a snagpuller called the *Samson V* that worked to clear the lower Fraser waterway of debris. The boat was retired in 1980, and now serves as an excellent maritime museum in New Westminster, B.C.

This story is my homage, my love letter, to the people of the Fraser Canyon, past and present.

ABOUT HARVEY CHUTE

Harvey Chute was born and raised in the Fraser Canyon village of Lytton, British Columbia, a town rich in native culture and colonial gold rush history.

In his high school and university years, Harvey spent his summers guiding whitewater raft trips on the Thompson and Fraser rivers, relating historical lore and legends to his rafting guests.

He received a Bachelor of Science degree from Simon Fraser University in Vancouver, where his elective studies included the history of B.C. and of western Canada. He currently works as a program manager for an Information Technology consulting firm.

Harvey also created the web's largest independent Kindle user forum, KBoards.com, which is popular with both readers and authors.

Harvey lives in Bellingham, Washington, with his wife, three daughters, a lovable golden retriever, and a stern cat. He enjoys walking mountain trails, learning blues guitar, and being surrounded by great books.

His previously published works include five technical guides in the "For Dummies" series, by Wiley Inc. This is his first novel.

ACKNOWLEDGMENTS

I am forever grateful to my parents, Joe and Peggy, for many things, but foremost for your love for me and my brothers and sisters. I appreciate the quiet, faithful way you've served your community, your caring for the people around you, and your curiosity of and respect for our local history. All of this gave me a strong sense of "place" as I grew up in the tiny and ancient community of Lytton, B.C. Thank you, Mom and Dad.

Thanks to Lyn, Heather, Ross, and Roger for your love and support. I'm proud to have you as my brothers and sisters.

I'm thankful for the First Nations friends I grew up with, especially Tommy Brown, my best buddy in high school, whose life ended tragically and too soon.

Thank you to the faithful few who safeguard the history and lore of British Columbia, especially the volunteers and devotees behind the museums in Yale and in Lytton; to Dorothy Dodge, for her generosity in listening to my questions and for sharing her knowledge of this area's history; to Bernie and Lorna Fandrich of Kumsheen Raft Adventures, who introduced me to the thrill of the Fraser and Thompson rivers; to the many authors and history-philes listed in the bibliography; to my teachers at Kumsheen Secondary and Lytton Elementary Schools, and to my History and English professors at Simon Fraser University.

A big thank you to Betsy, Carrie, Celeste, Dorothy, Hannah, Heather, Joe, Kermit, Kip, Laura, Lyn, Mary, Peggy, Robert, Roger, Ross, Sarah, Scarlet, and Ursula for reviewing drafts of this book as beta readers. Also to my wife and daughters for indulging me with my readings of selected passages; and to the readers and writers of KBoards.com, who have shared so generously about their love of books and the craft of writing.

One of the best writing decisions I made was to submit my work to Red Adept Publishing. A huge thank you to Lynn for believing in this book. I've been privileged to work with Michelle, my content editor, who helped me breathe life and spirit into a sixteen-year-old girl from the 1860s. Your care and patience and instinct for what makes a good story improved the telling of this tale in countless ways.

I'm indebted, as are so many, to the native peoples and the pioneers who forged an existence out of this wild, unforgiving, and incredibly beautiful province of British Columbia. Thank you to the people of Lytton. In ways both warm and wondrous, you shaped me from my earliest days to my adult years.

My three daughters: you make me laugh, ponder, or just quietly exult in simple joys, every day. This book, with its young female lead filled with compassion, strength, and creativity, is inspired by you and written in the hopes that you'll enjoy the story.

Finally, in this writing project and in countless other ways, I've been blessed with the love and support of Carrie. It all begins and ends with you, girl.

BIBLIOGRAPHY AND REFERENCES

The books and references cited below were invaluable, and often fascinating, resources for me in learning about the gold rush years in the Fraser Canyon.

Akrigg, Helen, and G.P.V. Akrigg. *British Columbia Chronicle: Gold & Colonists.* Vancouver: Discovery Press, 1977

Barman, Jean. *The West Beyond the West: A History of British Columbia.* Toronto: University of Toronto

B.C. Heritage Digital Collections. *The Gold Rush Town of Yale.* http://bcheritage.ca/yale

B.C. Heritage Digital Collections. *First Nations Fish Processing Techniques.* http://bcheritage.ca/pacificfisheries/techno/natpro.html

Boas, Franz. *The Indian tribes of the lower Fraser River.* London: Spottiswoode, 1894.

British Association for the Advancement of Science. *Tenth Report on the North-Western Tribes of Canada.* London: Spottiswoode, 1895.

British Columbia Legislative Assembly Archives. *Contract and Charter for Construction of Alexandra Bridge.* February 1863. http://archives.leg.bc.ca/EPLibraries/leg_arc/document/ID/LibraryTest/828378581

Christophers, Brett. *Positioning the Ministry: John Booth Good and the Confluence of Cultures in Nineteenth-Century British Columbia.* Vancouver: UBC Press, 1998.

Dawson, George M. *Note on the Occurrence of Jade in British Columbia, and its Employment by the Natives.* Early Canadiana Online, 1887.

Downs, Art. *Paddlewheels on the Frontier, Volume One.* Evergreen Press, 1967.

Early Canadiana Online. *Native Studies.* http://www.canadiana.ca

Good, John Booth. *A Vocabulary and Outlines of Grammar of the NITLAKAPAMUK OR THOMPSON TONGUE; The Indian language spoken between Yale Lillooet Cache Creek and Nicola Lake; Together with a Phonetic Chinook Dictionary Adapted for use in the Province of British Columbia.* St Paul's Mission Press, 1880. Source: http://books.google.com/books?id=gvVIexelLLQC

Ibid. Portions of the Book of Common Prayer in Nlaka'pamux or Thompson. Victoria, BC: St. Paul's Mission Press, 1882. http://justus.anglican.org/resources/bcp/Canada/thompson.html

Hauka, Donald J. *McGowan's War.* Vancouver: New Star Books, 2000.

Hayes, Derek. *Historical Atlas of Vancouver and the Lower Fraser Valley.* Douglas & McIntyre, 2005.

Historical Map Society of British Columbia, University of British Columbia Library. Plan of Fort Yale, Royal Engineers, 1858. http://hmsbc.library.ubc.ca/browse/map/id_2182/

Langley Centennial Museum. *First Nations Baskets.* http://www.langleymuseum.org/baskets/

Livinglandscapes.bc.ca. *1881 Yale Census Data.* Royal B.C. Museum, http://www.livinglandscapes.bc.ca/thomp-ok/census/index.html

Livinglandscapes.bc.ca. *1877 Indian Reserve Commission Census (IRC), Southern Interior of BC.* Royal B.C. Museum, http://www.

livinglandscapes.bc.ca/cgi-bin/census?db=ind1877&pg=br&inc=50&n=151

Lytton History Museum. *The Lytton Museum and Archives.* http://lyttonmuseum.ca/

Marshall, Dan. *Claiming the Land.* UBC Ph.D Thesis, 2002 (unpublished).

McLean, John, M.A., Ph.D. *The Indians of Canada: Their Manners and Customs.* London: Charles H. Kelly, 1892.

MemoryBC.ca. *Fonds—All Hallows' School (Yale, B.C.) fonds.* http://memorybc.ca/all-hallows-school-yale-b-c-fonds;rad

M'Gonigle, Michael, and Wendy Wickwire. *Stein: The Way of the River.* Talon Books, Vancouver, 1988.

Morton, Arthur S. *A History of the Canadian West to 1870-71, Second Edition.* University of Toronto Press, 1973 (first edition, 1939).

New Pathways to Gold Society. *Hill's Bar: Gold Rush Ground Zero.* http://www.newpathwaystogold.ca/geocache/route/1/hills-bar, New Pathways to Gold,

Ormsby, Margaret A. "Richard Clement Moody." In *Dictionary of Canadian Biography Online*, 2002

Royal Engineers & Associates Living History Group. *THE ROYAL ENGINEERS In Her Britannic Majesty's Colonies of Vancouver's Island and British Columbia.* http://www.royalengineers.ca

Samson V Maritime Museum, City of New Westminster. *Early Days of Fraser River Transportation.* Operated by The Royal Agricultural and Industrial Society of British Columbia. http://www.nwheritage.org/heritagesite/orgs/samson/Fraser history page.htm

Simon Fraser University Museum of Archaeology and Ethnology. *A Journey into Time Immemorial*, 2008/2009. http://www.sfu.museum/time/en/enter/

Teit, James Alexander. *Memoirs of the American Museum of Natural History, Volume II.I.IV: The Thompson Indians of British Columbia.* New York: The Knickerbocker Press, 1900.

Teit, James Alexander. *The Thompson Indians of British Columbia.* Memoirs of the American Museum of Natural History, Volume II, Anthropology, The Jesup North Pacific Expedition. 1900.

Teit, James Alexander. *Traditions of the Thompson River Indians of British Columbia.* London: D. Nutt, 1898.

Teit, James Alexander; H. K. Haeberlin; and Helen H. Roberts. *Coiled Basketry of British Columbia and Surrounding Region.* Forty-first Annual Report of the Bureau of American Ethnology, 1919-1924, Washington, DC: 1928.

Yale and District Historical Society. *Historic Yale, Boomtown on the Fraser.* http://historicyale.ca

Made in the USA
Charleston, SC
08 September 2014